A year of winter

1984 in the Durham coalfield: the year of the strike, of pickets and scabs, of father against son, of housewives with pinched faces, and bankrupt local businesses. 'It feels', says a girl in the pit village of Belgate, 'as if it's been a year of winter...'

And yet life goes on, amid the distress, the anger, the fear. Fran Drummond, a young widow, has found her feet and rebuilt her shattered life after her husband's sudden death; busy with her teacher-training course, her small son, and her gentle lover, Steve, she listens to her neighbours' conflicting arguments about the strike, and watches it affect their lives. 'One day', she thinks, 'there'll be an issue on which I'm a hundred per cent certain where I stand' – but she cannot decide the rights and wrongs of this strike which some miners reject and others crave. She can only see that, between the warring forces of Government and NUM, a community is suffering and being crushed.

Denise Robertson, who has lived all her life in the Durham coalfield, fills her story with a kaleidoscope of the authentic opinions and feelings – wry, humorous, violent, sad – which characterized that difficult year. An accomplished novelist, she creates a world of memorable characters revolving around Fran: sturdy, quick-tongued Bethel, the char; Min with her perfect fingernails and fuschia-pink Capri; feminist Margot with her saggy, mud-coloured clothes; militant Terry Malone; doggedly independent Bill Fenwick. This evocative and absorbing novel recreates Durham's 'year of winter' with vivid immediacy and moving intensity.

By the same author

Land of lost content (1985)

Denise Robertson

A year of winter

Constable · London

First published in Great Britain 1986
by Constable and Company Limited
10 Orange Street London WC2H 7EG
Copyright © 1986 by Denise Robertson
Photoset in Linotron Ehrhardt 11pt
and printed in Great Britain by
Redwood Burn Limited, Trowbridge, Wiltshire

British Library CIP data
Robertson, Denise
A year of winter
I. Title
823'.914 [F]   PR6068.018/

ISBN 0 09 467230 X

'Not only men but nations must realize that the human family is thus so linked together that we must work together in a co-operative spirit if civilization is to endure.'

Peter Lee

1

Wednesday, 22 February 1984

In summer the car-park would be a sea of cars, red, blue and yellow, disgorging families eager to enjoy the beach. Today it was empty, except for a man wheeling a bicycle in through the gate. Fran looked toward the sea. There was a tiny blob on the horizon, a cargo ship or a rig drilling for coal. She felt a glow of pleasure. It was nice to stand here, warm in her sheepskin coat, and look at the grey North Sea.

Behind her, in the trees, Nee-wan was dashing about, winter twigs cracking beneath his paws. She bent to pick up a branch and threw it in an arc. He went past in a flash of black and white, and returned with the branch in his mouth. It was his new trick and he was proud of it.

The pit stood above the cliff, its wheel and headstock almost dwarfed by a mountain of stockpiled coal. Each day the papers were full of an impending strike, but everyone knew you couldn't strike with so much coal already on the ground. She had come late to the life of a pit village, but even she knew that.

There was an impatient bark at her feet. 'Another stick?' She bent to fondle the dog's ears but it jerked away its head. 'Slave-driver!' She threw another brittle twig and moved forward out of the trees.

As she drew near she recognized the cyclist. It was Fenwick, a miner who lived a few doors away from her. There was a wicker basket strapped on the back of his bicycle and he was studying his watch. She slowed, knowing he was engaged in serious business and must not be interrupted. Pigeon flights were carefully timed, recorded, and checked, and Fenwick's birds were prizewinners. She had taken Martin to see them once, not long after they moved to Belgate. David had arranged it over a drink in the club. *'It's all right, Fran. Your precious son'll come to no harm. Birds don't bite.'* Martin had been eight then. They had taken him by the hand into the aviary and heard a soft coo of protest at their intrusion.

Now, as she watched, Fenwick lifted the lid of the left-hand basket and a bird flashed up. Close to, it would be grey and white and iridescent blue, beady of eye and red-legged. At a distance it was a black speck hurtling skywards. Another followed. She imagined the other birds waiting for release, light filtering in through the wickerwork. Did they dream of freedom or wait, docile, for whatever came? Impossible to be sure. But she knew that a finger planted at the base of their neck would encounter endless feathers – down, down and never a hint of spine. Fenwick raised the right-hand lid and they were free!

All four birds reached their zenith and hung there, marking time. They started to circle, small sweeps at first and then wider, as though searching. From that height they would see the tower blocks of Sunderland to the north, the spires of Durham to the west, Middlesbrough a smoky blur in the south. Were those their markers, or was it some indefinable scent that pointed them home? Whatever it was, they found it, taking wing to the south, Indian-file. A moment and they were gone.

'Were they the bed-socks birds?' she asked when she came up to Fenwick.

He grinned at the remembered joke. When they had visited his aviary there had been a pair of birds with feathered feet. 'They look as though they're wearing bedsocks,' Fran had said in amazement and they'd all laughed. She felt tears prick her eyes at the memory but Fenwick was shaking his head. 'They're not mine, Mrs Drummond. I'm letting them go for another fancier. They're on their way to Stockton now. Time trials.' He cleared his throat. 'I haven't seen you since ... well, not to talk to. I was sorry about your man. He was a canny bloke.'

Fran nodded and smiled, and saw his relief that she was not

going to cry. 'Yes. He was nice.'

They fell into step towards the gate, he pushing the now empty bike, she fumbling to put on Nee-wan's lead. 'We used to have a crack at the club,' Fenwick said. 'You know, just a quiet pint. He liked to hear about the pit.' His grey jersey was shapeless but clean, and the hands clasping the bike handles were huge and weathered, flecked with the blue marks of the collier. 'I would've come round when it happened, but you never know what to do for the best. I came to the church. Anyway, like I said ... how's the lad doing?' This was safer ground.

'Martin's fine. He's ten now. He misses his father but he's accepted it. At least, I think he has.'

Fenwick's mouth drooped. 'Aye.' They walked on in silence for a moment. 'I don't remember my dad. He went in the war. Burma jungle. They say I saw him, but I don't remember.' Fran made a rapid calculation. If he was a baby in the war he must be middle forties now. 'Then me mam went in 1962, and me sister married. I've been on me own since then.' He chuckled. 'I've never wed ... but I've had plenty birds ... feathered variety.' Fran was about to say that there was time for the right woman to come along, but refrained. He seemed perfectly happy as he was.

'Are you having a rest day?' she asked.

He shook his head. 'I'm tub-loading. Came up at six. I'll get me dinner and then have a bit kip before I go in tonight.' Before them the pit loomed.

'Is there going to be a strike?'

He shook his head. 'I doubt it. The lads'll not go for a strike. They can't afford to lose money – too many commitments. There'll be a ballot and I'll vote to take action, but they'll not get a majority.' He sounded regretful.

'You would strike then?' Fran asked.

'If I had to. They'll finish off this coalfield if we don't watch out. If we give the executive a mandate to take action, it gives them more clout in negotiations. But there must be a ballot: that's an NUM rule.'

He sounded so determined that she looked at him enquiringly. 'There's some as wants short-cuts. Hot-heads. But NUM

[9]

history's based on the ballot, you can't get round that. Any road, if this overtime ban lasts much longer there'll be no need to strike – they're not keeping up with maintenance and safety work. There's a few pits round here'll be shut down before long. It's gone on for months, you know.'

They had reached the gate and he watched her try to subdue the dog before they came out on to the road. 'By, it's a handful, that one. What's it called?'

It was Fran's turn to chuckle. 'Nee-wan.' He waited, scenting a joke. 'When we got it I asked what kind it was and someone said, "Nee-wan knaas." So we christened it that.'

He shook his head at her folly. 'Nee wonder it's daft.' His grey flannel trousers were wound round his calves and fastened at the ankles with clips. He swung a leg over the saddle and felt for the pedal. 'I'll be off then. Send the lad round any time he's a mind to see the birds.'

She was almost home when she saw Treesa Carruthers ahead of her. She was obviously pregnant now, the lines of her figure blurred, and when she turned at Fran's greeting her face was puffy. 'Hallo, Mrs Drummond. I thought you'd be at college.'

Fran fell into step beside her. 'It's half-term.' It was difficult to know what to say to Treesa. She liked her so much, but conversation was a minefield. In a few months Treesa would give birth to the child of her dead lover: was that a matter for congratulation or commiseration?

'It's cold, isn't it?' Treesa's shoes were pink patent-leather scuffed at the toe and oddly down at heel, as though they ached. 'Can you still manage the standing in the shop? I know they'd be sorry to lose you.'

Treesa's thin fair hair had blown across her eyes and she tidied it behind her ears before replying, 'I've got a chair out the back. The boss is canny about things like that. If he's not watching the ovens he pops out and serves. So I can manage a bit longer.'

They parted on a corner where ice glinted on drain covers and the edges of the kerb. 'Come round to tea when you have a day off,' Fran said. If Brian Malone had lived she would have gone to their wedding, bought a gift, drunk their health. Instead he had died in the pit, crushed between tubs, and Treesa was left alone. 'Don't forget. We'd be so pleased to see you.'

'I saw Treesa today,' she told Martin when he came home to lunch. 'She's coming to tea one day.' Before then she would have to explain about the baby. He had idolized Brian Malone, which meant he had a right to know. But not yet. This afternoon she had to write an essay on the educationally subnormal child. Sufficient unto the day!

'It isn't fair, you being off when I'm not,' he said when it was time to go back to school. 'College should be just the same as school.'

Fran pulled a face. 'Jealousy gets you nowhere.' She wanted to reach out and hug him until his bones creaked, but it wouldn't do. Since his father's death he had been wary of too much emotion. It was enough that he liked her. More than enough! She pulled up his socks and helped him into his anorak. There were times when he seemed not to mind dependency, and she treasured them. She watched from the back door until he was lost to sight, then scuttled back into the warm. This was the moment when she would have liked a cigarette, but they could not be afforded. Besides, there was work to be done.

She laid out pens, paper, reference books and dictionary. Outside the window the backyard wall blotted out the sky. She always worked here because there was nothing to distract. And she was so easily distracted! She selected a piece of paper and picked up a pen. In two years' time, if she got down to work, she would be a teacher, an expert on the educationally subnormal child and half a dozen other things besides. A year ago she would have thought that an impossibility. She had been simply David's wife and Martin's mother, only existing in relation to someone else. She had never realized that before but it was true. Daddy's little girl, David's loving wife, Martin's doting mother. In a sense she had never just been Fran until the day that David died, suddenly, of a cerebral aneurysm, leaving her a widow at thirty-two.

They had been in Belgate for three years by then. David had come to an engineering works to be Production Manager and they had moved from their pleasant suburban semi to a house on a street that ran down to a railway shuddering with coal trucks. And then David was dead. 'So there's no earthly reason to stay there,' Eve and Min, her lifelong friends, had chorused. She had looked for a house in Sunderland, even begun to pack, and then something had changed her mind. Some instinct had made her say, 'Here I stand!'

It didn't make sense. The house was too big for one woman, one boy and one small dog. It was miles away from her teacher-training college and she couldn't afford the rates. But she loved this house, built long ago for an eccentric GP, still with a 'Surgery' sign at the side door. Besides, it was near to the pit, the pit that throbbed with life around the clock. And there was Bethel, dear Bethel who made all things possible. She looked at the clock. If Bethel arrived and found her shirking there would be trouble. She uncapped her pen and began.

When she had filled a page she flexed her wrist, rotated her neck, and allowed herself a moment's escape. Tonight she was meeting Steve in the Saracen. For a drink, no more; she mustn't go back to his flat. Not tonight. She was happy in his bed but afterwards the guilt was all-consuming. A night out that did not end in love-making would be a demonstration that she was in control. She had gone to him to buy a second-hand car, and had wound up in his bed. It was incredible!

She was dying to know if making love with Steve was adultery but there was no one she could ask. They were both free, but did that make it right? She had looked up 'adultery' in the dictionary and it hadn't helped: '*Sexual unfaithfulness of husband or wife.*' But was she a wife? She was a widow, but was she still a wife? Or Steve a husband? His wife, had rejected him, had left him impotent in the wake of that rejection. So did that make it right?

Bethel arrived as she was writing the last paragraph. 'Nice to see you doing a bit work for a change.' She was unpinning her hat and placing it upside-down on the dresser. Her wool gloves went inside, followed by her nylon scarf, carefully folded.

[12]

'Get the kettle on,' Fran said.

They settled either side of the table, papers tidied away. 'By, it's cold,' Bethel said, eyeing the boiler. 'Let it go out again?'

Fran shook her head. 'I can work it now. It's simple.'

Bethel cackled. 'That's about your level, then.' They drank their tea, each enjoying the other's presence.

'Any gossip?' Fran said at last. Bethel was officially a char, in reality a town crier.

'Nothing much. Mind, I've never been across the doors till I came here.' She looked round the kitchen. 'If you get out of me way I'll bottom this place before tea-time. It's a mass of dog hairs.' Nee-wan pricked up his ears. 'Yes, you. You have a good right to cock a lug. You're more mess than you're worth.' Her voice was the voice of the doting grandma and the dog's eyes narrowed in ecstasy.

'I saw Treesa today,' Fran said. 'I couldn't help feeling sorry for her.'

Bethel sniffed. 'You make your bed in this life ...' The grey hair was scraped back from a weathered brow, but the pale blue eyes were kind.

'She's only a child,' Fran said.

Bethel pounced. 'Exactly! Only a child, but she's been playing with grown-up toys, hasn't she? Not that I blame her – or him, come to that. He knew no better, and he's dead and gone. No, it's the upbringing he had. You can't grow up straight in a mad-house.' Bethel's feud with the Malone family, her next-door neighbours, was long-standing but fervent.

'Be fair,' Fran pleaded. 'I know they're a big family and a bit untidy, but they do no harm.'

Bethel's eyes rolled. 'No harm? I hope you don't live to rue those words, miss. Letting your Martin run the streets with their Michael, in and out of that house. You don't know what he might pick up. As for that oldest lad, he's a communist – no more, no less! He's down on his knees praying for a strike. Begging for it.'

'He is a bit militant,' Fran said, 'but he's still a nice boy. Very willing.' Last week Terry Malone had located the stopcock for her and prevented a flood. She would not have him maligned.

'Anyway, there's not going to be a strike. Fenwick says so.' She knew she sounded smug but she couldn't help it. Usually it was Bethel who had the gen; today it was her turn. 'I met him today, setting off some pigeons. He says there can't be a strike without a ballot, and a ballot will say no.'

Bethel shook her head. 'I heard he's been making his mouth go. He wants to watch out. They don't like anyone that thwarts them. You should get Walter on about the militants...'

Fran seized on a change of subject. 'How is Walter? Set the date yet?'

Bethel bridled, drawing her folded arms to her ample breasts. 'No, nor yet likely to, Miss Impudence.' Her eyes twinkled. 'We're just good friends. And now get out of my way. The bairn'll be in next, and nothing done.'

Later they all sat down to tea together in front of the television. Martin had perfected the art of finding his mouth without taking his eyes off the screen. Fran worried about it but couldn't bear the thought of making him eat in the silent kitchen. When David was alive, meal-times had been fun. Now they needed a spoonful of media to help them down.

'What rubbish is this then?' Bethel asked.

Martin grinned. 'It's a quiz, Bethel. It's good.'

Bethel emptied her mouth. 'Good for nothing. And less of the Bethel if you don't mind. Show a bit respect.'

Martin raised his hand in mock-salute. 'Yes, sir!'

Bethel glanced at Fran. 'Remember what I said about who he was mixing with? He's picking up cheek.'

The local news programme began with pictures of jostling miners, demonstrating at the visit of MacGregor, the new National Coal Board supremo. The portly American came into view, incongruous in a donkey jacket. Fran saw a face loom up in the crowd, a man in a cap enjoying the mêlée. His hand came up, seemed to clutch the elderly man, and then MacGregor was sprawling backwards, the camera was swinging. 'Did you see that?' Bethel was outraged. 'He knocked him down. The young thug!'

Fran was watching the inert body on the screen, sprawled over a fence. 'I don't think he meant to knock him down. It happened so quickly.'

Bethel stood up. 'Where's me hat? If I listen to your excuses much longer, I'll be no more good. If you lunge at someone like that it doesn't matter what you meant, it's what you've done that counts. Well, if they've killed him I hope they hang. I've got no room for Yanks, but that was disgusting.'

When she had made her exit Martin grinned. 'I love it when she gets mad.' He searched for words. 'When she does, her thingies shake.'

Fran looked at him. 'You mean her boobs?' He was blushing now and she laughed. 'Yes, they do. You're quite right.' On the day of David's funeral Bethel had worn a bra, but her breasts had escaped above and below and made interesting little bulges beneath her dress. Fran had wanted to share the joke with David, but they had shut him away.

The phone rang. 'It's me ... Min. Did you see that on the box just now? Those rampaging miners? We told you not to stay there. You can't say we didn't warn you.' She assured Min that Belgate was in no immediate danger of insurrection and then tried to get away. The clock was ticking round and she wanted to look her best. 'I rang Eve this afternoon,' Min said. 'She feels vile, and there's still three weeks to go. Still, this might have taught her a lesson. It's easy enough to conceive, but that's not even half of it.'

When Min had put down the phone, Fran sat still. *It's easy enough to conceive.*' Tell that to the strained faces in the infertility clinics. *'Don't give up, Mrs Drummond,'* the consultant had told her a year ago, *'we've still a few tricks up our sleeve.'* She had longed to give David another child, would willingly have dangled from a chandelier to bring it about. Now he was dead, and it was too late.

Steve was waiting in the car-park at the Saracen, uncoiling from the seat of his car at the sight of her Mini. The street lamps sparkled on his dark hair and threw his eyes into shadow. He

[15]

looked thin and intense and strange, and she felt a frisson of excitement. 'Hallo,' he said and leaned to kiss her cheek.

He smelled different, an exotic but definitely male odour. She sniffed appreciatively. 'That's nice.'

He had taken her keys from her and was locking the door of the Mini. 'Do you think so? It's some stuff Jean sent for me at Christmas – we keep up a front for the kids. It's a touch of the casbahs, isn't it? Still, might as well use it.'

The pain burned in the centre of her chest as they walked towards the pub door. It was there while he found them a corner seat, and remained while he stood at the bar for their drinks. Jean, Jean, always Jean. For the hundredth time she wished she could see her rival in the flesh. For the hundredth time she reminded herself that Jean was not a rival but Steve's divorced wife, part of the past. But the pain remained.

'There you are,' he said, putting her sherry in front of her. 'Now, tell me about your day.'

It was what she usually said to him, and they both smiled. 'Nothing much,' she said. 'I took the dog out this morning.' He listened while she told him about the pigeons. 'You could see they were getting their bearings, and then off they went. It was marvellous. He's a nice man, Fenwick.'

They talked of the strike. 'I hope it doesn't come off,' Steve said. 'I get a lot of trade from the mining community.'

She had never thought of the knock-on effect of a strike. It would not just cripple Belgate and the other mining communities – the ripples would widen. 'Well, if it's any consolation he's sure it won't happen.'

Steve was looking at her quizzically. 'Penny for them?' she said.

He leaned towards her. 'I was thinking we could be back at the flat now, just the two of us.'

She looked at the clock. 'There wouldn't be time.'

He smiled. 'That's not the point.' She enjoyed it when they had this sort of conversation, and at the same time she was horrified by it. It was funny to be out in the world again after years of marriage, to be sitting in a pub with a man and carrying on a flirtation.

'What is the point?'

He leaned closer. 'You know.'

She shook her head. 'I don't.'

He smiled again. 'Then I'll spell it out. Do you want me?'

She dropped her eyes. 'You know I do.'

He leaned back. 'That's all right then. That's all I need to know.'

They talked of everything and nothing then. She asked questions and gave answers, but all she could think of was the intimacy of his question. How stupid to worry about Jean's gift of after-shave when he was here beside her in the flesh. She felt euphoric on the way home. There was nothing like being virtuous for cheering you up. They had wanted each other, but they had stood firm. 'Next time,' she'd whispered when he kissed her good-bye. He had nodded and hugged her closer, then handed her into the car.

She started to sing, 'I'm getting married in the morning ...' That was Freudian. She had only seen the film once but the song remained. She changed gear and turned into her own back street, parking in the right place to turn once she had the garage doors open.

She had just climbed out and was fumbling for her keys when she heard the noise of feet. Her heart lurched and then steadied. Muggers didn't hunt in packs, and besides she had nothing worth mugging for. The next moment they were passing her, young men in dark clothes. One brushed past so close that she smelled the male odours of sweat and tobacco. 'Sorry, mate ... I mean missis.' Her smile began and then froze, for his eyes had gleamed at her from slots in a mask. It couldn't be – except that it was. As they passed beneath a street lamp she saw that they were wearing ski-masks. Their heads looked like malevolent pumpkins. They had smelled and sounded normal, but they had not been nice. She knew that by the pricking of her thumbs.

She mustn't mention them to Martin. It was not that he would be afraid – no, his eyes would widen with curiosity. *'Who were they, mam? Where were they going? Why did they have masks on? I bet*

[17]

they didn't. You always get things wrong.' But this time she had not been mistaken. Here, in Belgate, in 1984, a gang of men had run by her, much as the rum-runners must have run from the customs men two centuries before. An old poem was coming and going in her mind . . . '*Watch the wall, my darling, while the gentlemen go by.*' As she went up to bed she decided they had probably been joggers, wrapped up against the cold. Half your body heat was lost through the head, she had read that somewhere. She relegated the joggers to the safer recesses of her mind while she said her prayers; and only remembered them when she drew back the curtains for a last look at the stars and saw the blue light of a Panda car winking as it raced past the end of the street.

2

Thursday, 15 March 1984

It was still dark in the bedroom but Fran could hear the clamour from the pit-head. The shift must be changing, tub-loading over, back-shift going down. The Durham coalfield had been officially on strike for three days, but still the Belgate men were going doggedly to work. Yesterday there had been Yorkshire pickets waiting. A car had been overturned and stones thrown. A few Belgate men had turned back but the majority had gone through with Fenwick as their leader. Thinking of Fenwick she turned on her side, trying not to remember. It was useless. She would never be able to forget! Even now, three weeks later, the memory made her cringe.

Bethel had brought the news. 'It's Fenwick's pigeons. Gone, every one of them. Necks wrung, feathers all over the place. He's just sitting there holding the cock bird. It's dead as a dodo, but he won't admit it.'

Fran had gone round to offer condolences. 'It was too late when I saw them, Mr Fenwick. Even if I'd dialled 999, it was all over by then.' The birds were laid out in rows in front of the cree, limp bundles that had once flown free, heads dangling from the wrung necks. It was windy, and the fine breast feathers stirred. Impossible to believe they would never again soar and circle and head for home.

Fenwick had not moved or spoken, and it frightened her. She had wanted to provoke him to some emotion, even grief. 'I'm so sorry. I know how much you loved them. People are saying it's because you were demanding a ballot before you would come out on strike – but I can't believe anyone would do such a thing. Not for such a trivial reason.'

As she waited for a reply he stood up and began to gather up the birds. Methodically, showing neither reverence nor contempt. He was packing them into a box that bore a garish label: 'Canary Island Tomatoes'.

Fran felt her face twitch. She felt out of her depth. 'Well, I must go now. I just wanted to say I was sorry.' Mustn't mention replacements. That was the ultimate insult to the bereft.

As she reached the yard door he spoke. 'Thanks for coming round.' His voice was flat. When she was through the yard gate and into the back street she had heard him clear his throat. While his birds had lived he had cradled them in his hands, preening the breast feathers with a forefinger. 'Aye, bonny lad. Aye there, cocker.' When they were dead he had had nothing to say. But he still went to work. She had seen him only yesterday when he had passed her window.

Remembering his pinched expression she decided to abandon sleep and lifted herself on her pillows. It was resolution time! In half an hour she would leap up, let out the dog, stoke the boiler, cook Martin a nutritious breakfast, wave him off to school, and sit straight down to her essay. Until then her time was her own. She felt goose-bumps rising on her bare arms and snuggled down again. Ten to one the boiler had gone out and would need resuscitation. Bloody clinker. Bloody, bloody clinker! The one sure thing was that she mustn't let coke or clinker or anything else interfere with her essay. She still felt guilty about skipping lectures. If she didn't make good use of the time she would be consumed with guilt and end up as clinker herself, consigned to some Hadean scrap-heap.

She flung back the bedclothes and dived for her dressing-gown. A car sped by in the street, gathering speed. That was what they did each morning now, tried to dash through before anyone could stop them. Sooner or later there would be an accident. She lifted the curtain and looked out. The street lamps were still on, lending a ghostly glow, and a kind of freezing fog hung in the air. Her bare feet were cold and she was about to hunt her slippers when the man came into view. He walked hands in pockets, hunched like a Lowry figure, all browns and blacks and misery. A cap was set forward on his head, his bait box tucked under his arm.

As he came near, the noise from the pit-head grew louder. She saw the man hesitate. His hand came up and drew his collar about his throat. Fran clutched her own neck in sympathy. The man was frightened! He walked on a step or two, and then turned back. She watched him out of sight before she let the curtain fall.

The strike couldn't last. What had the *Echo* said on the first day? '*Coal mountains at pit-head and power station, summer almost here ... the miners are cutting off their nose to spite their face.*' There was more traffic in the street, tub-loaders going home, gunning their engines to escape. Once they had gone there would be peace again until the first shift came up at noon. It had taken her a long time to work out the shifts and learn their names. Sleepless after David's death she had begun to listen for the first foot-fall in the street: 4 a.m., first shift. Now that she was coming to terms with life again she was grateful to those tramping miners, and she grieved for them in the grip of a strike that some of them didn't want and some of them craved.

She carried her radio through to the bathroom and listened to the news as she washed and dressed. Every colliery in the North-east was idle, according to the newscaster. So the men of Belgate didn't count! They would continue to work until they got the ballot that was their right – but if the media ignored the fact of their working, what hope was there? What point in their making a stand? She cleaned her teeth to the details of violent picketing in

Nottingham which had left a Yorkshire picket dead on the ground.

'Aunt Eve might have her baby today,' she told Martin over breakfast. She made a determined effort to sit down to meals with him now. In the beginning she had dined on cottage cheese eaten from the carton, unwilling to sit at a table David had shared. But she was braver now. Not hungrier, just braver. She pushed her half-eaten toast aside and sat back.

'She wants a boy, doesn't she?' Martin asked. Fran nodded and he gave a smirk. 'That's sensible.'

Fran rolled her eyes. 'I don't know about that ... girls have their good points.' She felt love for him well up and hurried to school her face. At ten you were embarrassed by shows of emotion. It was enough that they had shared a joke.

When he had gone she took another look at the boiler. The coke she had put on first thing was still silvery and unconsumed, the glow behind it even fainter. 'Burn, damn you. Or at least keep going till Bethel comes.' Bethel would fettle the boiler, bring up-to-date news of the strike, and restore the house to harmony. If she ever became a fully fledged teacher she would split her salary with Bethel. Except that Bethel would push it away and tell her not to be so daft.

She gathered her notebooks and sat down to begin her essay. '*The Value of Audio-visual Aids in the Teaching Situation.*' She underlined the title and then filled in the holes in the letters. '*The value of audio-visual aids in the teaching situation.*' She added a firm full stop, and then turned it into a flower. She would have to write the whole thing out again anyway. She began to embellish the title with leaves and flowers on a trellis until the importance of audio-visual aids was lost to view. She was seeing Steve tonight and would wear her flowered velvet skirt.

Everyone knew she was seeing Steve but no one could be sure how far they went. She could see the question in their eyes when they reassured her. '*I* don't blame you, Fran.' The emphasis on the 'I' implied that everyone else thought you a whore. 'David wouldn't have wanted you to shut yourself away.' That was what they said out loud. '*But you needn't have gone this far,*' their eyes

[21]

said, and flicked nervously away.

'*I am too sensitive.*' She wrote it on the pad and circled it with a balloon emerging from the mouth of a skirted matchstick man. So that was how the day was going to go: doodling and dawdling and no essay to hand in tomorrow. She got a fresh sheet of foolscap and began again. The trouble was, she wasn't cut out for adultery. Or for dissembling. She might have kept quiet about Steve but she couldn't stand the strain, so she had told them at a girls' night. 'There's this man ... it's not a grand passion. It's really quite platonic ... but he's lonely and so am I, so we go out.' She didn't add 'so there' but it hung in the air. They had all looked back calmly as though it was nothing out of the ordinary, but the relief when she went to the loo had been almost tangible.

By eleven Fran had filled three foolscap pages and was running out of steam. She put on the kettle and watched the clock for Bethel's arrival. Dear Bethel, who smelled of soap and nutmeg and told you not to be daft if you got too sloppy. She would never have survived David's death without Bethel. She wrote '*I love you, Bethel*' on the Shopping Memo, and wiped it out before she mashed the tea.

'You smelled it,' she said accusingly as Bethel came through the door.

'Never mind the cackle ... get it poured,' Bethel said. The gleam in her eye foretold news. 'By, there's been trouble there this morning!' 'There' always meant the Malone household. 'Bawling and shouting, thumping tables ... you can hear them at it through the wall, hammer and tongs. And her ... I've always said she was daft, but she stands there, wringing her hands, saying ... "Come on, now, dad; come on, our Terry." She wants to clash their heads together, never mind "Now dad."'

Fran poured tea as a way of evading reply. She hated it when Bethel criticized the Malones, and this was a particularly vexed question. The Malones, father and son, were miners but there the resemblance ended: Terry was for Scargill and the strike, his father for the NUM rule book and the ballot. 'I'll come out when I've had my say,' he'd told Fran last week, and that was what most of the Belgate men said. That was why they continued to work.

[22]

But how much longer could they hold out?

As if Bethel had read her thoughts, she spoke. 'They'll be out by the week-end, it stands to reason. Maniacs like Terry Malone putting themselves about, and worse coming from Yorkshire. They'll come out, they've got no more sense. And then they'll feel the pinch.' Her face shadowed as she remembered other strikes. 'We pulled together in the old days. We always managed. Well, we had nothing to start with so there was nowt to lose. But this lot, with their videos and their dishwashers ... mark my words, they'll be crying their eyes out in a fortnight.'

Bethel had another piece of news. 'Treesa's given up her job, and not before time. Standing in a shop with a bump like that. I don't know what we're coming to.'

Fran drained her cup before she answered. 'She didn't have much choice, did she? How else would she have managed? – And don't say they get everything given nowadays because they don't ... you get something from the State, but it's never enough.' As Bethel sniffed her disagreement Fran thought of her own widow's pension – if she hadn't started teacher-training, they'd have starved. 'Anyway, I expect it makes sense for her to give up now. The baby's due in June, isn't it?'

They fell into a discussion of giving birth. 'She's always a bit pasty, that friend of yours,' Bethel said in tones of foreboding. 'She has a chance to have a hard time.'

It was true, Fran thought, Eve was pale – but how much did that mean? The phone rang in the hall and she scampered to answer it.

'It's only me.' Min's voice was apologetic, as though she had known Fran was waiting for news. 'I've just rung Harold. He's tearing his hair. She hasn't had a single pang yet ... nothing. She'll have to have an induction. They stick a drip in your arm, and out it pops.'

Fran sat down to her essay when Min rang off, but it wouldn't come. Damn Min. Damn thoughts that lay comatose for months and then were resurrected to torment you. They had wanted another baby, had tried so hard ... '*I love you, Fran ... I love you ...*' In her mind David's arms, David's body turned into Steve's.

Steve alive, sweating with effort, loving her. '*Oh God, Fran, I do love you.*' She felt her face flush. Guilt, that was what it all boiled down to in the end! She had felt guilty after David's death, ashamed of breathing, eating, laughing ... especially laughing. And now, less than a year after his death, she had a lover and a life of her own, and didn't turn up for lectures into the bargain.

She went back to her essay, ignoring distant rumblings from the pit as the shifts changed. 'First shift's out,' Bethel said when she brought in lunch, 'and that lot's still hanging about for the back shift to come up. They want to fetch the pollis in.'

'That's all we need,' Fran thought. Aloud she said, 'I expect it'll be over soon.' If it went on she would have to take sides. Eve and Min were always on about the miners – '*Salt of the earth? I know what I'd do with them ...*' Well, if it came to the push she was on Belgate's side. One day, if she lived to be ninety, there might be an issue on which she could be 100 per cent sure of where she stood. Until then, she would have to make do with Hobson's choice.

Min rang up again at two. 'I'll go up there and drag it out shortly,' she said with feeling. 'Why can't they give her something and get it over with? My God, they talk about advances in medicine and we're all sitting waiting like aborigines squatting under a bush.'

Fran laughed. 'Maybe we should organize a fertility dance.'

Min's reply was tart. 'Harold did the fertility dance nine months ago ... that's why we're all suffering now.'

As Fran put down the phone she wondered once more about Min. '*Harold did it.*' Not Eve and Harold together, making love, making a baby. Just Harold. In Min's eyes the woman was used by the man.

'I'm going through to Sunderland,' she told Bethel. 'I'll take the dog out before I go, and finish my essay tonight. Min says Eve's in the dumps so we're going to cheer her up.'

Bethel's leer was a masterpiece. 'By, they're soft, those friends of yours. The least little thing upsets them and you've got to go and hold their hands. What a pity!'

[24]

Fran was still laughing when she emerged from the back gate with Nee-wan on his lead.

She had passed the allotments when Terry Malone joined her. The red hair curled around a naturally rebellious face, but he smiled at the sight of her. 'Who's taking who for a walk?' She tried unsuccessfully to bring Nee-wan to heel. 'He doesn't improve, does he?'

They fell into step. 'So you've come out on strike?' She knew the answer but she was curious to hear his views.

'Aye, I've been out from day one. We'll have the rest out before long ... once they see sense. It's do or die now, Mrs Drummond. We can lie down and let the buggers walk over us – excuse the language – or we can stand by Arthur and fight.' The speech had obviously been made before but was no less sincere for repetition.

Fran chose her words carefully. 'Are you sure a strike's the right way?'

His eyes were fervid. 'It's the only way. The *only* way. We won't be pushed around, not any more. Maggie Thatcher's met her match this time. She's wiped out British Steel, she won't cripple us. Not a single pit goes, and that's our last word.'

Fran wondered if he knew about world recession or the sad faces on the streets of Sunderland where one man in four was out of work. Could miners demand a safer world than other workers? Half of her said yes; the other half rebelled. Life should be fair. Except that fair shares of misery was not fair at all, and if a pit died the village died with it – or so they said.

They had reached the parting of the ways. 'Well, I hope it's over soon for everybody's sake. And I hope there's not going to be any more beastliness.'

She was thinking of Fenwick but his reply chilled her. 'I don't want trouble, Mrs Drummond, but this is war.'

Fran shook her head. 'You're wrong, Terry. It's an industrial dispute. You won't solve it with your fists. Look at Fenwick ... he was all *for* a strike till they killed his pigeons. Now he'll keep on working till he drops.'

His face had winced at the mention of Fenwick. 'That was

wrong. Senseless. Not that it was definitely our lads – it could've been cranks or someone with a grudge. But if it was to bring him into line ... well, it was wrong, but you must understand how they feel.'

As she walked away, Fran felt a sense of despair. Left to himself, Terry Malone would not harm a fly. Now he was at least half-way to condoning something that was vicious and wrong.

Harold was waiting in the drive, dressed as usual in neat pin-stripes. Fran had left her Mini at Min's and accepted a lift in her new fuschia-pink Capri. 'It's good of you both to come round,' Harold said, almost wringing his hands. 'She can't seem to find a resting-place and I haven't liked to leave her, but there are a few things at the office ...'

Min was pushing him towards his Audi. 'Stop being a wally, Harold. It's too late to agonize now. The damage is done.'

He cast a pleading glance at Fran. 'Off you go,' she said. 'You'll be all the better for a break, and we'll take care of Eve. Twenty-four hours from now it'll all be over. It's worth all the aggro.'

'You're far too soft,' Min said as they watched him drive away. 'He's had his pleasure, now poor Eve has to pay the price. You shouldn't pamper him.'

They were both shocked at the sight of Eve. Her face, usually pink and rounded, was pale, with blue shadows beneath the eyes. There was a line of moisture along her upper lip and her fore-head gleamed beneath lank hair. But it was her body that had changed most in the last few days. 'Yes, it has dropped,' she said, following their eyes to her belly. Her arms and legs looked stick-like, and when she tried to get up she resembled a struggling beetle that has fallen on its back.

'For God's sake sit still,' Min said. 'What is it you want? If it's anything except a pee, I'll do it for you.'

Eve subsided. 'I was going to make some tea.'

Fran went off to the kitchen to see to tea and Min opened her handbag. 'What you need is an uplift. Come to Aunty Min.'

As she waited for the kettle to boil, Fran thought about the two women in the adjoining room. They'd all been friends since their first day at the grammar school. By mutual consent Eve had been leader because she knew how to keep in with the staff. Min had been thin and shabby and never had money for extras. She had married Dennis for his money, and now even her bra and pants were designer models. She was still thin but she had the gait of a mannequin and a haircut that turned heads wherever she went.

Eve ... Eve was still Eve. Miss Goody Two-Shoes who never got order marks and had name tabs in all her clothes. She had wanted this baby desperately, a son to add to her two daughters. She had planned it down to the last detail. But even the best-laid plans could go awry. There had always been something of the saint about Eve, a Maid of Orleans quality that would burn at the stake for an ideal ... or a son. 'Please God, let her be all right.' As Fran scalded the tea she prayed, 'Let things stay as they are, God. No more missing pieces. I want peace!'

When she got back to the living-room, Min was showing off her handiwork. 'There now, that looks better, doesn't it?' She had looped up Eve's hair at the sides and taken up the back in a French pleat. Now she produced a small onyx case containing cosmetics. 'A little shadow. Green, I think. It's more you. And a little blusher there ... and there. And some lipstick. That's it ... lips together. There you are, that's more like it.' The lipstick looked incongruous on Eve's strained face and her hair had already begun to straggle. As if she sensed her efforts were less than adequate, Min produced a slim gold container and sprayed Eve lavishly from head to toe. 'Madame Rochas, you can't beat it. I try other things but they never measure up. Here ...' She pressed the phial into Eve's hands. 'Keep it. It'll do wonders for your morale and I've gallons more at home.'

Normally Eve would have refused such a gift. Today she was too weary. She took the cup of tea Fran offered and raised it to her lips. Her fingers had the spotless but unclean look of an invalid's, and Fran felt a sudden terror. Surely it *was* going to be all right? They never lost mothers or babies now. Not in 1984.

'I hope he's pleased with himself,' Min said again, as Harold,

[27]

newly returned, waved them good-bye. 'And I hope he's going to get a snip before he does any more damage.'

Fran couldn't let the injustice pass. 'Oh Min, you know this baby was Eve's idea. I don't think Harold even wanted it, much less forced it on her.'

Min lifted her hands and banged them down on the wheel. 'I know, I know. But it doesn't make any difference, Fran. I wish you wouldn't be so bloody reasonable!'

She refused Min's offer of a drink, and made for home. Poor Eve ... it *was* the woman who paid in the end, although she wouldn't admit it to Min. As the pit came into view she thought of the women of Belgate who would be crucified if the strike lasted any length of time. Last week a group of them had given Scargill a noisy reception when he came to Sunderland. They were demanding their husbands' right to a ballot, but he had dashed from his black Rover without speaking to them. And yet they were as involved as their men.

She had five minutes to spare before she needed to get ready to meet Steve. 'I've made the tea,' Bethel said. 'Get something eaten. You look peaky. I'm coming back when I've seen to me fire, but if you ask me you want to get your feet up. All this rushing about ... it wouldn't do for me.'

Fran pecked at Bethel's cheek. 'You're an angel, but if I have a cup of tea I'll be fine.'

She opened the evening paper – details of the death on the picket line that had featured in the morning news, and further trouble in Nottinghamshire. The Durham mechanics had rejected the strike call and Union activists were making threats. 'I've told you,' Bethel said. 'They'll not be content till they've drawn blood.'

Fran put the paper aside. Belgate had seemed the safest place on earth, a bolt-hole to hide in after David died. Now it was getting ready to erupt.

Harold's phone call put paid to her premonitions, substituting real fears for imaginary ones. 'Her waters have broken ... just after you left. They're taking her in now, she's in a bad way. Eve's mother's coming round to see to the children but if you're not busy ... well, I might be at the hospital a long time ...'

His unspoken plea could not be denied. 'I'm on my way,' she said and put down the phone.

She explained to Bethel and dialled Steve's number. 'Of course you must go ... I hope everything goes well ... I'll miss you ...' She shrugged into her coat as she ran for the car. If anything happened to Eve it would be more than she could bear. 'We've been friends since school,' she said to Bethel by way of explanation.

'I know, I know. Get yersel' off and stop slavering on.'

Harold was waiting outside the labour room, wearing the look of a convicted felon. 'We shouldn't have done it, Fran. I've been thinking that all along, but Eve had her heart set on a boy.'

It was a time for stern measures. 'Stop wingeing, Harold. In an hour or two they'll both be fine. Eve knows what she's doing.' She was amazed at the confident sound of her own voice. It was strange to be in command – strange, but not unpleasant. She went in search of coffee for Harold and made half-hourly enquiries as to Eve's progress.

'She's fine, Harold. Getting regular pains. And there's no sign of foetal distress.' He was still wearing his office suit but he had light-coloured loafers on his feet and it made her want to laugh. She had never seen Harold improperly dressed before ... in all the years. At school he had worn the uniform correct to the last button. Dennis had been the one who broke the rules with six-foot Dr Who scarves and olive-green chukka boots. And David ... David had always had style – or else she had been so in love that she had endowed him with some special grace.

'Do you think she's all right ... it's been ages.' Harold was leaning forward, his eyes fixed on her face. There was a blueness along his upper lip and around his jowl.

'I'm sure she is but I'll go and ask.'

The nurse was suddenly noncommittal. 'We'll let you know.' After reassuring Harold, Fran offered up a silent prayer: '*Take care of Eve. It isn't much to ask.*' When the doctor emerged and

[29]

decreed a Caesarian section, she gave up praying. It never worked anyway. Eve would live or die according to the script ... or the director's whim. She and Harold were merely the audience and had no say in the plot.

She rang Min from the call-box in the corridor. 'I couldn't bear it if anything happened to her, Fran. I know she's a pain sometimes, but she's always there when you need her. If she gets through this I'll never talk about her again ... not behind her back, anyway.'

Fran smiled into the telephone. Oh the power of good intentions. 'She'll be all right, Min. Now stop being silly and get on with Dennis's meal.'

At 10.45 Eve was delivered of a son. Seven pounds four ounces and apparently perfect. 'You're sure it's a boy?' Harold asked, incredulous.

'Fairly sure,' the midwife said tartly. 'I've delivered a hundred and three, so I hope I know by now.'

They were allowed to peer at the baby through a window. 'He's wonderful,' Harold said, his breath frosting the glass. The baby's eyes were closed but his face was troubled, as though he was angry at being brought into such a world. 'He'll still be at school in the year 2000,' Harold said suddenly and then, apologetically ... 'Sorry, I must be rambling.'

Eve was only half returned to consciousness. 'I'll wait here,' Fran said. 'They only allow the husband on the first day.'

A trace of Harold's self-importance returned. 'It's different in here,' he said. 'It's private.'

So Fran followed in his wake, and saw him lay his lips to his wife's flaccid fingers. 'Thank you, darling, for being a clever girl.' If she had given David another child he would have been grateful too. Fran wondered how much more pain she would be called upon to bear.

'I'm so happy for you, Eve,' she said. Eve still bulked huge in the bed, although a frilly nightie had been pulled over her head and down to meet the bedclothes in honour of the visiting husband. A line of white flesh showed, but all traces of gore had been tidied away. When David had come to her after Martin's birth he had put his lips to her cheek and whispered, 'Hallo mother.'

She left them alone and went to give Min the good news. 'Thank God. I've bitten my left little finger down to the quick. It's a good job I'm due for a manicure tomorrow. Still . . . as long as it turned out all right.' She made the contribution of her little fingernail sound as important as Eve's incision and stitches.

'Min,' Fran said, and her voice was fervent, 'don't ever change.' She put up a finger and wiped a tear from her eyes.

'What do you mean?' Min said.

'Exactly what I say,' Fran answered and put down the phone.

'There now. It's over,' she said as she bundled Harold into his car. She couldn't accuse him of insensitivity in asking her to be in on the birth. He meant to be kind, to make her feel wanted. He couldn't see inside her mind, her jealous seething mind that begrudged Eve the new life lying neatly in the blue-tagged crib.

'I couldn't have coped without you,' he said and held her wrist to his cheek.

'I wouldn't have missed it for the world,' Fran lied cheerfully, and waved him on his way.

She pulled into the car-park on the cliff when she got back to Belgate. The pit was tranquil, the wheel still. Only lights in cabins and walkways betrayed men working. In a few hours there would be all hell let loose, but for a little while there was peace. She laid her head against the side window. A baby. A life for a life. David gone, the baby safely arrived. 'I *am* glad,' she told herself. 'And if I'm not, I must try to be.' She turned on the engine and let out the clutch. She would have to finish her essay before she went to bed, disentangle the audio-visual aids from the flowered trellis. That was real life. Small and pedestrian and safe.

3

Wednesday, 21 March 1984

'Well, they've done it!'

The smell of new bread was filling the kitchen but Bethel was flushed more with the light of gossip than the exertion of baking. So it had happened: after ten days of conflict the die was cast and Belgate was on strike!

Fran dropped her books on to the table and sank into a chair. 'When did they decide?'

Bethel was filling the kettle, words spilling faster than the flowing tap. 'The Union men came down from Durham this morning . . . "Come out or else," they said, and the daft buggers just downed tools and walked out.'

'Even Mr Malone?'

Bethel's satisfaction rose in the air like steam. 'Oh yes . . . "Our Gerry won't come out," she says this morning. "Not without a national ballot," . . . an' the next minute he's slinging his pit-boots in the back passage and off down the club. She'll feel it now! Debt? They're up to their eyes . . . three wage-packets coming in and it's tick this, tick that. Her back garden'll be that full of clubmen next week, they'll think she's growing them.'

Fran smiled to acknowledge the joke but her thoughts were elsewhere. Tomorrow there would be no angry clamour from the pit-head but no reassuring footfalls either. She had listened for those feet in the days after David's death. Now, for a while at least, they would be silent. Still, it was probably for the best. The pickets' mood had been getting uglier every day – the *Echo* head-lines had told the story: '*Blue Army Keeps Peace at Pits*' – and the streets seemed full of Panda cars and sinister blue vans.

'Has Fenwick come out too?'

Bethel nodded. 'Him as well. They've cut their throats, throwing the rule book out of the window. They'll pay for that.'

Fran had long since given up trying to understand the ballot argument . . . national ballot, pit-head ballot, area ballot . . . Belgate's air was thick with jargon. She would have to ask someone to explain it to her.

Bethel was still in full spate when Martin arrived. School had been OK, playtime had been OK, but 'Grange Hill' was on the telly and could he have some Ritz crackers with marge not butter? While she filled his order, he told her about Michael Malone. 'He's off sick. Something he ate. Their Anne brought a note and she says the priest's been round again about them not going to the Catholic school. He won't have to leave, will he?'

Fran tried to make a non-committal answer. 'I don't know. I wouldn't worry about it until it happens.' It was not enough.

'What do they want a different school *for*?'

Fran could feel Bethel drawing breath to do her Ian Paisley impression. 'I don't know but take these biscuits and we'll go round and see Michael later on. You can take him some comics.'

'It's not Michael now. It's Mike.' He was examining the biscuits as though inspecting them for weevils and she struggled not to show irritation.

'Since when has he been Mike?'

Martin shrugged. 'Search me. He just decided. If anyone calls him Michael now, he thumps them.'

Bethel drew in her breath. 'The impident little monkey. Still you can't blame a bairn . . . it's what he learns at home. Religion? They don't know the meaning of the word. That's what's the matter with them . . .'

Fran knew what was coming next and she wasn't in the mood. 'Take your biscuits and off you go,' she said. 'And don't get marge on the chairs.'

When Martin had gone, Fran turned. 'Don't start about religious segregation, Bethel, because I haven't got any answers. Besides which, it's the Malones' business, not ours. So drink your tea.'

Bethel obeyed, but managed to turn defeat into victory. 'Aye, they've got bigger troubles than schools. Four young bairns there, all impressionable, and a girl having a baby out of wedlock that their brother fathered. What'll their Michael ... or Mike, as he calls hisself ... make of that?'

'I expect he'll understand. After all, he's ten. They know everything at that age, nowadays.' Suddenly Fran was filled with fear. If Mike knew about free love, so did Martin. They shared every thought. She would have to tackle him about it in case he got the wrong ideas. But what were the right ideas? Was she qualified to enlighten him, she who never knew her own mind from one moment to another?

'Mind, I'm sorry for that Treesa,' Bethel said. 'She's not getting on with her mam and dad. They're upset about her not being wed. Still, they had every intention if it hadn't been for tragedy. And the lad would've stood by her, I'll give him that. He was the only one of that family with any gumption.'

Fran hid her smile. Alive, Brian had been a Malone with all the dreadful implications of that name. Dead, he was beatified.

'If she has to get out, I hope she gets a place of her own ...' Bethel's eyes rolled upwards. 'If she goes in with that lot ... Hell'll freeze over before Winnie Malone sees sense ... She's having wall lights put in now!'

Obviously Fran was supposed to react to this ominous news. 'Wall lights?'

'That's what I said. Wall lights in her front room, and half the time there's nee bulbs in the upstairs. I can hear them groping around through the wall trying to find the bed.' Fran could not hold in her laughter. The picture of Bethel, ear to the wall, listening to the Malones' nocturnal ramblings was irresistible. 'All right, miss ... you have a good laugh, but if this strike keeps up she'll know what's what. You can't eat wall lights.'

Once again Fran was torn by divided loyalties. She loved Bethel and hated to cross her, but the Malones were special too. In their funny, haphazard way they had comforted her in the worst moments after David's death. Michael – no, Mike – she must remember to call him that – had come and gone, cheering Martin, chivvying him, making her laugh. And Brian ...! She reminded herself that dead people must not be elevated to the sainthood. Not straight away, anyway. But the Malone ménage produced happy, well-rounded human beings – in spite of wall lights and importunate clubmen and disapproving neighbours! She decided to speak out but when she looked up, Bethel's eyebrows were jutting ominously. 'I expect they'll manage,' she said sheepishly, and afterwards felt ashamed.

Belgate's decision to join the strike was front-page news in the evening paper. The Union leaders were relieved: '*By voting to strike Belgate is paving the way for the county's miners to speak with one voice for a national ballot.*' The Durham officials were notifying National Executive Headquarters in Sheffield that the Durham men wanted a national ballot as soon as possible. Fran felt a surge of optimism: a national ballot would settle things, one way or another.

Her good cheer was short-lived. A small paragraph revealed that the DHSS were setting up temporary offices to deal with the rush of claims. So somebody somewhere thought it was going to last! An uneasy vision of soup kitchens and hungry children lasted all through tea and put her off her poached egg.

They took Nee-wan for a walk after they'd eaten. Martin ran hither and thither, whooping with delight, an ecstatic dog at his heels. Ice glinted from the rutted track. Winter was unwilling to give up its grip – that should help the strike! Once more she wondered about her own allegiance. They were striking over job losses ... but no one would be losing a job. It would all be done painlessly by voluntary redundancy or moving to other, more productive pits. Lots of men would give their eye-teeth for a chance like that. But if the pit went, if the men were bussed away, what would happen to the village? Would it wither bit by bit until all that was left was a husk?

She had lived in the Durham coalfield all her life without thinking about the pit. Even when they moved to Belgate and she had gone down on a visit, she had seen it as a curiosity, something remote. And then David had died and she had lain sleepless, listening to the miners' footfalls, her mind following them into the cage and down to the caverns and passages, bringing the pit alive for her, building the rhythm of her new and frightening life around it. If they closed it down, she would lose that rhythm, those reassuring footfalls.

'Boo!' Martin leaped out at her from behind a fence and she chased him, laughing, all the way home.

She paused at the Malones' gate while Martin knocked, and asked after Mike. Mrs Malone appeared in the lighted doorway and beckoned. 'Come out of the cold, pet. It'd freeze the brass balls off a monkey.' Inside the single living-room a huge fire burned, an abandoned fire leaping up the chimney. Mr Malone was toasting his socked feet in the hearth and Mike lay on the settee under a quilt. He fell on the comics with cries of joy, and Mrs Malone pressed Fran to a chair. 'I've just brewed up ... it's nee trouble.'

Mr Malone was renewing acquaintance with the dog. 'He's twice the size.' Mrs Malone gazed at them fondly. 'Our Brian loved that dog. He was that pleased when it went to you. If it hadn't been for the cat, it could've stopped here.'

On the windowsill the battered tom closed its eyes in disgust and Fran smiled. 'I wouldn't be without it now.'

Mrs Malone sighed. 'I wonder what our Brian would've made of all this trouble. There's his brother upstairs in a freezing bedroom 'cos he won't share a fire with his own father. And if he does come down, it's a slanging match.'

Mr Malone spoke. 'That's enough now, mother. Mrs Drummond hasn't come here to be entertained to our troubles. Besides, it's a storm in a tea-cup. They'll see sense soon.'

Fran could hear Bethel's voice in the hall as she and Martin let themselves back into the kitchen, and then a tinkle as the phone was replaced. Bethel was rubbing her ear as though contact with the hated instrument had somehow defiled her. 'It was that friend of yours. That Minnie.' Bethel insisted on calling Min after Micky Mouse's partner.

'She'd kill you if she heard that,' Fran said, grinning.

[36]

A trace of a smile crossed the older woman's face. 'Well, she shouldn't call herself after a furniture polish, should she? Any road, she says she'll see you at the hospital. There'll only be you and her there. The husband's laid out apparently. Less than a week of coping on his own, and he's exhausted. What a shame!'

Poor Harold! Fran knew she should stick up for him but she didn't have time. Instead she scampered upstairs to get washed.

Min was already there when she arrived at Eve's private room. It was heady with flowers and festooned with cards, all of them depicting babies with large heads and bright blue eyes. The real baby was remarkably like its paper images, but the eyes were shut. 'He's gorgeous,' Fran said, and wished she could have thought of something original. Unless her memory was failing, that was what she'd said last time.

'You're looking better.' This time her words were sincere. Eve was sitting up now, hair tidied, a trace of lipstick and a powdered nose.

'Min's telling me about Vivienne ... she thinks she's pregnant.'

Fran's spirits lurched. Another baby to be glad about; it would probably be more than she could bear.

'It's your fault, Eve.' Min was peeling herself a grape with perfect scarlet fingernails. 'It's like a disease ... it spreads. One person goes down with it and the rest become broody. Well, it won't strike me!' She reached for another grape. 'I'm never going to be caught in that trap again. I want some fun. There's no earthly reason now why a woman should serve a nine-month sentence for a little bit of fun. No reason at all.'

Fran couldn't put her finger on it but she felt there was some significance in Min's words that was not immediately apparent. She looked across at the bed, but Eve seemed oblivious of any hidden meaning.

'Is the strike over yet, Fran? You're hot from the scene of the crime ... have they seen sense?'

If she made a joke of it the conversation would fizzle out and she wouldn't have to take a stand. For a moment she wavered, but the sardonic tilt of Min's eyebrows tipped the scales. 'No, it's

[37]

not over, Eve. And not likely to be. They've got a grievance ...
well, they feel they've got a grievance ... and they're standing
firm. The Belgate men joined the strike today. They want a
ballot but they're still solid behind the Union.' She was going
over the top with her defence: the Belgate men were not solid for
the strike, they were split in two. But she was not about to tell that
to Eve and Min, not when they were being so smug.

Min removed a pip from her mouth and wiped the corners just
in case. 'They can strike till they're blue, as far as I'm concerned.
We have gas central heating and the cooker's electric. Coal's a
fossil fuel anyway. It's time it was done away with. Then you
could come back here and be sensible.' Min had never forgiven
her for staying in Belgate. 'You could have been in Greenways
now, nicely settled in with ducted heating. Instead you're stuck
out there with that ghastly boiler, surrounded by left-wing
loonies. Well, don't come to me for sympathy.'

Eve detected a note of acrimony and moved to deflect it.
'Would anyone like a cup of tea? They're awfully good here ...
you can have anything you like, within reason.'

While they waited for tea to be brought Fran looked around at
the room. Laura Ashley curtains and the crib trimmed to match.
A television on a swivel stand, and cotton rugs to take away the
hardness of the rubber floors. Treesa's baby would lie on a paper
sheet in a NHS ward, and Treesa would be sent home after
seven days.

She was deflected from the unfairness of life by Eve's voice.
'Did you hear what I said, Fran? We're calling the baby David
Ian. It'll be Ian for everyday use but the David will be there just
the same.'

David, David, help me David. I don't want them to use your
name, to give it to this small, strange alien. Aloud she said,
'That's lovely, Eve. David would have liked that.'

Afterwards, driving to Steve's she tried to gauge her feelings.
They were doing it to please her, to honour their friend, to keep
his memory alive. One day they would tell the baby the origins of
his name, praise David ... that was nice. So why did she feel
such anger? Soon she must sit in the library all day and read

[38]

Freud – and when she had come to a decent understanding of the workings of her mind, she would throw herself under the first passing bus!

The laughter was still on her lips when she reached the flat. 'You look happy,' Steve said and bent to kiss her mouth. She was entitled to this, she reminded herself as she kissed him back. She was an animal, no more – with animal needs and animal desires. As long as she remembered that there was no need to feel ashamed.

He had set the table in style, down to a candle in a brandy snifter. Watching him as he dished up the lasagne, she could see that his face had filled out, there were fewer lines around the eyes, the shoulders were less slumped. She had done that for him. Made him a man again. But what had he done for her?

'Penny for them?' He was looking at her, brows raised.

'Nothing important.' She reached out and covered his hand. She still had the power to bring him down, that was certain, and it must never happen.

They carried their coffee to the fire and switched on the nine o'clock news. Domestic coal stocks were already running down but the power stations were safe. Pressure was building up for a miners' national ballot, but Scargill was standing firm. 'I hate that man,' Fran said and was surprised at her own vehemence.

'It all depends on the triple alliance,' Steve said when they switched off. 'If Scargill reactivates the steel and railway workers, he's got a chance. Without it ... well, spring's on its way, the power stations are stocked to the gunwales – Maggie's seen to that. I think he's in for a hiding. He hasn't even got his own men behind him. North Wales has rejected a strike two to one, Lancashire's split down the middle, the Midlands is three to one against, the Notts men are drifting back, and Derbyshire won't be far behind them ... No, he's had it.'

She still felt self-conscious with his arms around her. Even after he turned on the lamp and doused the centre light, she felt uncomfortable. To ease things she turned in towards him and

[39]

buried her face in his neck, knowing as she did so that it was the wrong thing to do. They moved to the bedroom slowly, unwilling to disentangle, tied together more by embarrassment than ecstasy. 'I love you Fran.' She felt a tenderness for him, an awareness of his vulnerability that made up for lack of passion. He needed her. She moved with him, tailoring her movements to his, trying hard to meet his every requirement. 'I love you, Fran.'

She laid her lips to his forehead, moist now with fulfilment. 'I know, I know.'

While he slept she thought about those magic words, 'I know.' The formula for all situations: 'I know how you feel.' Except that no one ever did. You were alone from the moment of birth, alone in all the things that mattered. When she and David had been together she had believed they were one. She had loved David, really loved him. Now, though, she realized that their love had not been infinite, it had had parameters that had been hidden until his death. Now she loved Steve, even cherished him, but that love too had limitations. Perhaps desire shifted as you moved towards it, so that you never really achieved complete fulfilment. Perhaps that was the secret of the universe, that the goalposts were ambulant. She chuckled silently and smoothed the hair from Steve's forehead. In the darkness the alarm glowed green: 10.30. In fifteen minutes it would be time to take the Belgate road, but meanwhile she would enjoy the comfort of another body breathing close, and try to tell herself that all was well.

4

Saturday, 31 March 1984

'I'm taking the dog out.'

Martin was glued to 'Dr Who'. 'I'll come if you want.'

She declined his reluctant offer and let herself out of the back door. Nee-wan strained at his lead and tugged her towards the allotments. 'Not there,' she said, struggling to restrain him. 'Not when I'm on my own.' It was a dark night, no trace of moon or stars. The orange street lamps glowed through a fine mist of rain. Her hair would frizz, but it didn't matter. There would be time for a bath before she went to Min's and she could use her heated rollers in the steam.

Another 'ghastly girls' night'. Every five minutes, or so it seemed, Min said, 'It's time we had a do.' Sometimes Fran enjoyed them but tonight would be awful. They would all get on about the strike and look at her accusingly, as though she were coal incarnate. 'I live in Belgate, I don't own it,' she'd told Min last week. 'Don't blame *me* for the strike.' But she had thrown in her lot with the miners the day she elected to stay in Belgate. For ever more, Eve and Min would hold her responsible for the price of coal.

And the price was escalating, it said so in the *Echo*. Up 86p a bag in Sunderland, and stocks fast running out. It wasn't just money either: the getting of coal had always exacted a toll in blood, and even with the pits idle that toll continued. A striker had already died on a picket line in Nottingham. According to the papers there was a breakaway group within the Union, and NUM leaders in Durham were under police protection after anonymous threats. The radio said Durham was solid behind the strike, but it wasn't true – Durham was struggling in torment and the strike not a month old. There were mutterings of protest but everyone was watching their tongues. 'It's hateful,' she said out loud to a passing lamp-post, and almost jumped out of her skin when a man loomed out of the mist.

He was trundling a wheelbarrow piled high with wood. To her horror she saw it was saplings, slender young trees chopped off at the base and shorn of branches. He looked at her as they drew level. 'I'm not going without a fire.' His tone was defiant.

She smiled non-committally. 'I expect it'll be over soon.'

His reply was thrown over his shoulder. 'Nee chance! The bugger'll drag on for months.'

Fran stood watching the white-lettered NCB on his donkey jacket until it faded and was lost to view. He was stocking up for a siege! Horror-stricken, she whistled up the dog and turned for home.

She had nearly reached the back gate when she met Treesa on her way to the shop. 'I'll walk along with you.' Treesa was moving awkwardly; breasts had merged with belly, coat buttons strained, her face looked swollen and tired. 'Not much longer now,' Fran said hopefully.

'Eight weeks ... well, eight an' a bit.' The voice was almost tearful and Fran looked at her with concern.

'You're not scared, are you? We go on about it being awful ... well, we have to, don't we? ... but it's not so bad.'

Treesa shook her head. In the lamplight, gleams of mist showed in her hair. 'No ... I'll be glad to get it over.'

Fran felt panic. Perhaps it was grief, plain, unadulterated grief for a dead lover. And if it was, and if Treesa expressed it, how would she, Fran, cope? 'Selfish, selfish bitch!' she told herself. 'Always thinking of yourself.' They walked in silence for a second, and then she took the bull by the unacceptable horns.

'I expect you miss Brian terribly?'

She couldn't look at Treesa but she could feel the quivering lip, the filling eyes. Except that when she turned the eyes were dry, the lips composed. 'I miss him, Mrs Drummond. I expect it'll be worse when the bairn comes – knowing he'll never see it grow up.'

There was only one reply. 'I know.' Somewhere back in time, Neolithic man must have grunted those same all-embracing words.

But Treesa was continuing. 'It's being at me mam's. It's not working out. I'm still sharing with our Dawn and our Mary. There'll be no room for a cot or anything. Me mam's already creating about the nappies and things I'm laying by. I'll have to move out ... I've got me name down with the council but you can wait months.'

'You couldn't go to the Malones, just for the time being? No, of course, they're crowded too.' But willing. What had Mrs Malone said when she first heard of the pregnancy? '*I'm doing out the back room ... our Brian's girl's got a bairn on the way.*' It had

[42]

been a cause for rejoicing then, with Brian alive and earning. Now it was a problem that must be accommodated. 'I hope you find something soon, Treesa. I'll ask Mrs Bethel ... she has her ear to the ground.' The shop doorway was open, spilling light. She followed Treesa inside, unwilling to abandon her just yet.

The shop was run by a husband and wife, together with one or two part-time assistants. Usually it was a hive of activity but to-night the atmosphere was subdued, the faces on both sides of the counter gloomy. Fran recognized the woman being served – she had a daughter in Martin's class, and they had chatted at sports meetings and open days. Botcherby. Angela Botcherby's mother. A bit of a gossip, but nice.

Tonight, though, she kept her head averted, her shoulders hunched. Her hand clutched and unclutched her big leather purse and the knuckles showed white. She was buying sparsely ... two pounds of potatoes, a sliced loaf, two ounces of chopped pork. She eyed some ageing tomatoes, then turned back. Her voice dropped. 'I think that's all ... can you mark them down?'

The shopkeeper was already reaching for his ledger, the 'tick book' about which Bethel was so scathing. He began to write, then looked up. 'You can have those tomatoes half price if you want them. They're not selling. Everyone's in the same boat, pet. I've cancelled the usual order till this lot's settled.'

As Mrs Botcherby eyed the tomatoes again he raised his brows to Fran. 'It's a right carry-on, isn't it, Mrs Drummond? I don't know how they expect us to manage.' His customer's face was scarlet. He leaned forward and patted her hand. 'I don't mean you, pet. You're like the rest of us – puppets. Do this, do that ... Arthur's running round in his Daimler organizing the troops, Maggie's on her high horse, and I'm sitting here watching a good little business go down the drain.'

Mrs Botcherby shrugged, obviously lost for words. Her yellow hair had black roots, the first time Fran had noticed them, and the pores on her cheeks were obvious, stained with rouge. She was packing her purchases into a string bag with fingers that trembled slightly and were brown with nicotine. 'Let me help you,' Fran said, and held open the mouth of the bag.

[43]

Even when Treesa had made her purchases and they were out in the street Fran was remembering Mrs Botcherby. It was all very well for Mrs Thatcher to talk about standing firm. There was room to do that in Downing Street. It was not so easy in the corner shops of the Durham coalfield. 'It's terrible, isn't it?' Treesa said suddenly. 'That's half the trouble in our house. Me mam doesn't know where to turn and it's making her ratty.'

Fran touched Treesa's arm and bit back the sympathetic 'I know' that had rushed to her lips. 'It can't last for ever, Treesa. And I won't forget about somewhere for you ... I'll ask Mrs Bethel tonight. I know the muddle over Brian's compensation is awful but they'll sort it out eventually – and then you can get a proper home.'

As she walked away she thought about her own house. Seven rooms for two people: space to swing a tiger let alone a cat. And Treesa's baby would share one room with three. '*You* could do something about it,' her conscience said tartly ... 'but you won't. You never do.'

The phone was ringing when she came into the kitchen. 'Fran?' She recognized the voice. It was Edward, a fellow-student until he had dropped out of the teaching course at Christmas.

'Hallo, Edward. Nice to hear from you.' Her voice was cautious. Last year, when she had still been reeling from the shock of David's death, Edward had been an assiduous though unwanted suitor. Now she assured him that she and Martin were well, and waited to hear what he had to say. If he asked her out she would plead pressure of work, or tell him Steve had a prior claim.

'I'm ringing with some news ... good news. Perhaps you can guess?' Fran's mind was suddenly running on six cylinders. Linda! Edward and Linda! She had introduced them, and they had seemed to click. Over-protective Edward and poor little Linda, single-parent Linda with money troubles and legs like matchsticks. Poor little Linda whom she, Fran, had vowed to befriend and had later forgotten. And now Edward was going to marry Linda and Fran's guilty conscience could be laid to rest.

[44]

'Oh Edward, I'm so *glad*!' She had never meant anything more.

When she got to college on Monday she would tell Gwen. Dear, comfortable happily married Gwen, who would be the best teacher ever. Her eyes would widen in amazement: 'Edward? Getting married?' Fran realized she was wriggling with pleasure at the thought of Monday. It was lovely to hear a bit of news when it was good news; even lovelier to impart it.

Lying in the bath, she thought about Edward and Linda. Edward was fortyish and middle class, O-levels, insurance policies, the lot! Linda was twenty-seven with not a CSE to her name and a passion for off-licence draught sherry. She had three children hardly out of nappies and a sheaf of unpaid bills, and Edward would revel in his new-found responsibility. But would they love?

She sank lower in the water and pondered love. She had loved David totally. Or so she had thought. Losing him and then meeting Steve had shown her other dimensions – not better dimensions, just different ones. She had adored David, set him on a pedestal. Towards Steve she felt protective, even maternal. But for neither of them had she felt passion – she had only just realized that. Perhaps it didn't exist except in Harold Robbins ... or, sanitized, in Barbara Cartland. She was definitely a Cartland character, knees pressed together, buttoned to the neck. Except for Steve. And adultery! She rested her head on the rim of the bath and thought about Steve, trying very hard not to think about adultery. It was no good. Seizing the loofah, she began to scrub her legs as if by exfoliation she could banish the last lingering trace of sin.

She wore her new shirt for the girls' night – jade polyester crêpe de Chine, and simply cut. She had put on weight in the last few months so her hip bones no longer jutted, but the face in the mirror was still gaunt. Probably always would be, now. She was thirty-three years old, two years off the point of no return, and it was beginning to show. All the same, she felt good as she walked into Min's hall and deposited her bag on the monk's bench. 'You look marvellous, Fran ... fabulous ... now come and see who's here.'

The usual faces turned to smile a welcome. Sally, Valerie, Dot ... no Eve, because she was still recuperating. 'I miss Eve,' Fran thought. Her heart sank as they resumed their chatter and the hum of totally feminine conversation engulfed her. She never got asked to mixed do's now. She was a widow, an oddity, a terrible reminder that marriage might not be for ever, so there were no intimate dinner parties, no groups to play badminton or go dancing ... just ghastly girls' nights, where lepers could be accommodated without too much pain.

Her moral indignation at society's treatment of widows fizzled out as she recalled that in ten years of happy marriage she had not once invited a single woman to her home other than for morning coffee. If she married Steve and was readmitted to the magic circle, she would make sure she changed her ways.

She looked around at the other girls. A bunch of exotic flowers in their boutique clothes, walking adverts for Estée Lauder, who was spreading through the British departmental store like wildfire. She had nothing in common with them now. They spent their days filing their nails and operating their microwaves, waiting for husbands with incipient beer-guts to come home from the office. Only with Eve and Min did she feel a rapport, and that was based more on nostalgia than compatibility. They had been too close as girls to be sundered now.

Min was leading her to a sofa. 'Look who's here ... you remember Margot? I ran into her in town and insisted she come tonight.'

Of course Fran remembered Margot. Manky Margot of the greasy hair and spectacles and the regulation school uniform down to the last durable item. Always top in RK and the last one to get a bra. 'Of course I remember you, Margot. You haven't changed a bit.'

As she sipped her wine she hid a smile. Min had more faces than a town-hall clock. She had never been able to stand Margot, especially since she became a social worker, and presumably had invited her tonight so that she could be suitably stunned by Min's lifestyle.

'Min tells me you live in Belgate?' Margot's eyes were strangely opaque. Contact lenses.

'Yes. We moved there for David's work, and after he died I decided to stay.'

Margot nodded. 'I heard about David. I was so sorry. He was nice.'

Fran wanted to feel grateful to Margot but she couldn't. Her condolences had a professional touch to them, like a key sliding into a well-oiled lock. 'You must feel very involved with the strike,' Margot was continuing, a note of envy in her voice. 'Have you made contact with the women's support group?'

Fran shook her head. 'I don't think we have one. As a matter of fact . . .'

She never got a chance to tell Margot that no one in Belgate was keen on the strike, for Margot was launched, riding on waves of enthusiasm. 'It's so marvellous to see them making a stand beside their men. I'm doing my bit of course . . . I can put you in touch with their fund-raisers if you haven't got the address. Someone has to call a halt to this government. Not that it'll be easy. They've made very sure of the police; they're up to all those tricks. It's economic nonsense to close pits. When we wake up to the dangers of nuclear power we'll need coal. There's no such thing as an uneconomic pit . . . investment, that's all it takes . . .'

'She doesn't know what she's talking about,' Fran thought, letting the tirade wash over her. Pits got old and tired, ceased to be fertile and bring forth. But Belgate's was safe, hardly middle-aged even. Sunk in 1928 – that was no time at all.

'They've established a worker's collective at Barfield . . . we've promised total support . . . total. They must stand firm!'

'*No matter what the cost!*' Fran was thinking about the corner shop, strain on both sides of the counter and two ounces of chopped pork to give protein. 'I must see if Min needs a hand,' she said, rising to her feet. Yesterday she had seen *Scab* painted white on a gable end – like a war-time newsreel: '*Juden*'. Only a word, scrawled large. Only a word, but deadlier than a knife-thrust.

[47]

They were talking about sex in the kitchen, uninhibited because Eve was not there to disapprove. Fran busied herself with the cups and saucers, and smiled non-committally from time to time. In an hour or two she could escape to the car, drive back to Belgate, sit for five minutes in the car-park and watch the moon on the water, the lights at the pit-head. Pretend there was no strike, no ripple on the suface. '*Please God, let it be over soon.*' If it went on, she would have to take sides, form opinions, stand up for her beliefs. Panic stirred ... and then Min was bearing down on her, exuding Madame Rochas and self-satisfaction in equal proportions. 'What did you think of her, Fran? That hair! She had it landscaped by Incapability Brown. And the brooch is a gallstone, I swear it!'

5

Monday, 2 April 1984

'It'll never work.' Gwen licked in the last morsel of chocolate pudding and shook a regretful head. 'Edward'll organize the poor girl until she can't take any more, and then she'll put prussic acid in his muesli and be up for manslaughter.'

Fran grinned. 'We could give evidence. "She was driven to it, m'lud ..."' She was about to expand her performance when shame overtook her. 'No, Gwen, we're being mean. There's a lot about Edward to admire. He'll never let her down ... and he'll do his best for the kids ... and anyway, Linda's nobody's fool.'

Gwen's eyes lit up. 'Perhaps she'll organize him. Turn the tables. Oh, I'd like to be around to see that.'

Once more Fran's conscience smote her. Edward had shown nothing but kindness to her ... and to Martin too. 'He wasn't really bossy, Gwen. He was trying to be protective.'

Gwen's eyes rolled in pain. 'Fran, you can't have forgotten! He was the bitter end. We used to sit in this refectory and will him to sit at another table. And it never worked. He nearly drove you crazy with his attentions, and almost put me off teacher-training for life. If he hadn't left when he did, I'd have been in jail now for GBH.' Her face softened. 'Still, he did have his good points. I used to borrow his notes sometimes if I missed things, and all the lecturers used to pick on him so we got off scot-free. But better Linda than me. Actually, it's quite brave of him to take on someone else's kids. Lots of men wouldn't.'

Fran bit down on her cracker, trying not to show she minded, but Gwen was too quick. 'Come on, why the hurt face? Anyone would be willing to take on Martin, he's a pet. Besides, he's almost grown-up. He'll be off and away before you know it.'

Usually Gwen was tact personified but today she seemed to be losing her touch. 'I don't want him to be off and away. I know it'll happen, but that doesn't mean I want it to.'

Gwen burped gently and tugged at her waistband. 'God, I've got to stop eating. I'm frightened to get on the scales. Lewis ... all ten stone of him ... keeps saying it's my nature to be plump. If I ever leave him, I'll cite that as unreasonable behaviour. Anyway, enough of me.' She patted her midriff. 'More than enough of me.' She raised her coffee cup. 'Here's to good old Edward – may he live happily ever after. And may Linda be given the strength to endure it!'

They talked about the respective strengths of Edward and Linda until it was time to gather up their books and head for the next lecture. 'You put me off, telling me the news about Edward,' Gwen said as they settled in their seats; 'I meant to ask about the war zone. Are they fighting in the streets yet? Lewis says there's a steady drift back in the Midlands ... p'raps it'll be over soon?'

As she half-listened to a dissertation on the teaching methods of Montessori, Fran thought about the strike. Belgate seemed quiet now that all the men had come out. There was only a token picket and apart from the odd rumble about Fenwick everyone seemed to be bearing up. But there was strain beneath the surface. Yesterday she had waited in the bank as man after man queued to cancel his standing orders. Cars and mortgages and finance-company loans were all suspended, pending a return to

[49]

work. As each one had finished his business and turned away she had seen bewilderment in his eyes, and anger, and the beginnings of fear.

There was a group of miners outside the pit as she drove home, huddled in the gateway, woollen-hatted and mufflered against the cold, but still shivering. A tattered banner proclaimed *Coal not dole* and someone had sprayed *Maggie out* on the left-hand gatepost. It was a relief to leave them behind and drive into the back street. Here, at least, normality reigned.

'I'm dying for a cuppa,' she said as she entered the kitchen.

'It's already masting.' Bethel's tone was smug. She loved being one step ahead. 'Get that down you,' she said as she pushed forward the cup. Her tone implied that this was the good news, the bad news was to come. 'You're out of coke. As good as, anyway.'

Fran sighed. 'How many days left?'

Bethel grimaced. 'Two ... three if you damp it well down. And there's none to be got – folk cannat get a fire, never mind central heating. There'll be power cuts an' all, if the deputies come out.'

Fran groaned. NACODS, the deputies' union, were meeting on Friday. If they decided to come out, the strike would be 100 per cent effective. Not even safety work could take place without a deputy present. 'Don't fret yersel',' Bethel said, drawing on her cigarette. 'They're only holding a meeting, an' that'll be hot air.'

'Do you think they'll come out?' Fran asked.

'Nee chance. They'll sit on the fence till their bums grow corns. Oh, they'll huff and puff, but they'll not give up their pay ... not that lot. Too many airs and graces to keep up.'

'I suppose you can't blame them,' Fran said. 'It's easy for us to talk, but it can't be easy for any of them to decide ... one way or another.'

Bethel's snort spoke volumes. 'It wouldn't take me long. They had a rule book ... if they'd stuck to that, they could've decided the way they've always done: by the ballot box. Still, they'll learn the hard way. Some of them's seen the light already. Fenwick's going back on Monday if they haven't fixed up for a ballot.'

Fran shook her head. 'I suppose he's desperate. He won't qualify for social security, will he ... not having any dependants? But he can hardly go back by himself. They won't let him.'

'He says they won't stop him ... he's always been a peaceable lad but his dander's up now. You don't persuade a man like Fenwick with rough stuff.' As Martin came through the door, demanding instant heat and food, Fran remembered the day she had seen Fenwick on the cliffs, a pigeon-basket strapped to his pillion, a smile on his face because he was out in the open air to fly his beloved birds. And now he was girding his loins for a fight with his marrers. Truly the world had gone mad!

When he had changed his shoes and raided the biscuits, Martin went off to watch TV, Nee-wan devotedly at his heel. 'More tea? I've watered the pot.'

Bethel pushed forward her cup. 'I shouldn't but I will. Have you seen Treesa lately? By, she has a poor look. The sooner her time comes the better ... though how she'll bring a bairn up in that house I'll never know. She's holding water, you can see it in her face. I never like that in a lass. Aye, it's easy enough makkin' bairns but carrying them's different.'

The *Echo* plopped through the letter-box. 'More good news,' the old woman said with sarcasm. 'You want to stop that paper before it cheers you up!'

As she collected the paper, Fran looked in on Martin. 'What do you want for tea?'

'Anything. Except sausage and beans.' Last week sausage and beans were the only things he would eat, and she had laid in a store.

'Oh God, the joys of motherhood,' she said and reached for the eggs.

There was a sudden toot from outside the door. 'That's Walter.' Bethel made no move.

'Let him in,' Fran said. Bethel's boyfriend was an impatient man.

'Hold on,' Bethel cautioned. 'He wants us to rush to the door, then he'll drive away just to show who's boss.'

[51]

Fran grinned. 'What shall we do, then?'

Bethel folded her arms across her chest. 'Sit tight.'

A few moments later there was a shout from the door. 'Howay, let me in. You pay a visit, you ask for a bit help, and you get ignored.'

Bethel was arming the wheelchair over the step. 'If I'd come when you called, Walter, you'd have buzzed off round the block leaving me on the pavement like a tin of milk.'

His howl was anguished. 'Me? Now I know you're senile, Sally. I've never done a thing like that in my life.'

She had lifted off his cap and was tugging at his muffler. 'You want to think on what you're saying, Walter. God's listening.'

Fran cracked more eggs into the bowl. Having Bethel and Walter here was the best thing she knew. 'Will you stay to tea?'

The bushy eyebrows shot towards the hairline. 'If it's not begrudged. If you'll keep this geriatric hooligan off me back. If I get a cup of tea that's not stewed.'

Bethel passed him a cup and he drained it. 'It's a bit past it, but it'll do.'

A heavy sigh issued from Bethel. 'One of these days you'll say something's all right and I'll drop dead of shock.'

Walter's grin was wicked. 'That's why I grumble, Sally. I want to keep you healthy.'

'I love them,' Fran thought as she tipped up the pot. 'I love having them here arguing, fighting, scoring points.' When they were here they filled the house, made it a home again.

Bethel moved to set the table and Walter accepted a second cup. 'Hear the news?' His tone was sombre. 'There's a Wheatley Hill lad tossed hisself in front of a train. They reckon he got punched at the club last night 'cos he wanted to work. The poor bit lad was saving up to get wed, and she was the ambitious type. Well, he's out of it now, poor bugger.'

Fran turned the first omelette on to a plate and put it in the warming oven. 'How long is it going to last, Walter?'

He shook his head. 'As long as it takes, bonny lass.'

Bethel bridled. 'Listen to that. "As long as it takes" – never mind the worry and the pain of it, never mind the suicides, as long as you score points. No wonder the young 'uns is daft, if you can't get sense from an old man.'

Fran intervened. 'I wish you'd explain something to me, Walter. The rule book says there must be a ballot before there can be a strike. There *hasn't* been a ballot but the men *are* on strike. How can that be?'

Walter's fingers plucked at the tartan rug that covered his knees. 'Aye, well, there you are ...'

Before he could continue, Bethel chortled. 'Hit you on a sore point, has she, Walter? You're as upset about the ballot as anyone, but you try to put a good face on it. Why don't you tell the truth?'

He glared at her for a moment, then his jaw came up and he turned to Fran. 'It's like this ... listen and take it in 'cos I'm not saying it again. The NUM's a federation. Each area's separate but they come together in a federation. So you can have a national ballot ... countrywide. Or an area ballot, in your individual coalfield ... or a lodge ballot. That's at the pit-head.' He looked round, daring them to question.

'Go on then,' Bethel said. 'Finish off.'

He held up his hands, strong from manoeuvring the wheels of his chair. 'Well, that's it ... they had lodge ballots ...'

Bethel let out a howl of triumph. 'And they voted not to strike. Come on, say it!'

Walter hit the wheels of his chair, causing it to buck. 'Shut up, you silly old woman. I'm coming to that. They voted not to strike, but then they changed their minds.'

Fran could stay silent no longer. 'Because they were lied to, Walter. The Union men promised to press for a ballot if they came out. But then they didn't ... they voted *against* a ballot. They broke their word!'

Walter adjusted his rug. 'It wasn't exactly like that ... they had a delegate conference ... oh, I'm not going on with this! Am I getting fed or not? Just say.'

Fran served up the omelettes, chattering brightly to cover his confusion. She knew what he was so shy of saying. The delegate conference had over-ruled the wishes of the miners. The men

[53]

had not been given their traditional right to decide, and no amount of huffing and puffing could disguise it. Even Bethel seemed to sense that she had drawn blood. Honour satisfied, she was prepared to talk amicably, her subject Martin's wish to eat in front of the TV.

'Aye, times is different now. It's another world. We had time in the old days. Leisure? This lot don't know the meaning of the word. We had days out in the hay-field, your bait in a tea-towel. Down the beach round a driftwood fire ... They're like yo-yos now – if they move too far from the telly the elastic snaps them back.'

Fran nodded. 'I know what you mean. And yet there never seems to be enough time.' The absence of time in a world of mod-cons had long puzzled her.

Bethel nodded. 'Two days a week we washed – round the poss tub all Monday, starching and ironing Tuesdays. No drip dry, no permanent pleats, no steam irons. Just Robin Starch and a good flat-iron. Now all they do's press buttons, and they're still running to catch up.'

Walter laid his knife and fork on his empty plate and wiped his mouth with a spotless hanky. 'Aye, you're right, Sally. It's nowt like the old days. No means test, no workhouse, no diphtheria, no standpipes on the corner, no night-soil men to empty the privies. The march of progress has a lot to answer for.'

Bethel turned to Fran. 'Ignore him, he's addled. The trouble today is, no one waits for anything any more. It's all live in advance. You can get everything on tick, so they're up to their necks in debt. It's the new disease round here, credit. And more money lenders than garden gates. They get loans at 60 per cent, and hand their family allowance books over.'

Fran was horrified. 'That's illegal!'

Bethel smirked. 'There you go ... it can't be true because it's illegal. It's a fact, miss. They live on the never-never and the very first week their man doesn't make bonus, the whole world falls to bits.'

As she washed up, Fran thought of Bethel's words. It was true. If you lived on weekly pay your world did fall apart in the first week of deprivation. Mrs Botcherby was proof of that. If you were salaried, you were cushioned for a little while. Nothing had really changed in the weeks after David's death, except for Harold's constant reminders that she must cut her spending.

The rates bill, tucked out of sight behind the clock, sprang into her mind's eye. If she paid it in full, even with the rebate, she would have nothing left. Well, almost nothing. The upkeep of the house was beyond her: Harold had said it from the outset, and he was right. Bloody Harold! It was a relief when the phone rang and interrupted her thoughts.

'How was your day?' Steve sounded weary.

'OK. How was yours?'

His day had been quiet. No actual sales, two prospective customers. 'Though I doubt if they'll clinch. No money, that's the trouble. No one has cash for the deposit. Did you see the paper yesterday? Sunderland's in line for EEC help as a poverty-stricken region – there's something to be proud of.'

Fran was taken aback at the bitterness of his tone. 'I'm telling you, Fran, Tyne and Wear's near the bottom of the European prosperity table, so if we bow and scrape nicely we'll be thrown a few pennies. Not that I care, as long as some of the loot comes my way.'

She tried to cheer him. 'I'll miss you tonight.' They had agreed not to meet that evening, but if he asked her, she would go.

'Well, mustn't keep you,' he said. 'I expect you've got piles of work.'

She put down the phone and sat on the bottom stair, hugging her knees. Did she love Steve? Or he her? Did she know him? Or he her? They conversed, they coupled, but did they comprehend? At last, weary of speculation, she rose to her feet and returned to the washing up.

6

Saturday, 7 April 1984

Martin's interest in shopping flagged after five minutes. If David had been alive he would have taken him to the park to see the crocuses, or even the football match. Sunderland were locked in yet another relegation struggle; father and son could have gone along to give support. Briefly she wondered if she should go herself and make an effort, but it didn't take a moment to decide against the idea. She would be terrified in a football crowd. The first shout of 'Howay the lads' and her knees would go! She would just have to file football away for the moment and hope for a miracle. That was what Sunderland football club were always hoping for, so it was quite appropriate.

'Do you remember Linda?' she asked as they sat in Dunn's, having pastries and fizzy drinks.

'Carl and Damian's mam?'

Fran nodded. 'And Debbie ... you remember Debbie?'

He wrinkled his nose. 'She's a girl.'

Fran pulled a face in return. 'That's not a crime ... not any more. Anyway, she's getting married – Linda, I mean. To Edward. You remember Edward?' This time Martin just grinned and Fran felt herself blush. So he had been aware of her feelings towards Edward.

'He was OK,' Martin said condescendingly. 'I expect they'll get on.'

While she told him about the cheeseboard she had bought as an engagement present, Fran pondered that last remark. What would he have said if she had suggested she and Steve might marry – '*I expect we'll get on*'? Or would the bottom lip have jutted, the brows come down? He was growing up and she could not be sure of his reactions.

By mutual agreement they called on Linda. The stairs were

still steep and dark, the carpet paper-thin, but Linda was strikingly different. Her face had filled out, the long hair was ear-length now and curled about her face. 'Fran! Come on in, we were only talking about you last night. And Martin ... wait till Debbie sees you. She'll go berserk.'

Fran looked apprehensively at Martin but he looked quite chuffed and certainly able to take adoring toddlers in his stride.

When the children had grouped round the toys, she settled with Linda on the settee, both of them clutching mugs of coffee – bone china instead of pottery with 'Oxo' on them, so Edward was already making his presence felt. 'I'm so happy for you Linda. And Edward. It'll be nice for him to have a family again.'

Linda grimaced. 'There's no "again" about it. He never had a family, as far as I can make out.' So Linda knew about Edward's unhappiness. It was funny, but Fran had never thought he would tell Linda about his mother's death. As if Linda had read her thoughts, she spoke. 'He didn't tell me, you know. Not a word. It was his cousin. She's really nice ... a bit posh, but you can't hold that against people.' She grinned and patted Fran's arm. 'You're a bit posh, but you're OK. Any road, she told me his mam always idolized his brother, had no room for Edward. Then his brother got ill and died, and she killed herself – as though Edward didn't matter. I'm not much of a mother, Fran, but I wouldn't do that to a dog, let alone one of the bairns. Did you know about it?'

Fran nodded. 'Someone told me. Yes, it was awful; but she must have been sick. It's not as though Edward wasn't a good son – according to this friend of mine, he idolized his mother. And he's a good friend. I never meant to let so much time slip by before I saw you both again. We were expecting Edward back at college after Christmas...'

Linda nodded. 'He was coming back ... I mean he was keen on teaching ... but this job came up that was too good to miss. Not his old trade: he's in insurance now. So he took it.'

It was Fran's turn to nod. 'I'm sure it was for the best.' Edward had been a fish out of water on the teaching-course but this was not the time to say so. Anyone who criticized Edward, however slightly, would probably be hung, drawn and quartered by his wife-to-be.

'We heard about that young lad,' Linda said. 'The one who was dancing at your party. It was such a shame ... dying like that in the pit. How's his girl-friend? Has she had the baby?' They talked about Brian Malone's death and Treesa's baby, and agreed that Treesa had a hard row to hoe. 'Being a single parent is hell on earth,' Linda said. 'No other word for it. Hell on earth.'

Fran's voice was rueful. 'Well, you won't have to endure it much longer.' If she had had patience with Edward she might be making wedding arrangements herself now, preparing to load half the burden of single parenthood on to a willing shoulder. Except that you couldn't marry where you didn't love. It never worked. Did Linda know that? Or was she scheduled to find out the hard way?

Fran looked round the room. The moquette three-piece suite was still shiny, but there were new velvet scatter-cushions on it and a thick pile rug at the hearth. Edward must have bought them to give comfort to the bare room. She looked at Linda. Still thin with yard-long legs, but the tension had gone from her face, her bones no longer jutted like prows. 'She's happy,' Fran thought, and was faintly mortified by the discovery.

'Have a tab?' Linda said, proffering a packet of Benson and Hedges.

'I've given up,' Fran said; 'too expensive.'

Linda nodded. 'I know. I'm trying. It worries Edward ... not the money, but I'm a bit chesty. I've told him I'll pack them in when I get the wedding over. Wedding! Even the word makes me mouth go dry.' She looked at Fran. 'What are you smiling about?'

Fran shook her head. 'Nothing. I've just noticed your bullfight poster's gone.' What had she said to Gwen last year when she had introduced Edward to Linda and seen them click? '*I bet he takes down the El Cordobes.*'

'See you in church,' Linda trilled as the Mini drew away. The children clutched Martin until the last minute and had to be forcibly detached. 'I think they like you,' Fran said, and received a smug 'I know they do,' in return.

Nee-wan was ecstatic when they let themselves into the house. 'Steady on,' Fran said, trying to keep her tights away from his raking claws. 'We've only been to Sunderland, not Australia.' They put him on the lead and set off through the dusk, pulled behind a dog mad for freedom. 'I think he likes living with us,' Martin said.

Fran puffed. 'As long as we're doing what he wants. I know some boys like that!'

Martin ignored the jibe. They had reached the safety zone, the dog could be let off the lead, and boy and dog ran, whooping, into the blackness.

After a moment Fran's eyes adjusted to the dark, and familiar shapes appeared. Light was reflected from puddles and glinting cold frames, even the occasional greenhouse. The fences around the allotments were cobbled together from whatever had come to hand, railway sleepers and old doors, corrugated iron and chicken wire. As she passed one plot she heard the soft cluck of hens disturbed by Nee-wan's presence. There was something about a new-laid egg, brown and dirty and feather-strewn – something safe. Except for cholesterol. Bugger the experts – sooner or later they'd destroy the enjoyment of everything!

They had turned for home and were nearly back to the street lamps when they saw Terry Malone in the distance, hands in pockets, shoulders hunched. Since the strike he seemed to be always walking the streets. To get out of the house and away from his father presumably.

'It's a cold night, Terry.'

His face in the lamplight was pinched. 'Aye, Mrs Drummond, I think winter's set to stay. Someone wants to tell the bugger it's spring-time.' He fell in beside her. 'Have you heard about Treesa?'

Fran's heart lurched. 'There's nothing wrong, is there?'

He shrugged. 'She's in hospital. They talked a lot of stuff about tension – blood pressure and all that...'

Fran comprehended. 'Hypertension, was that it?'

'Aye, that's it. Any road, she has to stop in bed. Her mam

wasn't keen, so me mam said she could lie up at our place, but there's no rest there ... not with a houseful of bairns. So the hospital took her in. It's all for the best, I suppose. Her mam's a bundle of nerves, what with the strike an' all.'

'It'll be a good job when it's over.' Fran's tone was tentative, for Terry was nothing if not militant; but his reply was cheerful.

'It won't be long now, Mrs Drummond, not with the deputies balloting. Once they're out, that's it.' He seemed to have no doubt that the deputies would vote for a strike; no sense of the irony of men denied a ballot of their own being so dependent on the ballot of others.

'Give my love to Treesa,' she said when they parted. 'I'll go in and see her myself before long.'

She would go in. Sunderland was a long way off if you didn't have a car and she could easily pop in one evening before she met Steve.

She collected the *Echo* from the doormat and glanced quickly through it. She was meeting Steve at 8.15 and time was running out.

NUPE was calling nurses into the picket lines and there was the usual controversy in the letters column. According to one writer, striking miners had only struck so they could carry bags of logs to coalless OAPs. Another letter blamed the whole thing on a 'vociferous minority'. But it was the account of the Kent men's march on the Nottinghamshire coalfield that took Fran's attention. The march had begun at Dover four days before, and would reach Nottinghamshire on Friday. The former general secretary of the Kent NUM explained, *'We are marching into the Midland coalfield to defend jobs. We removed Heath in 1974. Now is the time to remove Thatcher.'* Was he defending jobs or pursuing a political aim? Or were they one and the same? Not that it really mattered about the aims: Belgate and other villages like it were being crucified, and nothing could justify that.

Steve was waiting for her in the Saracen. He shook his head when she told him about Treesa. 'Poor kid. She needs a man and

[60]

a settled home, that'd do more for her blood pressure than a stay in hospital. It makes you wonder...'

Something in his tone made her look at him sharply. 'You think she was wrong to keep this baby?'

The shaking of his head was vehement. 'I never said that. But it's not straightforward, is it? Kids were meant to come into a happy home with two parents. Sometimes it can't be helped – take you and me – but if you have a choice...'

Fran felt chilled, too chilled to point out that Treesa's pregnancy had been advanced when Brian died, or that she had loved him and probably wanted to bear his child. Too chilled to say that babies were lovely and well worth any amount of suffering, and that she would change places with Treesa right now. She had done nothing about contraception, and infertility was fickle protection.

What if she were pregnant? Would Steve marry her or give her another little speech about abortion?

The thought niggled all the way back to the flat and lay between them in the bed. It was only banished when another more uncomfortable thought came to oust it. 'That was good, Fran.' He lay on his face, his arm heavy across her belly. 'Good for you too?' She squeezed his arm in reply. 'I wish you didn't have to go home. It spoils things.'

She spoke indulgently. 'I have to go home ... I live there.'

Suddenly he was sitting up, reaching for her. 'That's what I mean. You should live here, you and Martin.'

She kept her tone light but her mind was hitting the fan. 'Are you proposing to make an honest woman of me?' How would she tell Martin? Face other people? Face David on the Day of Judgement? Would he be good to David's child? He loved his own children to distraction, but would Martin equal them? Questions. Always questions.

He whispered, 'I suppose I am,' against her ear, and she turned it into a joke.

'I never accept proposals on Saturday. Ask me again on May the 32nd.'

He seemed happy enough to end the conversation there, and

suddenly she was peeved. What sort of proposal fizzled out when treated with frivolity? And what sort of a woman froze with fear at such a proposal and then took offence when it was not pursued.

The questions stayed with her. 'Frances Mary Drummond, you don't improve,' she said as she swung the car towards Belgate and saw the moon's path on the water as clear as the road ahead.

7

Wednesday, 2 May 1984

She could see the figure through the swishing wipers, head down, inadequately clad against the driving rain. She would have to pick it up, him or her. Thoughts of knives driven into drivers' sides intruded, but you couldn't leave a dog out on the open road on a day like this. As she slowed and drew level, she saw it was a woman. 'Mrs Botcherby ... what are you doing out here in this weather? Get in!'

The woman stood for a moment, apparently uncertain. Rain streamed down her face, her yellow hair was moulded to her head on either side of the black untouched roots. 'Get in!' Fran's voice was uncertain now, the situation beyond her. Mrs Botcherby put a hand to the door, then bent into the seat.

It was better with the door closed and the noise of the rain diminished. 'Are you going home?' Dignity was beginning to reassert itself; Mrs Botcherby had taken the sodden scarf from her neck and was wiping her face.

'Yes. Stafford Street. The end of the street'll do.' There was no gratitude, no explanation of her presence on the road between Belgate and Sunderland, inadequately clad, without handbag or head covering. Her bare legs steamed in the warm air from the heater and she stroked them with fingernails bitten to the quick. It was no time for polite questions and Fran kept her mouth shut.

She drove right up to the Botcherbys' door, half-way down a sloping terrace. She knew it was the Botcherby home because Angela was on the doorstep, soaked cotton dress protruding from a sodden anorak. She peered at the approaching car and then scampered back into the house, reappearing behind her father. He too was rain-soaked, a muffler crossed over his chest, his face drawn. 'Where've you been, lass? We've been frantic.' His eyes flicked to Fran and he smiled. 'Thanks for bringing her back. The lads are out looking; I had to come back to see Angela.' The nine-year-old, suddenly mature, had taken her mother's hand and was leading her into the house. Relief broke on the man's face. 'I thought ... well, never mind what I thought. She's back. Where was she?'

'Out on the Sunderland road. Did she miss the bus?' Damn you, Frances; still trying to keep the lid on things! Mr Botcherby's face closed as quickly as it had opened. He had been glad to see Fran, now he wanted rid of her. 'Aye, well, thanks very much.' He peered into her face. 'It is Mrs Drummond, isn't it? We know your lad, he's in our Angela's class. Well, thanks for bringing her home, I'd best be getting in ...' He paused, feeling something else was needed. 'It's this strike, you see – she takes things very serious, always has. Money's short, things have to go ... we're all in the same boat, I tell her, but she takes no notice. Any road, we'll have the doctor in. He'll give her something to tide her over ...'

Long after she had driven away Fran could see Mrs Botcherby's face in her mind's eye, blank almost vacant, except for the agitated eyes. The sight of that face had been almost as upsetting as the sight of Angela, old before her time, leading her mother into the house.

She called in at the corner shop on her way home, running from the car, her handbag held over her head to protect her hair. The bell jangled a welcome but the shop-keeper's face was sombre. 'Nobody's got any money, Mrs Drummond.' He was scooping potatoes into the scales. 'Every time that bell jangles, it's someone wanting tick – or else it's a support group wanting handouts. I'd like to say "Get lost", but I'd only lose me windows. So I shell out. I just hope I can keep going till they see sense.'

Fran looked around the shelves for something else she needed – anything to promote a little cash trade.

'Don't get me wrong, Mrs Drummond, I think they've got a case. Coal not dole. It'd be different if there was jobs for them to go to ... but there's nothing but the pits round here, is there? Not a blessed thing.' She bought two pounds of sugar and a quarter of PG Tips. You could never have too much tea and sugar.

'Never mind, love,' he said as she left the shop. 'It'll be over soon, and I'll be killed in the rush.'

'You know I'm going out tonight?' she said as they ate tea.

Martin nodded, eyes fixed on the screen. 'To an engagement party, I know ... you've told me twice.'

The invitation had come out of the blue: '*We've decided to have a small gathering, a few close friends ...*' Edward was trying to be nonchalant but she'd sensed the underlying excitement. 'Don't let him down, Linda. Please, please don't let him down,' she thought. She had bought them a cheeseboard as an engagement gift, flower-strewn melamine with a gilt ribbon through the handle. It lay, gift wrapped, on the hall-table, along with the card of congratulations. It was nice to be celebrating something.

She wanted to visit Treesa tonight, so there was only time for a quick skim through the evening paper as she dried the tea dishes. Howls of protest from the NCB about the American coal order, the first from the US in ten years. If Durham coal stocks remained strike-bound, the order would be lost. 'Fed-up Striker' wrote that the silent majority was suffering, and he wished it had the guts of the Notts miners; 'Fair Play' said Labour had closed pits but hadn't paid a pensioner to do it. Well, he had a point there! 'Back to Work' gave statistics: from 1960 to February 1984, ninety-five pits had closed in County Durham, fifty-five of them under Labour, forty under the Conservatives. With friends like those who needed enemies, he asked, and ended with a plea to buy British. £2 saved on a shirt meant the dole queue for someone. Fran looked guiltily at the tea-towel she was holding, nervous of seeing a 'Made in Taiwan' label. You could never be sure nowadays, not even when there was a Union Jack on the packet.

She turned the page. Durham's member on the National Executive was appealing to miners not to ring the Coal Board's redundancy hot-line: '*You are giving the NCB propaganda to under-mine morale.*' The suds were settling on the washing-up water and Fran's spirits were sinking too. If everybody left the pits, what price Belgate? Some villages in Durham already had 21 per cent unemployed. If the pits went, that figure would soar. Suddenly another item caught her eye – the Northern director of ACAS was warning against too much optimism on the jobs front!

Treesa's was the only unvisited bed in the ward, hers the only locker without a bouquet of spring flowers. She lay, eyes closed as though to shut out the attentive fathers and doting parents. 'Hello, Treesa.' Fran laid magazines and fruit on the jacquard counterpane.

'Mrs Drummond! I'm glad you came in.'

Fran drew a chair closer to the bed and sat down. 'How are you feeling?'

Beneath the counterpane there was a baby, boy or girl, arched in the foetal curve. Fran felt a sense of longing so intense that she had to shake her head to get rid of it. 'No, it's all right, Treesa. I'm OK. A bit of a dizzy spell, that's all. Now tell me about yourself.'

Lying there in the metal bed, Treesa looked even younger than her years. And clean. Amazing how people in hospital always looked so clean. 'So if you could take it, Mrs Drummond ... just until I get back home?' Treesa was worried about the layette, the things she had put by for the baby. 'There's that many bairns you see ... and me mam doesn't have much control. They'll have everything out and on their dolls if I'm not careful, and it's not as if I've got much ...'

Fran left, promising to collect the layette the next day. 'You're

[65]

sure your mam won't mind?'

'Why, no, Mrs Drummond ... she'll be pleased to see the back of it.'

Fran was out in the hospital car-park before she realized they had never talked about Brian. He had fathered Treesa's baby, provided the vital spark ... now he was shut out of their conversation for no greater crime than that of dying. 'Brian Malone,' she said out loud to the driving mirror, as though by speaking out she could redress the wrong.

The engagement party was being held at Linda's and Fran rather admired Edward for that. His own house in Queen's Crescent was a spacious three-bedroom semi. The old Edward would have jibbed at inviting his friends to Linda's threadbare flat. Or would he? Had she credited him with a snobbishness he did not possess, as she had credited him with so many other small defects? She was still trying to decide as she mounted the narrow stairs and held out her gift to her waiting hosts.

It was a lovely party. Edward's friends and relations seemed genuinely pleased at his new-found happiness and Linda's, relieved that at last she was out of the wood. 'She's done all right for herself this time,' one portly uncle confided. 'He was a bad 'un, that first husband of hers. Good for nowt but makkin' bairns. This one's a gentleman, you can tell from his shoes.'

It all came down to shoes in the end, Fran thought as she drove home. What had the sociology tutor said? '*You can always tell what sort of home a child comes from by the state of its shoes.*' And you were still being judged when you were turned forty and gone grey at the temples. All the same, it had been a happy evening. They had toasted the engaged couple and Edward had clutched Linda by the waist in a proprietory gesture and received a smacking kiss for his pains. 'I'm dead scared about the ceremony,' Linda had confided in the kitchen as they made a hasty second batch of sandwiches. 'I want to do it properly.' Fran had promised to procure a book on wedding etiquette and act as a consultant on protocol. 'You know about these things,' Linda had said trustingly. 'I knew you were classy as soon as I laid eyes on you.' They had laughed then about the 3 Rivers Social Club where they had met, and the Sybil Fawlty figure who ran it. '"I just need some per-ficks,"' Linda mimicked, and stuck out her flat chest to emulate Sybil's pouter-pigeon boobs.

Fran was driving along the coast now, the beach silver in the moonlight, the tide a white ribbon at its edge. She would have liked to stop the car and run barefoot along the sand to watch the sea-coalers filling their sacks at the tide-line, but she was scared of the deserted beach at night and the sea-coalers were gone, banished by the strike. Her eyes flicked to the dashboard clock: 11.30. In normal times tub-loading would just have begun, the night-shift men would be ascending in the cage. She put thoughts of the strike firmly out of her mind. It only made her miserable, and she needed to keep cheerful for what must be done before she went to bed.

'*It's not as though I have that much.*' Those words of Treesa's had haunted her all evening. Brian Malone's baby was coming into the world in style if she, Frances Drummond, had anything to do with it. When Bethel had handed over the reins and gone home, she went into her bedroom and kneeled down by the otto-man. Inside were those baby clothes of Martin's she had saved for a second baby, and the items she had bought from time to time while she prayed for another child. She fingered the voile and viyella, the broderie anglaise and terry towelling that had made up the fabric of her hopes. When she had repacked them in a case for Treesa, she put her head against the ottoman's padded lid and cried.

8

Tuesday, 5 June 1984

'And it's there in the window. It is, it really is,' Martin said as though he expected her not to believe him.

'What does it say?' She was peeling potatoes for lunch but she dried her hands and sat down at the kitchen table. As he quoted she realized the notice was imprinted on Martin's mind. '*To whom it may concern. If the strike is not settled by Monday 18 June I will be going in*. That's all ... and it's signed *W. Fenwick*. Someone's already smashed the window, and he's taped it up with sticking plaster. And Mike says if he scabs they'll expel him from the union, and that means he'll be finished.'

The child's eyes were gleaming with excitement and Fran felt a sudden distaste. 'Well, I think it's awful, darling – a man having his window broken just because he wants to go to work.' She was suddenly aware that she was making a political statement. It was wrong to indoctrinate your children, an abuse of parental power. 'It's not that I'm against the strike ... well, not altogether ... but if they've got the right to strike, then he's got the right not to strike. Hasn't he?'

Martin shrugged and she began to dither. 'Well, they shouldn't throw things at his window ... no matter what he's done ... and it isn't as if he's done anything yet. He's only saying he will if they don't sort things out...'

She might have been mistaken, but there was a faint smirk on Martin's face that might have been contempt. 'I wouldn't scab,' he said, 'not if I was a miner. I'd occupy the pit until they promised to leave it open for good.'

Fran looked at him. He was enjoying the excitement, the anger, the increased activity. It was only child-like, but it filled her with unease. And there was no escaping it. Bethel's latest bulletins filled the kitchen, TV and radio were obsessed with the picket line, the local paper read like a supplement of *Coal News*. North-east miners had already lost millions of pounds in wages, but their leaders were asserting that they could not afford to lose the strike ... 'the only way out is victory'. Once more the Falklands! No wonder Martin was confused.

Sooner or later she would have to talk to him about it, but first she would have to work out where she herself stood. There was right on both sides but eventually someone would have to give way. If it was the miners, there would be no holding Maggie Thatcher, and if the government was broken, anarchy would reign. Once more the Devil and the deep blue sea.

'Can I go down the beach?' Martin said, suddenly erupting back into the kitchen. 'It's a lovely day. And can I have some sarnies and an apple and some pop, and Mike says not to wear good shoes in case we have to plodge.' It was summer half-term and she ought to take him out somewhere, but the thought of five minutes' peace on her own was glorious. She gave him a bagful of sandwiches and a can of Coke, and warned him against drowning. 'I am getting better,' she thought as she waved him away. 'I am learning to let him go.'

She was thinking of afternoon tea when Bethel arrived. 'His lordship's on his way in. He says you'll be glad to see him, even if I'm not.' As usual when she spoke of Walter her face was poker-like but she turned to fill the kettle before she removed her hat. The next moment there was the ritual shout from the open door.

'Howay! Howay! Two of you in there gobbing on, and me stranded.' Fran left Bethel to manhandle the wheelchair, and got out cups and saucers.

'Aye, well ...' he said, when he was settled. His shirt collar was as crisp as ever, and once more Fran wondered if Bethel did his laundry. He spread his hands on the tartan rug that was strapped about his legs and regarded them solemnly, turning them palm upwards for a closer look. A heavy sigh followed and Fran could not repress a grin at the thought of what would come next. 'You'd think,' he said solemnly, 'that a woman of Sally Bethel's age would be above lying to a poor feller that's bound to a chair. But no, she's not. "Come in, Walter," she says, nice as ninepence. "The tea's all brewed. Biscuits ready, homemade." Gets you in with a nice little tarradiddle, and the bloody kettle's not even on. And I bet it's packet biscuits. Pap!' Bethel went stolidly about the tea-making as though she had not heard but Fran was willing to wheedle.

'What would you say to chocolate bourbons?'

He sniffed. 'They'll do. But it's tea I want. Now! I'm clammin'.'

He had lost the use of his legs in the pit twenty years before but he was still every inch a man. 'If he'd been nearer my age I'd have

[69]

given you a run for your money,' she had told Bethel once.

'You can have him,' Bethel had sniffed with a nonchalance that convinced no one.

Now, as they sipped their tea, she told them of Fenwick's notice.

'There'll be trouble,' Walter said. 'Still, he's made his row and he's hoeing it.'

Bethel's snort was a masterpiece. 'They'd better not cross my path. He has his rights ... a lad that's lived here all his life. Half of this lot causing trouble's incomers.'

Walter put down his cup. 'There's the Tory talking.' But he spoke automatically, as though he half-agreed.

'I'm no Tory, Walter, but I'll tell you what ... this carry-on has a chance to make me Tory. They're acting themselves like animals, some of them. I class myself better than that. Billy Fenwick would have stuck out if they'd left well alone, but no – it's do what we say, or else! So he's going to show them. And he'll not be the last. What else can single lads do? They've got no social to depend on – it's work or starve.'

'You do not scab, Sally. That's the miner's Bible, that. You do not cross a picket line. You might have doubts, you might not like the cause, but you *never* scab. You have your say in the meeting, then you accept the democratic decision.'

Bethel leaned forward. 'You don't fool me, Walter, not for a moment. You keep on spouting, but you don't like what's going on any more than I do, do you?'

His brows bristled. 'I don't like scabs.'

'Answer the question, Walter. You don't like what's going on any more than I do.'

He put his hands on the chair wheels and moved a little backwards. For once he was seeking words, and Fran was amazed.

'Well, no, I don't ... But that doesn't affect the issue, Sally. We can't all be ruled by slop. Oh, poor Fenwick, let's all have a sob for Fenwick – that's not the main issue. You've got a woman in Downing Street that hates the working class. You've got a Yank in the Coal Board that hates the human race. I've got no room for Scargill – he's a bloody fool, or else a bloody agitator –

and your average miner doesn't like him either. But they hate Maggie! And they despise MacGregor, for all his power! They'll not stick out for love of Arthur Scargill, they'll stick out to show her she can't beat the miners. They'll eat grass to prove that. If I had legs, I'd be out there with them, and don't you believe anything else.'

Long after they had gone and the tea things were washed and put to dry, Fran was remembering Walter's words, or rather the feeling behind them. The strike was escalating now, for all the papers might say about deadlock. Feelings were sharpening on both sides, you could sense it in the air. She got out her knitting and tried to concentrate on the matinee coat she was knitting for Treesa's baby – white with a touch of lemon.

She had collected the layette as Treesa had asked her: three polythene carriers and a soap-powder box containing a potty and some plastic bath toys. She had added her own store of baby clothes, and then looked through for omissions. Hence the matinee coat.

There was a visitor by Treesa's bed when she reached the ward later that day: Terry Malone, scrubbed till he shone, blue denim neatly pressed and red hair slicked down. He leaped to his feet when he saw Fran. 'Sit here, Mrs Drummond. It's good of you to come.'

Fran felt *de trop*, but to turn and go would cause further embarrassment. 'I wish I'd known you were coming,' she said. 'I could've given you a lift.' Treesa looked rested now, her hair brushed and looped up with slides. Only the swollen belly beneath the bedclothes betrayed maturity. 'Not long now,' Terry said, nodding at the bump and blushing furiously, when Fran caught his eye.

Treesa smiled. 'It can't come too soon for me.'

Terry was fumbling with his jacket pocket. 'I brought you these ... I forgot.'

Her eyes widened. 'Peppermint creams! Lovely.'

As they ripped off the cellophane, Fran watched them. Two

[71]

kids, still with the round faces of childhood. No trace of militancy in Terry tonight, but the scarred hands were surprisingly large and strong. He must be nineteen or twenty. She accepted a peppermint cream and wondered how to get away. 'I expect your mother's dying to see the baby. It'll be her first grandchild, won't it?'

For the first time, Treesa's brow clouded. 'I suppose she is. She doesn't say much.' Terry's shoulders hunched under the blue denim and he rubbed his chin on his T-shirt. 'You did get the baby things, didn't you?' Treesa asked.

Fran nodded. 'Yes, they're safe. And I've added a few things I'd been saving ... if you want them.'

She saw Treesa smile and then suddenly redden, realizing what lay behind the gift. There was silence for a moment and then Terry cleared his throat. 'How're you doing for coal, Mrs Drummond? If you've got nowt left I can get you a bag from the mineral line. It's wick with duff, that place. I'm digging it out for me mam, so you only need to say.'

Suddenly he was Brian ... '*It's nee trouble, Mrs Drummond,*' was what Brian used to say when she was down and desperate, and missing David.

'I'm fine at the moment, Terry. But I'll remember if I get stuck.' No point in telling him she needed high-grade coke to fuel the boiler. Why kick a gift-horse in the teeth?

She left them, leaning towards each other across the jacquard cover, and as she walked away she wondered how they felt about one another. Was it loyalty to a dead brother's child that had brought Terry here? Or gratitude that made Treesa's face light at the sight of him? If it was love ... or anything like love ... it was a fairy-tale, and those were thin on the ground in 1984.

Thinking about them disquieted her. That, or the thought of the coming baby. She sat behind the wheel, a hand against her chest, wondering if the burning sensation beneath her ribs was angst or indigestion. She felt flat and over-excited at one and the same time, unwilling to move and yet unable to stay still. In the end she switched on the engine and turned towards the town centre. She had not arranged to see Steve, had even vowed to

[72]

stay away from him tonight, but nothing less would still her agitation.

'Fancy a curry?' Fran said when Steve answered the door. 'Chicken Bhuna, double pulao, poppadums and a bindi bhaji?' She decanted them on to the table and took off her jacket.

She told him about Fenwick as they ate. 'It sounds pretty terrible,' he said.

'It is. How much longer can it go on – before something dreadful happens?'

Steve shook his head. 'It won't finish this month. Or next. Scargill's hanging on for the end of the summer, isn't he? That's when power cuts would bite. If he can keep going till October, he's cracked it.'

She pushed away her plate. 'You can't be serious? October! That's four months away.' If it went on until winter, there would be no trees left, no fences. Fenwick would have vanished beneath the onslaught and would never fly pigeons again.

Long after, when they lay together in Steven's bed, it was Fenwick's face she saw imprinted on her closed lids, the new, austere Fenwick, who had not a friend in the world. Soon he would leave his neat council house with its looped lace curtains and run a gauntlet of hate to the pit. Before the strike began, miners' wives had heckled Scargill when he visited Sunderland. Now those same women, or at least some of them, were supporting him. When a safety worker had been killed in the pit recently they had withdrawn the official picket, but one woman had declared it a fitting end for a scab. She would have told Steve about that too – but his mouth was sealing hers, cutting off breath, banishing unpleasant thoughts to some far-off box-room of the mind where they could stay until morning.

[73]

9

Sunday, 17 June 1984

She moved the car forward and got out to close the garage doors behind them.

'Hurry up, darling.' Martin was struggling with dog and lead, and shrugging into his anorak at the same time. Fran resisted the impulse to interfere; he hated it when she made a fuss. She was trying to look nonchalant when Bethel came round the corner, indignation in every line. Fran dispensed with formal greetings. 'What's happened?'

'What's happened? You might well ask.' Suddenly she cast an uneasy glance in Martin's direction and dropped her voice. It was too late. He was pretending to fiddle with the lead but his ears were cocked like Mr Spock's. 'Animals ... that's what they are. Not fit to live in a decent society.' Fran struggled to hold her tongue, knowing the penalties of interruption. 'Someone's nailed a dead pigeon to Fenwick's door.'

Fran shuddered. 'Who did it?'

Bethel's brows flew skywards. 'They've done it. *Them*! By, you're slow! He said he was going back tomorrow, didn't he, so they showed him. There's spray paint everywhere. "*Learn the scab*," it says on the door. "*Stop out or else*."'

Martin's face was grim, lower lip trembling and tears not far away. As Fran bundled him into the car, Bethel spoke. 'They've spoiled their bloody selves. He's no blackleg, he was only talking. But he'll go in now, all right, and God help anyone that gets in his way.'

The dog had got caught in its lead and was yelping discomfort. 'You're never taking it through the town?' Bethel reached for the squirming body. 'Give 'im here. I'll walk him down the allotments, but he better behave himself. You can't take a dog to a christening.'

Fran smiled her thanks and slid behind the wheel. Nee-wan would be better off with Bethel. She looked at Martin, who was still struggling with news of the pigeon's death. He was too soft-hearted, that was the trouble. And wanton destruction was hard to take at any age.

They were passing the pit when Martin spoke, the question she had been dreading. 'Whose side are you on, mam?' The pit was deserted and still, except for the police van in the entrance, a bored copper slumped behind the wheel.

'I don't know, Martin. But they shouldn't have hurt Mr Fenwick's pigeons.' That, at least, was clear.

'Who did it?'

She moved up a gear and shook her head. 'I don't know.' Mustn't tell him about the ski-masked men. 'Someone who was angry, I suppose.'

His tone was impatient. 'I know that. But I mean who would do it . . . no one we know?' It was a plea for reassurance.

'No, Martin, no one we know would behave like that.'

She hoped he was convinced by the lie. They knew everyone in Belgate – well almost everyone – so chances were they knew the pigeon-killers. Perhaps the one who had brushed by her was a neighbour, a fresh-faced boy who whistled his way to the pit and had 'Dire Straits' embroidered on his denim jacket. She was glad when they left Belgate behind and the pit could be forgotten for a little while.

They had almost reached the town centre when she remembered David. It was strange – for long periods now she didn't think about his death or the happiness that had preceded it. And yet she loved him more than ever. The trouble was that living reasserted itself, whether you liked it or not. Once she had been whole, single of purpose. Now there was one Fran who loved David, one who almost loved Steve, and one who increasingly loved no one and yearned to find something . . . but what? She indicated a left turn towards Eve's and resolved to stop philosophizing. She had no talent for it and it never got you anywhere, anyway. That was why she got such low marks for philosophy: it was like trying to hold water in a sieve.

As soon as she entered Eve's living-room she knew something was wrong. 'I'll tell you later,' Eve said. 'Does this dress look all right? I've had to let it out at the waist.'

Harold was holding the baby like a wand of office. 'Here you are, godmother. Over to you. Are we all ready? It's twenty past.'

Fiona and Elaine were dressed in Laura Ashley prints with wide pink sashes. They watched critically as she gathered their baby brother into her arms. 'This baby's going to be ruined,' Fran said, wiping a bubble from the fat pink mouth.

'He's gained four ounces,' Fiona said. 'That's an awful lot.'

She looked at Fran, defying contradiction. Fran pulled a face to indicate that she was suitably impressed and shifted the baby to her other arm. Elaine looked dubious above the pie-crust collar. Life was always difficult for a second child. Fran put out a hand and touched her cheek. 'He's lucky to have sisters like you.'

They trooped out to the waiting cars, Fran given precedence as godmother. The baby slept in her arms, gorged on milk. 'He should be OK till we get back,' Eve said anxiously. She smelled of milk, and suddenly Fran was reminded of childhood holidays, up in the hay-loft, cows lowing in their stalls, a nest of kittens under the eaves suckling from an alert mother cat.

And then they were in church and she was straining to catch every word so that she could fulfil her role. Behind her Min was tanned and elegant in white crunchy knitted cotton, and strangely enigmatic. Perhaps she was put out at not being chosen godmother – if so, they would certainly hear of it. And what had Eve meant when she said 'Tell you later'? The baby stirred in her arms and she rocked it gently. It was strange to be standing there before the blue and red stained glass, holding a baby that was not your own, making vows that were seldom if ever kept. 'I baptize thee David Ian.' She looked at the sleeping face, puckered as though with all the cares of the world, and made her own promises. She would love this baby, take an interest, never ever allow herself to envy Eve's possession of him. She would be good! Thoughts of all the other times she had vowed to be good rose up in her mind and were sternly put down. Church was a place for new beginnings.

[76]

She walked out into the sunlight and handed the baby to Eve so that the polaroids could have their fill. Fiona and Elaine jostled to get on either side of their mother and the new baby. 'He'll be a little prince,' Fran thought, 'adored by all his women.' Harold was doing his David Bailey act, coming on with the camera from every angle.

'Doesn't it make you sick,' Min murmured in her ear.

Fran kept on watching the display. 'I don't know, Min. It's a special day ... nice to have mementoes.' When Martin had been christened, David had made a ciné film and screened it ad nauseam. She turned to look for Martin. He was standing a little way off with Min's Althea, Peter and James. They all had a faintly deprived expression, as though Fiona and Elaine were getting an unfair share of the limelight. Min had followed her eyes. 'Jealousy gets you nowhere,' she called out, and when Althea, the eldest, scowled – 'Your face'll stick like that one of these days.'

Dennis moved protectively towards his children. 'Race you back to the car,' he said, ruffling Peter's hair and hugging the toddler, James, against him. He reached out and tweaked Martin's tie into place. 'That's better,' he said, and Martin smiled.

The fatherly gesture touched Fran. 'You're lucky to have Dennis,' she said, but Min had already turned away and if she heard she gave no sign. The cameras stopped clicking and people began to drift towards the cars. It was over and it hadn't hurt at all. Well, hardly at all.

Back at the house she handed out sherry, then wine, refilled buffet tables, acted the perfect godmother and best friend. Eve's thanks were fervent. 'I couldn't have managed without you, Fran.'

As they waited in the kitchen for coffee to brew, their eyes met across the hissing percolators. 'What are we going to do about Min?' Eve said suddenly. 'No good pretending it's going to go away. I've tried that. She actually wanted me to ask him here today. Here! With Dennis!'

'What do you mean?' Fran asked.

Eve put down the cream jug. 'You mean you don't know?'

Fran shook her head. 'I haven't a clue.'

Eve crossed to the door and closed it. 'We'll have to be quiet. Dennis is just outside the door.' She pursed her lips. 'You remember Hindson-Evans, the surgeon from the Infirmary? You met him at Min's.'

Fran nodded. She had met Richard Hindson-Evans and loathed him on sight, so it had been no trouble to refuse his invitation to dinner.

'Well, Min's having an affair with him. I wouldn't believe it at first ... when Sally told me I went down her neck. But it's true. And she wanted him here today! I thought you knew – Sally was simply broadcasting it! But of course you live in Siberia. I said no when she asked me to invite him here – she tried to look wounded and astonished, but I was quite firm. Harold nearly had a fit. He can't understand why Dennis doesn't twig. She'll get no encouragement from me. And if I *had* asked him ... well, Harold's foaming, I can tell you; I wouldn't put it past him to take Hindson-Evans by the lapels. Not that I blame *him* ... well, it's man's way, isn't it? They take what they're offered.'

So that was how Eve's mind worked. All men were natural marauders and not to be held responsible. It was up to women to be chaste. That was probably why she never took her eyes off Harold, in case he gave way to primeval impulses. The thought of Harold beating his pin-striped chest was so lovely that Fran smiled.

'It's no laughing matter, Fran. She'll never get away with it. And asking me to lie for her! I'm shocked. She's always been headstrong but this ... I hardly dared tell Harold. He says we should say something to Dennis, but I keep hoping she'll come to her senses.'

Fran held up a hand. 'Whoa. What has she asked you to lie about?'

Eve took a deep breath. 'She wants to go to a conference with him. A drug company's paying. Two nights at the London Hilton. She's cock-a-hoop about it. "Back me up to Dennis," she says. "I'll say I'm going to visit an old school friend, and you back me up."'

[78]

'She hadn't any friends at school, except us,' Fran said, 'and we're here.'

Eve nodded. 'Exactly what I told her. He'll be on to it straight away.'

Harold came into the kitchen then, and Eve made a great show of making coffee. They carried the pots out to the waiting guests, trying hard not to look at Min, draped elegantly across a ladder-backed chair.

'Coffee, Min?'

Min put out a languid hand. 'I'd rather have a drink, Fran. Has Harold locked up the rest of the booze?'

Fran had emptied her tray. 'I think there's some Asti in the kitchen.'

Min unwound from the chair. 'Lead on, MacDuff.'

They filled two glasses and consigned the empty bottle to the waste-bin. 'Here's to crime,' Min said and clinked glasses. Fran's cheeks felt hot. Was she supposed to know? Min's eyes were twinkling. 'Come on then, give me a rocket. Everyone else has. I'll rue the day and all that sort of thing.'

Fran shrugged. 'It's not up to me to criticize, Min. But I hope you know what you're doing.'

Min was examining her perfect oval nails. 'It's just a bit of fun. Richard's here at a loose end and Dennis is out several nights a week. I meet Richard now and then for a laugh, that's all.'

Fran wanted to ask about the London Hilton but didn't dare. 'Cheer up,' Min said, draining her glass. 'You've gone all goody-goody like Eve. I can't stand two of you doing a Saint Joan. I thought you'd understand.'

Fran was saved from having to reply by the advent of Valerie. Her eyes flicked from face to face, but she feigned nonchalance. 'We need another pot of coffee ... and Harold's aunty wants tea.'

As she filled the kettle, Fran wondered how long it would be before Dennis found out. Already half a dozen people were in the know, and a secret was something known by one person.

Harold buttonholed her when she appeared with the tea and grilled her about money. 'I hope you've had second thoughts

[79]

about the house, Fran? Get it on the market and move back here. You'd be far better off. I'm not saying anything against Belgate, but it's no place to bring up David's son – especially at the moment. And if you were nearer, I could keep an eye on your finances. No use having a friend who's an accountant if you don't make use of him.'

Fran tried to look as though she was paying attention, but she could hear the children whooping and hollering around the garden. Harold was proud of his flowerbeds: if Martin trampled the carefully planted annuals she would simply die! Her own garden had grown rampant with summer, straying over paths and straggling on walls. The garden had been David's province; now it was up to her.

'You will do that, won't you, Fran?' Harold was waiting for an answer and she gave him a fervent assurance. Anything for peace.

10

Friday, 29 June 1984

There was no one about as she passed the pit. Morning was the time for pickets, but the police van still lurked in the gateway, its occupants trying to look unobtrusive and thereby looking ridiculous. She felt hot and sticky, in need of a bath and a long drink and a seat in front of the telly to watch Wimbledon. When David was alive he had always made a fuss of her in Wimbledon fortnight, doing the chores so she didn't miss the good bits, and once bringing her strawberries on a tray.

It was over a year since David had died. Impossible to believe that. Last week, on the day itself, she had gone alone to the cemetery and brushed dirt from the stone with her fingertips. '*David Alexander Drummond, a beloved husband and father.*' There would be no strawberries on a tray for Wimbledon, and no watching either. She had a million things to do before she went to visit Treesa, and all of them urgent.

'Sit down. I've got the kettle on. The bairn's had his tea.' The light of a good tale was in Bethel's eyes and it was not long before it spilled out. 'You know the Botcherbys? Second house down in Stafford Street? Poor-looking little thing, dyes her hair? She was a Connor before she wed, and they were a funny family. Any road, she's taken this strike badly. A maniac for the house she was, HP here, HP there. There's any amount like her, but they're not taking it so serious.'

'What's happened to her?' She couldn't wait any longer for Bethel to spill the beans.

'Over-dosed!' Bethel's tone was triumphant, which meant Mrs Botcherby had survived. Bethel never gloated over real tragedy. 'Took a bottle of sleeping pills and brought them back up. Sick all over the place. Botcherby fetched the woman over the road – she used to work in the fever hospital. She says it was in the bedclothes, on the carpet, all up the wall.'

By night-time, Fran thought wryly, it would be dripping from the chandelier. 'But she's all right?'

Mrs Botcherby of the bitten nails and the untouched roots was indeed all right, and probably all the better for 'a good clear-out' according to Bethel.

'I'm going to visit Treesa tonight,' Fran said, glad to broach a more cheerful subject.

Bethel lit a No 6 and blew smoke. 'And that's another tragedy ... a bairn coming into the world to nowt. She'll get no help off her own family and even less off that sackless lot.'

Fran felt prickings of indignation. 'I suppose you mean the Malones. I think they'll be very supportive. Mrs Malone loves babies, and it will be her first grandchild.'

Bethel's sniff would have done credit to a water buffalo. 'Yes, God help it. Of all the nutty varmints to have for a grandma, *she* takes the biscuit. Any road, I don't hold with all this free love, having bairns to fulfil yersel'. I'd've liked a bairn after Tommy went ...' her words slowed as she thought of the young husband killed in the pit before his time, '... but I wasn't that selfish. You

[81]

hear them on telly now – "Ooh, I must have a baby ... I'm shopping around for a man to spark it off ... I can rear it on me own." Go out and buy a doll if you feel like that, that's what I say. Don't bring a live bairn into the world to have no dad.' Their eyes met, and she saw the dawning resentment in Fran's eyes. 'I'm not talking about people like you. You've been landed with a situation you had no hand in. I'm talking about women who say, "I want." Someone should tell them "I want" never gets.'

'Treesa's not like that,' Fran said defensively. 'She meant to get married ... the wedding was fixed.'

Bethel's retort was sharp. 'Then she should've kept her hand on her ha'penny till she left the church. Now look where she is ... flat on her back in a hospital, and no place for her or the bairn when she comes out. There'll be compensation when they work it out but God knows when that'll be ... or who'll get it. In the meantime, her mother'll take her in all right but she'll pay for it! You can be sure about that.'

As she drank her tea, Fran wondered what Bethel would say if she, Frances, were to become pregnant. Not that she would ever dare to confess it. She would rather face the Spanish Inquisition! She filed the worry of contraception away for later and asked for news of the strike.

The Malones, father and son, were still at loggerheads and Fenwick's windows had gone for the umpteenth time, although he was still only talking about going back to work. 'A lump of concrete that wide went clean through the quilt. His sister told me herself. Not that she's sticking up for him; she says he's caused more trouble than enough for her and her man ... by, she's bitter. She says he's always been awkward.'

'He was happy enough when he had his pigeons,' Fran said. 'All he wanted was to be left alone to go to work. I don't think that's asking much. He talked about breaking the strike, but he probably never would have done it if they hadn't killed his pigeons.' Remembering that night, the padding footsteps in the dark, she shivered. 'What kind of men ... young men ... can kill defenceless birds.'

They were deep in argument over the effects of a) TV violence and b) the demise of corporal punishment, when there was a call from the back door. 'Hallo?' It was Manky Margot.

'What on earth is she doing here?' Fran thought, and then, 'I must stop calling her Manky. We're grown women now.'

In spite of the heat, Margot was wearing a shapeless knitted sweater in an indeterminate sludge colour, her only ornaments two badges, one for CND the other *Coal not Dole*. 'I couldn't pass your door without calling,' she said, flashing Bethel a wide smile that said, '*We're all sisters, aren't we, and class doesn't matter at all.*' The trouble was that to think class didn't matter implied that you recognized its existence, which seemed to make nonsense of the whole thing.

'Come in and sit down,' Fran said, suddenly remembering her manners. 'Would you like some tea?'

Bethel was preparing to go but she reached for the kettle.

'No, ta ... I'm awash with tea. We've made gallons of it for the boys. I've been lending a hand at the support centre. You knew we had the welfare hall? It's marvellous to see them come in and get a square meal. We've all got to help, haven't we? I know it's a fight for pits and jobs but it's the class thing, too – that's why they must stick out to the bitter end. We must all give till it hurts; that's why I'm through here every spare moment – pitching in.'

There was a dry cough from the doorway. 'I'll just be going.' The set of Bethel's jaw told it all: she had had enough.

Margot was on to the subject of women now. 'There'll have to be positive discrimination in the end. We've tried to change sexist attitudes with subtlety but it hasn't worked, so it'll have to be direct attack. We've formed a collective in Sunderland ... you must come along one night ... and we're making strides; but there'll never be equal participation without positive discrimination.'

Wicked thoughts were rising up in Fran's mind. Positive discrimination was what Hitler had practised in favour of Aryan blondes, and Paisley in favour of Ulster Protestants. Positive discrimination was all right if you were doing it, and all wrong if it was the other fellow. She looked at the clock. Ten to seven: not enough time to enter into an argument, and she was not going to

[83]

be ashamed of her relief. 'I'm awfully sorry, Margot, but I have to dash. I'm visiting a friend in hospital . . .'

Margot went, in a rush of promises to call again. 'I'll be standing in whenever I can – I've told them at the office that I'm taking all my lieu days. They understand.' Her tone implied that any good liberal would, and, to her subsequent shame, Fran nodded to indicate agreement. Anything to get Margot over the step.

She had picked some flowers from the garden, and started looking for a sheet of wrapping paper. She had found the aquilegia among the knee-high grass. David had planted it two summers ago and called her out to see the first blossoms. She must find a way to cope with the grass and let the flowers breathe. It was the least she could do. And she mustn't be tempted to call on Steve again when she was in Sunderland. She was becoming a nymphomaniac . . . or she would, if she wasn't careful.

She gave up looking for the wrapping paper. Newsprint would have to do. She was rolling the flowers in an old *Echo* when some figures caught her eye. She looked at the date: 17 March, when the figures of the regional ballots had been coming in. South Derbyshire had been 83 per cent against, Northumberland 52 per cent for, but North Wales, Lancashire and the Midlands were all two or three to one against. There had been a gradual drift back in the Nottinghamshire coalfield and a call for a national ballot everywhere. With that degree of opposition, how had the strike ever got off the ground let alone lasted for four months?

As she drove towards Sunderland she realized how little she had done since she got home. She might as well have watched Wimbledon, for all she had accomplished. Next week-end she would let everything go and watch the finals. They wouldn't be able to go shopping anyway, for the money in the bank was dwindling rapidly: £998 at the last count. Less than four figures, and Martin would need kitting out completely for the winter. The thought depressed her so much she began to sing. '*When I'm faced with a day that's grey and cloudy, I stick out my chin and grin and say – tomorrow, tomorrow, I love you, tomorrow …'* When David died she had driven the roads screaming her agony, seeing startled faces as she flashed by. Now the same startled expressions greeted her vocal cords. She shut her mouth firmly on the last '*tomorrow*' and concentrated on the road.

Treesa's bed was empty when she reached the ward, but the young nurse was full of information. 'She's in the labour room. Her waters broke at three o'clock. Any time now, I should think. Her mother's waiting in the corridor. She'll probably be glad of some company.'

Treesa's mother was small and thin, a complete contrast to her daughter. 'Yes, we're not alike; she takes after her dad. They all do.' She looked as though the paternal resemblance gave her no pleasure. 'I don't know how it's going to work out, I'm sure. Thoughtless, that's what she's been. I've told her that. "It's all very well to be grown-up," I've told her. "You have to act grown-up. We've got no accommodation for a baby." Besides, I thought I'd put all that behind me – broken nights, and the clothes horse round the fire all the time – not that we have a fire at the moment, but that's another story. She'll have to buckle to and find somewhere. I've told her that. As soon as she's on her feet. I've told her that. And she'll have to chase up the compen. If the Malones get their hands on it, she won't see a penny for her or the baby. I've told her that.'

How awful to be told so many things when you were about to give birth, Fran thought. Poor Treesa. Poor little baby.

She looked at the wall and wondered why she was sitting in on a birth for the second time in weeks, she who had not been able to give birth at will. It wasn't fair. But life was never fair. It worked out how much you could bear and pushed you to the brink.

'It's a boy!' The baby was firmly wrapped in cellular cotton, a face like a pink walnut the only thing on show. The staff nurse held it in one arm and guided the foot of the trolley that bore Treesa with her free hand. The porter at the other end was whistling 'Memories', but he wasn't a patch on Elaine Paige.

'Are you all right, Treesa?' Her mother's tone implied that she

[85]

better had be.

'A bit sore, but that's all. Have you seen him?' Mrs Carruthers nodded grimly, unwilling to acknowledge that an illegitimate grandchild was anything else but a drawback. 'Yes. He's very nice.'

Fran leaned to squeeze Treesa's arm above the plastic name-tag. 'He's beautiful.' There was a streak of dried, bloody mucus on her arm and a terrible odour of antiseptic.

When Treesa was safely in the ward and the baby whisked to the nursery, they sat either side of the bed. 'How many stitches did you have? They won't send you home too soon, will they? I'm counting on a day or two to get put straight.'

Treesa's eyes were half-closed and there was a terrible resignation about her mouth. 'I don't know, mam ... I don't know how many stitches I had ... I don't know how they go on.'

Birth shouldn't be like this, it should be joyful! Fran made one or two efforts to deflect Mrs Carruthers, but she was indefatigable. 'You'll have to go round the councillors, Treesa. Tell them you've lived here all your life and you must have a place. Say we can't keep you.' No wonder Treesa had loved Brian Malone: like all the Malones he took life a day at a time, trimming his sails to whichever wind was blowing.

When the bell signalled the end of visiting time, they left the ward together. 'I wish I could give you a lift, Mrs Carruthers, but I'm not going back to Belgate yet.'

She waited till the other woman was out of sight before she ran back to the ward. 'I won't be a moment,' she told the startled staff nurse. 'It's something urgent I forgot.' Treesa's eyes were closed and sweat gleamed in the blurred sockets. 'Treesa, I know you're dying to go to sleep ... it's just that I've been thinking. We have so much room, Martin and I, plenty of room for you and a baby ... if you'd like to come?'

Treesa was nothing if not honest. 'Oh, Mrs Drummond ... I've been praying you'd say that!'

As she drove towards Eve's, Fran felt mingled delight and terror. To have a baby in the house again ... would that be unalloyed pleasure? Or exquisite pain? Treesa had promised to pay her way, so it wouldn't rock the financial boat and the company would be nice. And nice or not, she wouldn't have sent a hyena back to Mrs Carruthers' tender mercies. All the same – lodgers! When she'd suggested them after David's death, Harold had thrown up his hands in horror. However would she break the news to him?

She reached the corner that led to Steve's flat and turned resolutely in the opposite direction. Mustn't importune. The trouble was, she was not cut out to be on her own; she was meant to be half of a whole. She thought of him in bed, muscled forearms lying on top of the duvet, his hair rumpled on his brow. Gwen had said he was a bit like Richard Gere and it was true. If he proposed properly she would probably say yes. Except that people would disapprove, and she couldn't bear that. On the other hand, if she turned him down, could she live without him? Anyway, she didn't have to decide just now. Steven was preoccupied of late – bowed down with worry about his business probably. The strike was beginning to affect everyone. She shivered, remembering what Steve had said about it lasting till October or November. The sky was high and clear, the moon a kindly face. She banished thoughts of General Winter from her mind and opened her mouth to sing.

11

Saturday, 7 July 1984

'Well, I only hope you won't come to regret it.' Bethel's tone implied that Fran undoubtedly would, but she still bustled around the spare bedroom, making everything spick and span.

'It looks nice, doesn't it?' Fran said placatingly.

'All right,' Bethel said. 'At least there's plenty room.'

Fran had always loved the spare bedroom, with its white walls and blue and white curtains. Perhaps, subconsciously, she had made it a nursery for David's baby that was never to be. Anyway, it was perfect for Treesa and Brian Christopher. Bethel had snorted when she heard the chosen names: '*He'll need St Christopher to find his way round that lot.*' Nevertheless, she had worked hard to get ready for the homecoming. Fran said, 'I love you, Bethel.'

The older woman sighed. 'There you go again. Slop, slop, slop. That's why you get nowt done. Too much jaw.'

While Bethel peeled potatoes for lunch, Fran popped to the corner shop. For once she was not the only customer. Two women stood at the end of the counter holding on to a large cardboard box. The shopkeeper was packing it with goods – a plastic bag of potatoes, sugar, two packets of dried peas, a bottle of tomato sauce. So somebody at least had money. Behind Fran the doorbell jangled and someone entered the shop. One of the two women looked up and nudged her neighbour. The other woman turned her head, gold earrings swinging at the movement, and regarded the newcomer. Fran was dying to turn round, but it would look too obvious – and something was certainly up. The shopkeeper's professional smile turned into a fixed grin that suggested terror more than bonhomie. He looked appealingly at the women. 'Shall I just serve Mrs Mather?' He turned to the newcomer. 'Is it much, Mrs Mather?'

As she advanced to the counter, fumbling with her purse, the two women at the end of the counter began to converse. 'By, I could do with something nice for me tea. A nice bit of roast pig . . . I mean pork . . .'

Her stooge was quick to respond. 'It's the only way I do like pig . . . I mean pork. Roasted. That's what you do with pigs. Fry them.'

Fran couldn't resist a peep at the shopkeeper and his customer. She had pointed to a punnet of tomatoes and he was putting them on to the scales, fumbling in his haste to get her served and out of his shop before there was trouble. As Fran watched she saw that the woman's mouth was set to cover a tremble, and her hands clasped and unclasped her purse just as Mrs Botcherby's had done. But this was no striker's wife, not if she could afford tomatoes.

She paid for her purchases and turned, but the sight of the tomatoes had enraged the other women. 'It's all right for some isn't it?' They were talking to one another but their remarks were for broadcasting. 'Them as don't mind breeding pigs. Pigs can afford tomatoes. Snouts in the bloody trough. Still, we'll be the ones that's laughing before long. Fenwick got the message; he's seen sense. The pigs'll have to take the consequences, won't they?'

The bell jangled, the door closed. The shopkeeper turned back to the box and threw in two or three cans of food. 'There now, is that OK?'

The gold-earringed woman pulled a doubting face. 'We're short of washing-up liquid. All them dishes. Still, if you can't manage ...' He reached for a small Fairy Liquid, hesitated, and then chose the largest size.

They hefted the box between them and made for the door. Fran held it open for them and received a nod for her pains. The door closed and the bell ceased to jangle.

'By God, that's shortened my life.' The shopkeeper was wiping his brow, and Fran looked at him enquiringly. 'They're from the support group ... well, they are the support group, the rest's just followers. In here every week for a load like that, and I'm not taking twopence ha'penny.' He gestured to the shelves. 'This shop's getting galloping alopecia, bald spots everywhere, but I can't afford to restock. Try telling the wholesale you'll pay them when the strike's over. They'd laugh in your face! And I'm not the only one – we had a meeting last week, retailers from all over the coalfield. It's the same story everywhere. You've got your regular customers, good payers when they had the money ... you can't see them go without, can you? I've got women never ticked on in their lives. They come in here and you can see the pain of it on their faces. Humiliation. And then there's the other lot. If I want customers after the strike, I've got to keep them sweet now ... so I fill their box. Nobody's balloted *me* about the strike; it's pay your dues or else. There'll be wholesale bankruptcies before this lot's over.'

[89]

Fran nodded sympathy – she hadn't liked the look of the two women. On the other hand she would do murder to feed Martin, so how could she blame them for what they were doing? 'Who was the other customer? The one who bought the tomatoes?'

He shook his head. 'I'm sorry for her. She's a widow. One son. Her man was a miner, got dust, took his redundancy, and snuffed it. But the son's a copper. Bright young lad, used to do a paper round for me ... did it for years. Never missed a day, rain or shine. He was a police cadet and then he joined the Northumbria Constabulary.'

'So he doesn't work round here?' Fran said.

'No, but he visits. And they know who and what he is. Talk about Northern Ireland – they'd put a bullet in his back as soon as look at you.'

He put his hands on the counter and leaned forward, his face sombre. 'Mrs Drummond, I don't have political opinions. Half the time I don't bother to vote. It makes no difference who's in power; we suffer. I don't see how you can keep uneconomical pits open, and I don't see how you can shut them and toss whole communities on the scrap-heap. But I do know someone's to blame for this lot ... neighbour against neighbour, father against son, miner against miner, lads that have grown up in a community afraid to come back to see their mothers. Someone somewhere's to blame for that ... and I hope they think shame of themselves.'

It was a relief to get back home, even though she was immediately called upon to arbitrate in another row. 'He says the baby's more his than ours.' Martin was bristling with pride of ownership, and Mike was looking to Fran for justice.

'He doesn't belong to anybody ... he's himself,' Fran said, weakly, and then caught Mike's reproachful eye. 'Well ...' If she went into Mike's position as uncle she might get into deep water, but there was no escape. 'Well ... Mike is Christopher's uncle, because Christopher's daddy was his brother. So in a way it *is* more his.' Mike was looking decidedly mollified, even smug.

'But Christopher will be living here for a while, so you'll be sort of a big brother.' Pride stirred in her as Martin assumed a modest expression and did not gloat. It was incredibly easy to talk to children really: they never raised irrelevant issues like illegitimacy, they were more concerned with possession.

'I'm turning this oven off now,' Bethel roared from the kitchen. 'If you can't be bothered to eat it, I might as well not've cooked it.' They sat round the table, munching cheerfully, four sets of legs underneath to jostle. If she married Steve they would move away, leave behind this funny house with its even funnier kitchen. And then the ambulance was drawing up at the door with Treesa and the baby, and it was time to think of someone other than herself.

'Aye, he's a bonny bairn all right. I see his dad in him.' Bethel was being unusually magnanimous in admitting the Malone strain. Now she looked up at Treesa. 'You look peaky. You want to get yersel' built up. Calves-foot jelly, that's what you want, not this chemical muck they give you nowadays.' She extolled the virtues of Scott's Emulsion and stout, while she donned her hat and coat and left in a blaze of injunctions to the children. 'You'll have that baby a bundle of nerves if you don't stop your carry-on. And help your mam and Treesa.' Her parting shot was directed at Mike. 'You've got no home to go to, I suppose ... or not what most people would call a one.'

When the children had drunk their fill of the baby and zoomed out of the house, Fran sat down opposite Treesa. 'How do you feel? I remember when I brought Martin home, I felt so weak! How'm I going to manage, I thought. But I did.'

They drank tea and discussed the pros and cons of living together. 'This is nice,' Fran thought. 'Like having a sister.' When the baby cried she picked him up and soothed him, moving him instinctively to her shoulder where he hiccuped wind and tiny gobbets of undigested milk.

'He's marked your dress,' Treesa said apologetically.

'It doesn't matter,' Fran said. Nothing mattered except the unfocused blue eyes that fixed on her face as though it held the secret of the universe.

She was about to ask when Treesa's mother would be calling, when the phone shrilled in the hall. It was Linda. 'I'm just ringing to say your invite's on the way. Eddy's made it out for Fran and partner, so bring a feller.' Fran didn't know which was the bigger shock, the double invitation or the idea of Edward as Eddy. It conjured up a whole new persona. Eddys made saucy jokes, got holes in their socks, made love on the hearthrug or in the bath. Where had immaculate, precise Edward gone? 'Did you hear what I said? He'll be very welcome.'

Fran demurred. 'It's very kind, Linda, but I'm sure you've more than enough as it is. Besides, he has his children on Saturdays...'

Linda was not at all fazed. 'Bring them ... they'll be company for my lot and your Martin. He's included of course ... our Debbie's made sure of that.' Her tone changed, becoming less certain. 'Did you manage to get that book?'

It was time for a whopping lie. 'No. It's out of print. But I've got all the gen from one of the women on the course, so I'll pop over next week and fill you in.'

She *had* been able to get a booklet on wedding etiquette, a silver-backed volume packed with advertisements. She had looked for the section on second marriage and found it towards the end. It advised soft pedalling on everything the second time around. 'Discreet dress' obviously meant sackcloth and ashes; 'no ostentation at the reception' meant send out an apology with the invitation; and the final straw was a recommendation to dispense with bridesmaids and music. She had sent it spinning into the wastepaper basket. One marriage in three was second time around now, but no one seemed to have realized. There was no way she was going to cast Linda down when she was so happy. 'Gwen says you should do what you did the first time,' she said, 'but I'll give you the details later.'

She was about to put down the receiver when Linda cleared her throat. 'By the way, Fran, I've been meaning to say this ... ta for the introduction. I'm going to make him happy, you can be sure of that.'

When she got back to the living-room she found Mrs Malone

had arrived and was cooing over the baby. 'He's like his dad,' she said, pushing at one tiny fist with her forefinger. A tear gathered in the corner of her eye and ran down the fat cheek. 'He didn't have much hair, our Brian. But what a good bairn.'

Behind her Terry grinned. 'Not like me, you mean. I bet I was a right little sod.'

His mother looked at him indulgently. 'Still are,' she said. She turned towards Fran. 'It's a relief she's here, Mrs Drummond. We're not that well placed, but I wouldn't have seen her beaten. It'll be different when they get the compen. sorted out. It's the bairn's by right, no doubt about that. His and Treesa's. It's only a pity they want it proving.'

Fran nodded. The legal wheels were grinding slowly. No one knew what to do about a baby born to a miner long dead in the pit. 'Not that she needs to worry,' Mrs Malone said. 'If they reckon it's ours, we'll pass it straight on. No fear about that.'

Treesa was raising her arms, proffering the sleeping baby to Terry. 'I can't hold bairns,' he said awkwardly, but he took it just the same. 'There's a good lad,' he said to the sleeping head. 'You lie quiet for your Uncle Tel.'

Fran tiptoed away and made tea, carrying it in on a tray. 'You shouldn't've bothered,' Mrs Malone said, but Fran could see she was pleased.

'You didn't hear the news,' Treesa said. 'Terry's just been telling us – Fenwick's taking the Union to court.'

Fran handed out tea. 'Can he do that?'

Terry looked suddenly more mature, launched on to his favourite subject. 'Oh yes, Mrs Drummond, an individual member can take legal action. He won't win because he's got no case, but he's entitled to try. What the lodge wants to know is who's behind him. He didn't think that up on his own, and he won't be paying for it.'

'He could be getting legal aid,' Fran ventured.

Terry shook his head. 'I hope not ... seeing as none of our lads are allowed it.' His expression was bitter.

'I thought everyone got it, unless they were rich?' Fran remarked.

'It's like a lot of things, Mrs Drummond. They look all right till you come to rely on them.'

'Like being insured for everything except what got on fire?' Fran said, and he nodded.

'It's a pity he's done this. It'll only make things worse, prolong the dispute, cause more bitterness ... Still, like I said, he's got the right.'

Mrs Malone had been silent; now she sighed. 'I doubt things can get worse. I never thought I'd see a bairn of mine not speaking to his own father.' She looked at Fran. 'I'm not saying anything I haven't said already. There's no excuse for two grown men being at loggerheads under one roof.' She leaned forward and tickled the baby's cheek. 'I mind on when you were like this, our Terry, and your dad carried you everywhere. Our Brian was always my bairn, and you were your dad's. And now this.'

Fran looked at the young face, as resolute as the north face of the Eiger. 'He knows my views.'

Mrs Malone turned back to Frances. 'See what I mean?'

Long after they'd gone the unhappiness hung in the room. 'It'll get over, Treesa,' Fran said. 'When they get back to work, the bitterness'll go.'

Treesa shifted the baby to her other arm. 'I'm not so sure, Mrs Drummond. They feel it deep, both of them. Both sure they're right.'

'Who do you think is in the right?' Fran asked, but Treesa shook her head.

'It's too deep for me. I only wish Brian'd been here. They wouldn't have fallen out if he'd been between them.'

Steve rang at half past nine. 'Is she settled in? And you'll be drooling over the baby, I suppose ... We went to the park, then I fried chips for tea. It's far too hot for chips, but they won't touch salad. Julie didn't eat anything as usual, but Ian made up for it. He's shooting up.' There was always pride in his voice when Steve spoke of his children. 'Anyway,' he said at last, 'what's the news of your wayward friend?'

Fran laughed. 'You mean Min? Nothing new. She's still planning her illicit weekend and Eve's having kittens about it. The one good thing about it is it's stopped her having those ghastly girls' nights. She's too taken up with her boy-friend.'

'What about *your* boy-friend. When does he get to see you?'

She smiled into the mouthpiece. 'Boy-friend? I haven't got a boy-friend.'

His voice dropped. 'You have, you know. And he misses you. It's no cop, me here and you ten miles away.'

She tut-tutted. 'You're exaggerating, it's only eight miles.'

'Eight inches would be too much right now. I love you, Frances. I want you. I need you.'

She went into the kitchen and spread out the books she needed for her essay on 'The Learning Situation'. She tried to concentrate on Piaget, but her mind wandered. For some reason she kept thinking about Min. Nowadays she looked like the cat who was getting the cream – which was funny, really, because she had always moaned about sex: *'You have to go on with it, it's the price you pay for marriage. But that doesn't mean you have to like it.'* Now, if Sally were to be believed, she was at it like knives. Perhaps she was attracted to his being a doctor? Or forbidden fruit, the ultimate aphrodisiac? In any event, she wasn't suffering pangs of guilt. Not visibly. 'Not like me,' Fran said aloud and for good measure wrote it on her nice clean page.

Why couldn't she be permissive? Not promiscuous, just reasonably carefree? Instead hell and VD were ever-present threats. Her mother's teaching had been specific: if you were wicked, you went to rot and bits dropped off . . . but Min was visibly blooming, waxing on her sin. Life was one long enigma. She, who did like sex, tried to keep out of one man's bed; and Min, who did not, had taken not one man into her bed but two. The thought of Hindson-Evans getting into bed in his custom-tailored suits made Fran laugh out loud. Perhaps he did it in his white coat with a stethoscope round his neck? Perhaps Min was a surgical-mask fetishist? Or had to be given a general anaesthetic? Coitus nitrous oxide!

'You want to stop being hysterical and get some work done,'

Bethel said disapprovingly from the kitchen doorway. 'I'm on me way back from the bingo and I bought you some cod and chips. I nearly had the holiday flyer, but I needed one number. Still, I had a canny little win on me last card, so get them down you. And there's some for that Treesa. She needs a feed.'

When Bethel had gone and Treesa's cod had been carried upstairs, Fran took her own plate through to the living-room. The telly was switched off and she left it silent. She was tired of pictures of picket-line violence interspersed with American cops and robbers. She picked up the evening paper for her daily shot of the letters page. Dame Flora Robson was dead ... one more pillar of childhood gone. Arthur Scargill was saying, *'We are going to win,'* and the Bishop of Durham was quoted: *'I am going to do a Brer Rabbit now ... lie low and say nothing.'* Fran smiled to herself. The Bishop had the over-excited look of someone new to the limelight who, having found it, doesn't intend to be out of it for a minute. She munched her batter. The letters page was as productive as ever. *'1984 is coming true.'* *'Comrade Scargill will close more pits than MacGregor ever intended to.'* Another writer mocked Scargill's constant promise of victory: *'It's like Sunderland football team being two goals down and the manager saying "Keep it up lads, we're winning."'*

She was putting the *Echo* away when she saw the picture of a railway line where men were excavating for coal. *'NE Mineral Lines a Danger. Two men already killed in Scotland and Yorkshire in vain attempts to get fuel.'* She must show it to Terry Malone and tell him not to dig out the mineral line any more. If anything happened to him it would surely break his mother's heart.

She carried cocoa upstairs and knocked on Treesa's door. 'I thought you'd like a drink?' They sat on the bed to sup their cocoa. Treesa's nightdress was wet at the nipples and clung to her. She had the body of a woman but the face and hands were those of a child. 'Is this all right for you,' Fran said, gesturing round. 'Tell me if there's anything you'd like changed.'

'It's lovely, Mrs Drummond. It's so peaceful. I'll try not to be a nuisance ... well, we'll both try.' The baby slept soundly in Martin's crib.

'It's nice to have a baby in the house again. If David hadn't died, we'd have liked more children.'

Treesa nodded. 'You do, when you love someone, don't you? It's only natural.'

'We can talk,' Fran thought. 'We can talk about them without it hurting. As though they were both here.'

Treesa licked cocoa from her upper lip. 'I'm glad I've had the bairn. I know it's not right, not being wed and everything ... but at least I've got something out of it. It's not as though Brian didn't count.'

When they had paid homage at the crib and said their good-nights, Fran walked across the landing to Martin's room. He lay asleep on his back, his copy of *Bert Vegg's Nasty Book* open in an outstretched hand. She took it from him and laid it on his desk. There was a faint down on his upper lip and perhaps the hint of an Adam's apple in the childish throat. She put out a hand to the lamp. 'Thank you David,' she said, and plunged the room into darkness.

12

Saturday, 11 August 1984

There was a spattering of letters on the mat as Fran came down the stairs; bills and circulars and a DHSS envelope for Treesa. She carried them through to the kitchen and submitted to Nee-wan's onslaught of welcome. 'All right, all right. You'd think I'd been to Nova Scotia, not just upstairs in bed.' That was the best thing about dogs, they were eternally pleased to see you. The sun was shining through the kitchen window, and when she let the dog out into the garden a cabbage white was spiralling above the buddleia. At least Linda was getting a lovely day.

She carried tea and toast upstairs for Treesa. She was curled in the chair by the window, the sated baby asleep against her breast. His cheeks were puffed with satisfaction and milk dripped from the pouting mouth. 'He's lovely, isn't he?' Treesa said and transferred him to Fran's arms. As she put him down and tucked him in, Fran was proud of herself. She had come to terms with the baby problem. They were for other people, not for her, but she could still love them if she chose.

'I think that's your Giro,' she said. It was indeed the magic slip but the figure was still wrong.

'I'll have to go down again,' Treesa said. 'They never listen, that's the trouble.' While they drank their tea they talked about the DHSS. 'It takes at least three visits to get things straight. They never have time to get it right. Everyone else behind you is coughing and groaning, and the bairns are crying. You look at them through the grille and you see their eyes go funny. And then they say, "You'll get something in the post", and you know it won't happen and they know you know, but they still say, "Next please".'

Fran reassured her that there would be compensation money sooner or later, and gave silent thanks for her own teacher-training course. She had made a trip to the DHSS offices at the beginning of her widowhood, and the mingled odours of sweat and despair were in her nostrils still.

'You'll need a good wash and your things are laid out on my bed.' Martin had never been to a wedding before and excitement was exuding from every pore. She hoped he wouldn't be disappointed. He had looked forward to it for so long, but in life you got what you wanted and then waited for elation to strike, and it didn't.

Bethel arrived in time to do the washing up. 'No, go and get yersel' ready. It's not often you get a day out. I'll fettle this lot.' She looked at Nee-wan. 'And not a cheep out of you, mind. Or else.' The dog rolled on his back, paws languid. No matter the words, the tone told him he was loved.

'Fenwick's going in on Monday.' With a start Fran realized she had not thought of the strike this morning. How could you forget something so momentous, even for a wedding?

'Do you think he'll really do it this time?'

Bethel's nod was emphatic. 'Oh yes, there'll be no turning back this time.' Fenwick had been signalling his intention of going back for weeks. 'He's sat down there in the library day after day, head buried in law books, scribbling things down. He's never been the same since those pigeons. I reckon he's gone funny.'

And now he was going back to work, and there would be trouble. Fran reminded herself that this was Linda's wedding day. Time enough to worry about Monday morning when the wedding was over.

Bethel was standing up to the elbows in suds. 'I expect we'll have her round on Monday, wringing her hands and spouting rubbish. That friend of yours, I mean. That Margot! Solidarity? The only solid thing about her's her backside.'

Fran felt bound to put the other side. 'She means well ...' She got no further.

'Means well!' Reddened arms were withdrawn from the sink, suds flying. '"Means well" is the cause of the trouble. Thatcher "means well", I daresay. Scargill "means well". If they'd all stop "meaning well" and let the miners get on with it, all this trouble'd stop. Besides ...' The parting shot was half meant for Fran. '... she's only a townee. She doesn't know what she's talking about. Pits are for pitmen. And their women. She should keep herself to herself.' She dropped into a wicked imitation of Margot's accent. 'They must see it through to the bitter end. I've done my bit to see they're not starved out. Mrs Thatcher will never break the miners.' She reverted to her own voice. 'Mrs Thatcher won't break them but the do-gooders just might manage it.'

It was nice to be dressing for a gala occasion. Fran was wearing a suit she had bought just before David died and seldom worn, navy linen with red and white blouse and lapels. She spent a lot of time on her makeup, keeping one eye always on the clock. She had promised Linda that she would be there in time to give her a final inspection, and nothing must interfere with that. It was funny to think of Edward marrying Linda. She had met each of them in the aftermath of David's death, almost as a consequence of it. She had invited them to her Christmas party to salve a guilty conscience, nothing more. And now they were getting married. For every action in life there was a consequence. Sometimes you knew nothing about it, but it was there just the same.

When she went through to the bedroom in search of her red earrings, the stack of files and textbooks on her dressing-table was a reproach. She had taken to working in the bedroom lately, away from Martin and the TV. She would have to get down to some work next week. There were still weeks and weeks of summer holiday left, but she had a daunting list of essays to complete. She regarded herself in the mirror. She looked nice, but would she ever make a teacher. She consoled herself by listing some of the idiots she knew who had risen to senior posts in the teaching profession, and then went down to check on Martin.

He looked suitably clean, his hair plastered to his head and his tie knotted loose on the clean shirt. He protested when she made to tighten the knot. 'Nobody wears their tie like that now, mam. Except the fascist junta, and they want throttling.'

Fran looked at him. 'Is that the police you're talking about?'

He put up a hand in the Nazi salute and the other forefinger under his nose. '*Jawohl*,' he said.

Fran licked her lips. 'Do you know what it means?'

He grinned. 'No, but I know it's rude. They're like the Argies ... bang, bang.'

Fran sought for words. How could she explain the difference between the Falklands battlefield and the Durham coalfield when a British MP had stood at a miners' rally and demanded victory for extra-parliamentary action? Still, she mustn't over-react. He was only a child, after all.

'Yes. Well, we'd better get on. It'd be awful if we were late.'

Bethel waved them off, restraining a frantic dog. 'You don't look bad, quite classy. Behave yourselves.' And then, in an aside to Fran, 'If that feller of yours is there, it has a chance to be a double wedding.' It would have been nice if Steve could've been there, but she understood about his access day. She had told him of the invitation. 'Linda says bring them along, but I don't think you can. I'm not sure I should be taking Martin. Edward's paying for it all and Linda seems to have asked the world and his wife.'

He had shaken a rueful head, and today he would wander the park or the seafront, trying to wrap a week's worth of fatherhood into two or three hours, while she stood alone at Linda's wedding, trying to appear as though it was from choice.

They were almost at Linda's house when the traffic slowed. 'I bet there's been an accident,' Martin said, leaning out of the window for a better view. A flashing blue light could be seen in the distance and the faint beating of a drum. It was five minutes before the marchers came abreast of them, with familiar banners – *Coal not Dole* and *The Right to Work* – an effigy of Mrs Thatcher hanging from a pole and another that might be MacGregor or any other elderly gent. Margot was in the third rank, arm in arm with a girl in dungarees pushing a pushchair and a middle-aged man who looked like a union official. From time to time he tried to disentangle his arm from Margot's but she held cheerfully on.

Fran turned away, fearful of being seen, and caught Martin's eye. 'Do you see what I see?'

He nodded, grinning. 'It's that Margot.'

The traffic was beginning to move and Fran let out the clutch. 'We used to call her Manky when we were at school.'

His grin widened. 'What does it mean?'

Fran shook her head. 'I don't know ... but something awful.' The spectacle had put them both in a good mood. Even when she put out a hand and squeezed his knee he didn't seem to mind.

She had expected pandemonium at Linda's flat. Instead there was ordered calm. The children were resplendent in new clothes, faces shining, wearing an aura of importance. Debbie was clutching a silver horseshoe in a cellophane packet and the two boys had boxes of confetti. Fran fumbled in her bag and produced her own box for Martin. When the white-coated driver arrived and spirited all four children away, Fran had time to take stock of Linda. 'You look lovely,' she said. It was true. Linda's angularity had softened to slenderness, her bust looked fuller, her cheeks rounder. The cream dress with its neat collar looked exactly right for a second-time bride, the bunch of silk roses that formed her hat set off the long dark hair.

'Are you sure?' For a second the old Linda looked out, uncertain and afraid.

'I'm sure,' Fran said firmly and then, suddenly feeling responsible, 'Are *you* sure you're doing the right thing? There's still time.'

Linda smiled, suddenly at ease. 'Oh yes, I'm sure. You think he's funny, I suppose – I know everyone thinks that. I've seen the looks. He does fuss around and he likes everything just so. But he's thoughtful, Fran. He makes me feel I'm important ... even the kids, they know they count. I only hope I don't let him down, that's all.' She put up a forefinger and wiped her nose. 'My God, I'm getting bloody maudlin again and I've never had a drop.' She crossed to the wall unit and took down two glasses. A bottle of sherry was produced from the cupboard. 'I'm trying to give this up but I need one now. Bloody hell, you don't get married every day. I'm trying to give up swearing too, for Eddy's sake.' She sipped. 'Ooh, lovely!'

Fran held out her glass and they clinked. 'To marriage. May it be a happy one.'

They clinked again. 'I'll bleeding well make sure it is,' Linda said and drained her glass.

'Dearly beloved, we are gathered here ...' She had turned and smiled at David then, and he had reached for her hand and squeezed it. Someone had let out a sob behind and she had known it was her mother. Now she sat in the unfamiliar church and listened to the service. Linda and Edward were being married in the Reform Church which permitted the marriage of divorced people at the minister's discretion. She looked down at Martin but he was rapt. He was always rapt in church. Perhaps he would wind up a vicar. She was picturing her mother's celestial delight if such a thing came to pass when someone moved into the pew beside her. 'I made it,' Steve whispered, and bowed his head in prayer.

She felt a suddent exultation, a clutching at her chest that could hardly be borne. He was here, he cared! She was glad when the organ pealed out 'Love Divine' and she had to concentrate on her hymnbook.

She had accompanied Linda in the bridal car, leaving the Mini at the flat. Now she climbed into Steve's car for the journey to the reception. Martin had made himself part of the official bridal party and would ride with Linda's children. 'They looked happy, didn't they?' Steve said as they drove out of the churchyard. They had looked happy, both of them. Linda had looked cherished and Edward had kept a protective eye on the children as photographs were taken.

'He'll love being a father,' Fran said.

Steve laughed. 'I give him two weeks. It's not as easy as it looks.'

Suddenly Fran realized he was thinking of his own children; picturing them, if Jean remarried, walking down the aisle behind a new father-figure. She wanted to say something reassuring but as usual she couldn't find the words.

Linda had banished her family from the house before she left for the church but they were prominent at the reception – aunties and uncles and cousins by the dozen, all in the mood for a knees-up. Hilarity accompanied the speeches and the nudge-nudge, wink-wink telegrams, and grew to a peak when Edward rose to make his speech. Fran looked at him apprehensively. Poor stuffy old Edward ... how would he take all this?

Edward, a lock of hair falling on to his forehead, looked at least ten years younger. He was, he said, the luckiest man imaginable. Not only did he have the loveliest wife in Britain, he had the three best children in the world. Linda allowed him a fair measure of hyperbole and then gave a gentle tug to his sleeve. 'That's enough, dear.'

Edward looked round as if to say, 'See how gloriously henpecked I am already?' and sat down.

'I thought you told me he was bossy?' Steve whispered, and all Fran could do was shrug.

The couple were seen off in a snowstorm of confetti and silver horseshoes. Edward kissed all the children and promised untold

treasures upon their return, and the car clanked off in a flurry of
Ostermilk tins tied to the rear bumper. Linda's cousin was looking after the children. 'She says I can go too, mam. Four's no
more trouble than three. Besides . . .' Martin tried to sound nonchalant . . . 'she says I'm a good influence on them. She wants
me to come.'

Fran sought out the cousin and checked. 'Of course he can
come. They'll all have to bunk in, I've told them that. But he's a
proper little gentleman, isn't he? That polite! He's been here
before, that one.'

So it was arranged. 'It feels funny to be free,' Fran thought as
they left the hotel. Nothing to go home for except Nee-wan, and
Bethel was seeing to him.

'Where shall we go?' Steve said. 'Do you fancy a big night out?'
He had managed to persuade Jean to let him take the children
tomorrow, so he too was free.

'I'd like a cup of tea,' Fran said, 'and I'd like to take off these
shoes. There's something about weddings that goes to my feet.'

They talked of the strike as they drove to Linda's to pick up the
Mini. 'So he's really going to do it this time?' Steve said when she
told him about Fenwick. 'If one or two of them make a start it'll
open the floodgates. But they won't get in without a fight. The
mobile pickets are hit-men, nothing less.'

Fran shivered. 'Don't let's talk about it. I don't want anything
to spoil today.'

It was cool in Steve's flat, cool and dark after the heat of the
day. They stood in the centre of the room, mouths together,
fingers fumbling with buttons and zips. 'I love you, Fran.'

She wanted to say, 'I love you, Steve,' but some tiny mechan-
ism held her back – until he was moving with her and through
her, taking away her consciousness so that the dead man's handle
fell away and she could cry, 'I love you,' and feel no shame.

Beside her Steve stirred. 'What are you thinking about?'

She put out a hand and laid it on his belly. The flesh did not
quiver as it would have done before they made love. Now he was

[104]

at peace. 'I was thinking about them. Do you think they'll be happy?'

Steve considered for a moment. 'They've got as much chance as anyone else. More, probably.'

She turned on her side, sliding her hand further so that her arm was around his waist. 'Do you ever think about Jean? You know what I mean?'

Again he paused before answering. 'Sometimes. We were married a long time you know. You remember.'

It was not the answer she wanted. It was emphatically not the answer she wanted. Of course he would remember a wife of fifteen years' standing. Reason told her that, but instinct could not bear it. She wanted to get out of bed, pull on her clothes and rush from the house. Instead she laid her lips against his chest and moved her hand to fondle his cheek.

He groaned. 'Not again. I don't believe it. This woman is insatiable. Help!'

She giggled and started to tickle him, seeking the places where she knew he could not bear it. 'This is good,' she told herself. What did the experts say? '*A good laugh in bed is worth a thousand orgasms.*' They had loved and now they were laughing. It was all right.

But long after they were still she thought about that shadowy figure, the woman who had given him his children, and knew that she was right to be afraid.

13

Saturday, 1 September 1984

Long after she was back in the house the horror of the scene clung to her. She had come out of the shop and heard a clamour. At first the distant sound had not been frightening – a compound of excitement and laughter, children's voices, a barking dog ...

And then one word rose above the rest: 'Scab. Scab. Bloody scab!' She had stood, stupid, in the street, arms full of purchases, and wondered what was going on.

And then Fenwick had rounded the corner; Fenwick who now went doggedly to work each morning and returned in the afternoon from his permanent, lonely back-shift. Around him women and children swirled, taunting, mocking, spitting hate. Teenage boys, faces alight, lunged forward to aim a blow, or mouth an insult. But it was Fenwick's face that held Fran's eye. The lines of good humour were gone, the double chin was now a slack pouch, the eyes stone-hard and fixed ahead. He walked on steadily, not heeding the blows, the hard words. He walked as though the crowd around him did not exist, not even when their spittle flew through the air and landed, glistening, on his clothes. Some of the women in the crowd Fran knew from the school gates or the corner shop, but they were strangers now, fierce creatures exulting as though around the guillotine, wielding their pushchairs like scythes. Fran moved back against the shop window as they came nearer. 'Scab, scab ... fucking scab!' Children used the oath freely, recognizing it as a word that would not bring rebuke – not now, while Belgate was at war. Fran recoiled at the sound. No matter what the cause, it could never be right to teach children to spew out hate.

And then, as Fenwick drew level and she saw the tic at the side of his mouth, she was filled with a sudden and insensate rage. Who had a right to block anyone else's path? She moved forward, determined to fall in beside him, demonstrate solidarity. A woman's face loomed up, grinning: 'Get the scabby bastard!' Her eyes flicked over Fran's face and then back to it, sensing a stranger, someone out of step. Gold rings hung from her huge lobes, the holes of their insertion pulled down by the weight. It was the woman Fran had seen in the corner shop. Her eyes locked with Fran's and challenged: '*With us or against us?*' they said, without room for compromise.

Fran dropped her eyes and turned, clutching her shopping before her like an excuse.

The cock-crow sounded in her ears a thousand times before

[106]

she reached her own door and was safe inside.

The house seemed cold, or else what she had just seen had chilled her. She went through to the kitchen and checked the boiler. They were burning the dust from the coke house now. She put a poker through the bars, but there was no answering glow. She shivered and shut the boiler door. She could pile on cardigans when winter came, and anyway she was at college all day and Martin at school. But what about Treesa? If the unthinkable happened and the strike went on till Christmas, what would become of the baby? As she straightened up she resolved to keep Treesa and the baby warm somehow, even if she had to chop up the furniture. What else could she do? The whole area was picked clean of anything that would burn, even fences and park benches. Besides, she would never have the nerve to steal wood. But she would keep Treesa warm, one way or another! She looked at the calendar: 1 September. *Surely* this misery couldn't last till Christmas?

She put Nee-wan on the lead after lunch and went prospecting for fuel. She had hoped Martin would come with her but he was off on some jaunt with Mike. 'You find the wood or the coal or whatever, and we'll come and carry it later on.' He was turning into a thorough little procrastinator! Mike was more helpful: 'I could get you a bag of duff. Our Terry's digging tons out of the railway. Me mam says she can do without anything except a fire, so he gets it nearly every day.'

Fran felt bound to point out the dangers. 'The banks could cave in, Mike. I've seen warnings in the papers. It's happened in other places, and people have been buried alive.'

Mike's smile was pitying. 'Our Terry's a face-worker, he knows all about getting coal.'

Looking at his face, full of pride, Fran knew it was useless to argue. 'Well, I expect he has plenty to do, keeping your fire on. Don't worry about us, we'll manage.'

Martin was less tactful. 'Does your dad dig coal off the line?' For perhaps the first time, Fran saw Mike Malone nonplussed. His eyes dropped. 'No. Me dad doesn't go down the line.' Then the old spirit re-asserted itself. 'But he could if he wanted!'

So the conflict between Terry and his father was getting to Michael. As Fran got the car out she wondered for the thousandth time if Scargill and Thatcher had any idea of the havoc they were causing in ordinary people's lives.

People had changed in the last few months. They looked older, more determined – or perhaps her view of them had altered. She was certainly reacting to the coal strike. It was still summer, the air was warm, but she was possessed with the need for fuel like the rest of Belgate. She could heat water with the immersion heater but it would not do. She wanted a fire, a living flame, a symbol that life in the coalfield still went on. That was why men tramped the woods for sticks or flitted through the darkness with buzz-saws. It was a sign that they were not yet defeated.

As she drove toward the blast, she thought about the first time she had gone there. David had told her of the beach beneath the colliery where they tumbled waste into the sea, but nothing had prepared her for the sight. Now, as she crossed the mineral-line tracks, the landscape changed, as though someone were dropping grey filters one by one before her eyes. She drove between banks of rubble, a compound of earth and shale, with everywhere twisted wire and cable, and once the remnants of some ancient tree. The sea came into sight, and then the beach; but this was no Hawaii. A fine grey silt sloped to the sea, rising like smoke at every footfall, turning to slurry when the tide lapped at its edge.

On her first visit she had stood there horror-stricken, and known this was the landscape of the future, when man had blown himself out of existence. There were no birds, no blades of grass; no fish could swim through that sludgy sea. She had picked up a rounded stone from her feet and it had fallen to pieces in her hand.

Above them the pit had stood castle-like against the sky, the gantries of the tippers like Triffids, silent and watchful. She had shivered and turned to David. 'This is a place of desolation.'

[108]

Now she parked the car and walked forward, hoping to pick through the waste for enough to keep the boiler going for another day. Others were there before her. A man in a pork-pie hat went by, pushing a bike. A half-filled sack lay across its saddle. 'There's nowt left, pet. It's picked clean.' The beach came into view and she saw them, heads bent, scrabbling for nuggets in the blackened sand. As she watched, a woman straightened up, empty-handed, and shook her head in a gesture of despair. Fran turned away and went back to the car.

She parked above the allotments and let Nee-wan out of the car. He bounded ahead, stopping now and then for some extra-special smell. Everywhere she looked there were signs of de-forestation. The newly cut stumps shone white through the greenery, raw evidence of the search for fuel. And always the saplings. No one had time to take the old, dead trees that could be spared; they took easier prey, trunks no bigger than a man's wrist, logs that would flare up for a moment and then subside to grey ash. God damn Arthur Scargill, Fran thought. Thirty years from now his mark would still be left on the British coalfields.

She was turning for home when Nee-wan went into a frenzy of barking. The man was almost up to her before she recognized him. 'Hallo, Mr Botcherby. It seems we had the same idea.'

He had a bundle of twigs under his arm, small pieces that had been missed by earlier gleaners. His shoulders were hunched under the navy donkey jacket, and he needed a shave. 'Aye, it's a sad carry-on when a collier's reduced to this.' He had stopped to speak but he avoided her eye.

'How's your wife?' Suddenly she was afraid of intruding and hastened to give him a get-out. 'And Angela? I haven't seen her lately.'

He shifted his wood to a more comfortable position. 'The bairn's all right. The missus ... she's bearing up.' He sought to change the subject. 'You'll have run out of coal by now, I suppose?'

Fran was relieved. 'Yes, well, almost ... it's coke I use. I had the offer of some duff from the mineral line but I didn't think it would burn in my boiler?'

[109]

A trace of a smile crossed his face. 'I was all for going down the line till I got a look. It's Piccadilly Circus down there. There's that many backsides sticking out of them embankments, it looks like a Butlin's Bonny Bottoms contest.'

Fran laughed. 'Is it safe?'

He was getting ready to move on. 'Safe enough for them as knows what they're doing. Besides, safe or not, what else can they do? We're all living dangerously now, Mrs Drummond, and God knows what the end'll be.'

Long after he had passed from sight and she and Nee-wan were back in the car, she was trying to work out what he'd meant.

Treesa was in the kitchen when she got back and the kettle was on the boil. 'Tea! Lovely!' Fran subsided into a chair and opened the evening paper. There were the usual letters for and against the strike, and one from 'Industrial Democrat' who said the ordinary miner could truthfully say, 'I am the union', and, if he wanted to go to work, cross picket lines with a clear conscience. Mrs Thatcher was saying miners who returned to work would end the strike, which Fran felt would surely prolong it by another week or two. Every time the leaders of either side opened their mouths, it was a setback.

But it was the 'Quote for Today' that caught her eye and made her look across at Treesa, curled in a chair with a mug of tea clasped in both hands, her eyes fixed on nothing in particular. It came from the Director of the Population Institute: 'A girl who has an illegitimate child at sixteen suddenly has 90 per cent of her life's script written for her. Her life chances are few.' Treesa was not sixteen, but she was little more, and for the next sixteen years at least her role as a mother would over-rule all others. If Brian had lived it might have been different. Then again, it might not. Could you find undying love at eighteen or nineteen. Or would you wake up at thirty and find yourself married to a stranger?

She looked up to find Treesa's eyes on her. For a moment she was disconcerted, feeling Treesa must have known what she was thinking. But Treesa had something else on her mind. 'I've been

[110]

thinking ... now that the bairn's settled down and I've got a bit more time, I think I'd like to give the women a hand.' She looked at Fran apprehensively. 'Would you mind?'

'Of course not.' Fran's answer was swift. 'I know some of them go on a bit, and Margot's a pain, but I agree with what they're doing. Especially for the single men – I don't know how they're surviving.'

Treesa nodded. 'Brian would've been in there helping, wouldn't he? That's why I want to do my bit.'

It was true. Whether or not he had agreed with the strike, Brian would have pitched in, loyal, cheerful ... to the bitter end.

'I know he would,' Fran said, 'and I think you should help. It'll get you out a bit, too. You haven't had many laughs lately, have you? And I'd love to babysit when I'm here.' She was about to suggest Bethel as an extra babysitter when there was an urgent knock at the door.

'Let me in, Fran! Hurry up!' Min was shouting through the letter-box in her haste to gain admission. 'Oh God, Fran, I'm in such terrible trouble,' she was babbling all the time Fran was pushing her into the front room and closing the door for privacy.

'Shut up a minute, Min. I can't take it in if you talk like that.'

For the first time in years she saw signs of the old down-at-heel Min of their schooldays. Her nose was red with crying and mascara streaked down her cheeks. Her blouse clashed with her jacket and the sleek black hair was spiked with anguish. 'It's Dennis. He's gone berserk. Like a maniac! I've tried to explain but he won't listen ... you'll have to go and see him ... he's always had a soft spot for you, Fran. Tell him it was all a joke. I'd never have let it get out of hand, you know that!'

Fran took a deep breath. 'Min, sit down and pull yourself together. I suppose Dennis has found out about Hindson-thingummy. Well, it serves you right. Eve did warn you. I expect it'll all blow over....?'

She was about to suggest a nice cup of tea when Min began to jump up and down. 'Oh for God's sake listen, Fran ... blow over? *Blow over?* He's packed my bags! I'm out in the street. He's got it all worked out ... maintenance, access to the kids ... he's going to sell my Capri ... it isn't that I mind *that*, so don't say it is. I know you all think all I care about is money, and I admit it's important ... but I actually like Dennis. I like living with him. But he won't listen, he's shown me the door, Fran. I'm telling you ...'

Fran left Treesa to make tea for Min, and got out the car. What *was* she going to say to Dennis? She could hardly accept Min's picture of him as a raging bull, but she still wasn't sure how to handle it. '*Now look here, Dennis ...*'? Or, '*Before you speak ... I know you've got every right to be angry ...*'?

In the end it was Dennis who began the conversation. 'Come on in, Fran. I wasn't sure whether it would be you or Eve. Of the two, I'm glad it's you.'

He led the way across the parquet-tiled hall to the kitchen. A bottle of Blue Nun and two glasses stood on the table. He poured wine for them both, sat down, and swung his crossed feet on to the table. 'Come on then, get it over. The kids are at Mum's, so you can feel free. And I know what you're going to say, it's all been a misunderstanding, she's really a good little girl, and can she come back?'

Fran took a good swig of wine. 'Something like that.'

He held his glass to the light and squinted at it. 'Well, between you and me, the short answer is "yes".'

Fran felt a sudden desire to laugh. Surely it wasn't going to be this easy! She fumbled for the right words. 'I really think she's sorry, Dennis ... and after all, it didn't get that far. I mean ...' She was on dangerous ground here. 'Well, you know Min, it's more talk than anything else.'

He was grinning. 'Yes. She's big on promises but not so hot on performance.'

Fran felt herself blush. When all this blew over, she would murder Min for putting her in this situation. 'Shall I tell her to come home then?'

He looked at his watch. 'Not yet. We'll give her another hour, just to let it sink in.'

Fran looked at him for a moment and then took the bull by the horns. 'Dennis, I think you're enjoying this.'

He lifted the bottle and topped up their glasses.

'With a bit of luck, Fran, I am going to have the best year of my life out of this lot. When she comes back, I'll tell her she's on probation. I've told her I've seen a solicitor – I didn't tell her it was for a drink at the squash club. If she gives me a touch of the geishas, it'll stay on the file. Otherwise . . .' he tilted further back in his chair and smiled, 'it's out into the cold, cold snow.'

Fran began to laugh, wiping tears of merriment from her eyes. 'How long have you known?' she said at last.

'From the beginning . . . but there's always a psychological moment to intervene. You learn that in business.'

Fran reflected that Dennis had more nous than anyone had given him credit for. No wonder his family had made so much money out of their furniture business. They had the business instinct! As she left the kitchen, Dennis gave her an affectionate pat. 'Don't let her off the hook, Fran. It's for her own good.' So she would tell Min she could go back home on sufferance, and in all probability Min would be grateful to her for acting as go-between. It was a bit of a cheat but it was all in a good cause.

Fran sent Min on her way with a final word of warning. 'Don't forget it's hanging by a thread, Min. I talked him round, but it wasn't easy. You'll have to tread carefully for a long while.' When Min had gone, she sat down on the bottom of the stairs and hugged her knees. She felt devious and wicked. It was lovely to lie and not feel really sinful. She was wondering how much of the evening's events she should relay to Eve when the letter-box rattled. 'Fran?' Min stood on the step, still dishevelled but resolute. 'Look Fran . . . I don't think we need to tell Eve about this. You know what she's like. She'll be looking at me as though I was in the condemned cell for the next ten years, and as for Harold – he'd just gloat.' She pulled the collar of her jacket into place and touched up her hair. 'Dennis may have been a swine tonight, but I'd rather be married to him than a stuffed shirt. Actually . . . well . . .' A fatuous smile was spreading over her face. 'Well, Dennis has his points.'

When Fran subsided on to the stairs again it was to wonder whether Min really liked the new dominant Dennis, or whether she was simply convincing herself that she did.

She could see the light under Treesa's door and was about to knock when she heard Martin call out. He was sitting up in bed, eyes bright. 'What happened?'

She played for time. 'What do you mean?'

He gave her a knowing look. 'About Aunty Min getting thrown out. Are they getting divorced?' He had overheard some of Min's conversation and put two and two together.

'You mustn't say a word to anyone,' Fran said, and gave him an edited version. He seemed to appreciate being made a confidant.

'Sit down a minute,' he said, patting the bed. She felt as honoured as if she had been asked to share the throne. 'Do you think the strike'll last long?'

'I don't know. It's difficult to judge. They're still talking, so I suppose that's something.'

He was looking down at the duvet. 'I don't know which side I'm on.'

So that was it! 'I don't know either. I try to make up my mind, but then something happens to change it.'

He nodded. 'It's awful in the playground now.' She waited. 'We used to play Police and Pickets, and it was all right at first. But now it's not much fun.' There was an even longer pause. 'People cry sometimes.'

Fran nodded. 'I know. What does Mike think about it?'

Martin shook his head. 'He's the worst. He gets mad with everybody because his dad and Terry don't like each other any more. And he likes them both.'

When she had put out the light and was safely on the landing she let out her breath in a gust of anger. Whatever they were currently discussing in their political seaside hotels, it wouldn't be the agony of one small boy torn between loyalty to father and brother. And yet what could be more important?

14

Wednesday, 24 October 1984

The trees on the campus had shed most of their leaves by now and shivered in the east wind. Fran pushed open the refectory doors to allow Gwen to pass, and the mingled odours of coffee and over-heated fat enfolded them. The red-topped tables were mostly unoccupied, condiments still neatly grouped around a vase of plastic roses.

'It's quiet for a Wednesday.' Gwen put her books down to bag a table and reached for a tray.

Fran followed suit. 'No one's got any money.' That morning she had totted up the stubs of her cheque-book and total depression had ensued. Christmas was looming larger with each passing day and funds were dwindling in direct proportion.

Gwen looked around at her fellow students. 'Well, they haven't spent it on their backs. I know we were too subdued in my day but, God ...! Take any two items; if they clash, wear them!' It was true. The students looked bizarre, boys and girls alike. But cheerful!

Fran looked up to find Gwen's eyes twinkling. 'I'm showing my age, aren't I? And I'm jealous. Look at those waistlines.' She sat down, looked at her sausage roll, lifted it, and bit firmly. 'After today, no more.' She emptied her mouth and licked her lips. 'Heard anything of the newly weds?'

Fran shook her head. 'I must get over there soon. They've moved into Edward's house; Linda loves it. And him! She was on the phone at the weekend. She says she goes from room to room, counting.'

Gwen shook her head. 'I have to take your word for it ... that she loves him, I mean. Loving Edward! The mind boggles. When you think what we endured with him prosing on all the time. He knew better than us, he knew better than the lecturers

... he knew the lot!'

Fran nodded. 'Yes, he was a bit of a pain, but I think he was frightened. Uninvolved and frightened! He was out of his depth on the course, and then he went back to an empty house. He had to be pompous to keep his nerve. He's quite different now, he's always laughing. If you saw him with Linda's kids you wouldn't recognize him.'

It was true. Edward looked ten years younger, fatter, more muscular. 'In fact,' Fran reflected wryly, 'I half wish I'd nabbed him myself.' But Linda had done for Edward what Fran had been unable to do. Had she, Fran, done better by Steve?

'You're doing it again!' Fran looked up as Gwen spoke to find the other woman's eyes bright with affection.

'What?'

Gwen smiled. 'You know! Going moony. Thinking about that boy-friend of yours. You ought to set the date.'

Long after the conversation had turned to the coming teaching practice, Fran felt an uncomfortable flushing of her face and neck. It came whenever she thought of remarriage. She couldn't stand in a church and make the same vows. It would be a mockery.

'I'd like to get Broad Street again,' she told Gwen. She had done her first teaching practice at Broad Street Juniors and it had been the pleasantest of experiences.

'I shouldn't think you will,' Gwen said. 'They like to shuffle us round. We might get too happy if they didn't.' They grinned in mutual antipathy to their college authorities and began to gather their books.

'How are things in Belgate?' Gwen asked as they left the refectory. 'I keep forgetting you live in the battle-zone.'

As they walked back to the lecture room, Fran tried to explain what Belgate was like now. 'You think before you speak all the time. You stand next to someone you've known for ages and the subject of the strike comes up and you think ... Dare I speak? Are they for or against? It's awful. You want to say what you think, but you don't want trouble.'

As they passed through the lecture room doorway Gwen

pulled a face. 'That's how these things happen in the first place. The majority are afraid to speak out.'

All through the psychology lecture Gwen's words were uppermost in Fran's mind. Perhaps you should speak out, and to hell with the consequences. But if you did you'd be in constant hot water. And the issue of the strike was more complicated than most: even Walter was confused. He and Bethel had always argued over politics but it had been light-hearted, almost a game. Now their disagreement had a cutting edge. Yesterday he had lashed out at Bethel over the Christmas appeal that Wearside miners had launched. She had looked at him stony-faced. 'They should think shame on themselves. They've always had good wages, and now they're cadging. What about them as has no jobs? Who's begging for *their* bairns? There's some been out of work in Sunderland two or three years.'

Walter had bristled. 'There you go! They can't do right in your eyes, can they? They're in a war, you silly old git. Front-line troops. That's why we should see to their bairns ... because they're fighting our battle.'

'I'm not going to take offence, Walter. You've always been proud of the NUM, but you're seeing it dragged in the dust and it's turning you nasty. Well, I'm not going to crack back – although I could – because I'm sorry for you.'

He had glared at her for a moment and then booled his chair towards the door. It was the first time Fran had seen him lost for words, and she had not enjoyed it.

Fran was half-way between Sunderland and Belgate when an ominous thudding began. At first she thought it was the engine, but then the wheel began to buck in her hands and she realized she had a flat tyre. She was on an unlit section of the road and her heart sank. She knew the theory of changing a tyre, but would she have the strength? David had always grunted with effort when he loosened the nuts. And what about the spare? She hadn't checked the spare since she got the car. It rolled to rest at the side of the road and she switched off the engine. The lights of

Belgate winked through a mist of rain. She could lock up the car and walk, but the road lay between open fields. Anything could be in there ... anything! A car might come by and stop, but ten to one it would be driven by a psychopath. With her luck, that could be practically guaranteed!

She had opened the boot and located the jack when the car nosed in behind her. The sight of its blue flashing lamp was at first balm, and then full of terror as she tried to remember if all her documents were in order. 'Having trouble?' Inside the police car the dashboard crackled with tango messages as the driver stated their location. 'Looks like a lady driver in trouble. Yeah!'

His answering laugh to the dashboard's obvious quip brought out the feminist in Fran. 'It's only a puncture. I can manage.'

A young PC uncoiled from the passenger seat and put on his hat. 'Let's have a look...'

As he changed the wheel with minimum fuss, she recognized him. It was the young policeman whose mother lived in the wide back street, the woman she had seen in the shop that day being taunted by the strikers' wives. 'You come from Belgate, don't you?'

He nodded without taking his eyes from his work. 'That's right.'

Fran sought for a topic of conversation. 'Do you lodge in Sunderland?'

He shook his head. 'Share a flat.' There was a pause. 'Just as well, at the moment. I'm not too popular in Belgate right now.' His tone was bitter.

'But you don't do picket duty there?' Fran said.

He was swinging the spare wheel into place. 'No, I went down to the Midlands through the summer. It was quiet up here once they got all the pits out. There was plenty of trouble on the opencast sites with them being privately owned ... the men not in the NUM ... but our lads could cope; so we were sent to Notts and Derbyshire to help out. But since some miners have started going back up here, it's been all hands to the wheel. None of our lads can be spared – in fact we've got men from other forces coming in to help us. I don't do duty in Belgate ... that's the county force, and I'm Northumbria Constabulary. But you get your local hot-heads picketing away from home and word gets back.' He started to tighten the nuts. 'It's not too nice for the old lady, but I just shrug it off. According to them, I'll be able to retire on me overtime pay, so I suppose that's a consolation.' His tone belied his words.

His partner had left the car and come to inspect progress. 'They say we gloat about the pay; that they've got nowt and we're coining it in.' Suddenly Fran remembered Walter's tale of fat pay-packets waved in the faces of hungry pickets. 'But we don't need to rub it in. They're not daft, they know the score. What are we supposed to do – offer to do picket-line duty for free? I know what they'd say about that.' His tone was flat. 'Besides, you get sick. There's no time off. You're out there doing twelve on, twelve off, and you're covering for the men on picket-line duty. Either way, it's work, work and more work. As for days off . . . I've forgotten what they are.'

'You sound fed-up,' Fran said as the wheel was lowered to meet the ground. 'I don't know how to thank you. I was scared stiff till you came along.'

They stood as she climbed into her car. 'No need for thanks, pet. It's nice to be popular for a change!'

As she drove back to Belgate, Fran thought about the two policemen, both in their twenties, both local lads, but outcasts now. If anyone believed the 'fascist junta' was enjoying the strike, they were wrong.

The door was open when she got home, streaming light into the yard. Terry Malone appeared in the doorway, carrying a bucket full of rubble. His hands and forearms were black with soot. 'It's done, Mrs Drummond. Opened up and a good fire going.' She had forgotten about the fireplace! When the coke had run out, she had switched on electric fires to keep everyone warm. It was no good worrying about bills with a baby in the house. But still they had shivered. 'Open up the fireplace,' Terry had urged on one of his visits to Treesa and the baby. 'Open it up, it's only

[119]

filled in with hardboard, and I'll keep a fire going. Nee worry about that.' She had jittered about years of disuse and the capped chimney, but he had waved her objections away. All the same, she had never thought he would actually do it.

Indoors, a fire was burning brightly, duff coal piled on broken pieces of the timber that had framed the fire throat. The hardboard sheet which they had supported stood against the wall. 'I took it down carefully,' Terry said. 'We can put it back when things are back to normal. And I shinned up the roof and took off the cap. That can go back, an' all!'

Bethel was in the kitchen, Treesa's baby propped on one hip, tea-pot in the other hand. 'Sit down and get that door shut. This bairn's nithered with all the comings and goings.' She gave Terry a malevolent look. 'I hope he'll be around when the trouble starts. You can't open up a fire just like that. You'll get smoke pouring out of everywhere, bricks coming down, God knows what. The mess here today ...' Her eyes rolled upwards.

Terry gave a grin and sat down at the table. 'H'away, Sally, give the workers a cup of tea and stop slavering on.' Bethel snorted, but she poured his tea just the same.

'Is Treesa at the church hall?' Now that Treesa helped the support group, Bethel had come into her own. Not only a house to fuss over, but a baby too. It was nice, Fran thought. Nice to see them all getting on together. One good thing out of all the bad. Once it would have been impossible for Bethel and Terry Malone to sit down together and talk. Now they were doing it. Whatever the rights and wrongs of the strike, whatever your position, it was drawing communities together ... except that it was also separating families.

It was warm in the kitchen, heat flowing from the open oven. She had told Bethel to warm whichever room the baby was in, and the oven was the obvious answer. The immersion heater was ticking away upstairs, heating the water for the nappies. When she went to jail for debt, she would have the comforting feel of duty done.

They were on to their second cups when Treesa came in. She turned towards the baby but did not hold out her arms. She looked tired and the fair hair was lank. 'It's taking too much out of her,' Fran thought. 'It's too soon after the baby.' She pulled out a chair and Treesa sank into it.

Terry did not speak but there was satisfaction on his face as he looked at her. 'I'm not tired,' she said, taking the proffered cup of tea. 'Just a bit weary. I've peeled that many taties this week I'm ready to drop.' Her hands looked red and sore, with brown patches down the side of the left index finger. 'It's been a thin week, so we've been making stovies.'

Fran had never encountered stovies till she came to Belgate – layers of sliced potato and onion cooked with butter or marge and topped with cheese, if you were in the money. 'Is that all they get?' she said. She was always haunted by thoughts of protein. Miss your protein for a day and your legs gave way. She knew it was crazy, but she couldn't help it. And miners, used to four good meals, were now reduced to stovies.

Treesa had revived with the cup of tea. She held out her arms for the baby. 'Who's been a good lad, then?' He lay in her arms looking up into her face. She smiled at Bethel. 'I don't think he wants his mammy, he's happy with you.'

Bethel struggled to keep a poker face and lost the battle. 'He's a good bairn, I'll say that for him. It's nee trouble to me to keep an eye on him. Not that I agree with what you're doing, mind; don't think that. Dragging everybody back to the soup kitchens. It's a disgrace. They want to get back to work.'

Terry drained his mug and put it down on the table. 'Come on, Sally. It's the right to work we're striking for. We could take redundancy, sit back or get bussed to another pit. Then they close Belgate. What happens to your young lads then, the ones coming out of school? Where's their jobs? I'll tell you ... down the drain, because we sold them out. I'm not facing them year after year to tell them why there's nowt but the dole queue.'

He's right, Fran thought. They *are* fighting for more than their own jobs.

Bethel did not agree. 'Hold hard, there. You've got it all down nice and pat; Scargill's got you well trained. But stop and think a minute. Take your bad pit ... it costs you £90 a ton to bring coal up. You sell it for £30. Who foots the difference? The government? They've got nowt, only what they take off the people. So they take extra to keep your pit open. And the ones they've taken it off – what about them? What about their jobs? It's all very well to say, "Make sure I'm all right Jack." But what about the other feller? Look at the middle of Sunderland – it's getting to be a ghost town, with shops closing that can't afford to stop open for the rates and taxes. So they close, and a few dozen shop-girls get tossed on the street. Never mind, as long as the pits stop open! You'll face them, will you, and say "Hard lines"?'

Terry was shaking his head. 'That's half the trouble, you know. Everybody's an economist, they've all got a recipe. "Do it this way and it'll come up roses." Arthur's got the only answer: operate the pits for people not profit.'

Fran was trying to put her finger on the weakness she knew was somewhere in his argument when Bethel spoke, not in her usual sharp tones but a more measured way. 'You may well be right, Terry Malone. I am an old woman, and ten to one I see things too simple. But I know how to spot a bad 'un and I had Arthur Scargill spotted long afore he was elected to anything. He wants to play God and move a few mountains, and as long as you silly buggers let him get away with it we'll all have to suffer.' Suddenly the old fire flickered. 'He's set son against father. Don't tell me that's right.'

Fran felt her cheek flush. That was hitting below the belt. She saw Terry's Adam's apple bob, but when he spoke his voice was equable. 'I'll say this for you, Sally, you've got a wicked tongue on you sometimes.'

Bethel grinned. 'I can stick up for meself. Don't go forgetting it.'

Treesa launched into a hasty discourse about the support group, designed to pour oil on troubled waters. Fran drank her tea and gave thanks that the argument had gone no further. There was one thing about life in Belgate: it got down to the nitty-gritty. None of the dissembling of life in Sunderland – and no generation gap either. Terry was a third of Bethel's age, and yet they had been able to argue without any sense of strain.

Suddenly she realized Treesa was talking to her. 'Sorry, Treesa, I was miles away.'

Treesa smiled. 'It was nothing. I just said that friend of yours was there again today, the one with the CND badge. Nobody can stand her. I mean, it's good of her to come and everything, but ... well, she doesn't do much.'

'You want to tell her,' Fran said and Treesa grinned.

'Someone did. "Let's have less solidarity and a few more taties peeled." That's what they told her. Well, Ella Bishop did. She dares say anything.'

Fran looked enquiring. 'Do I know her?'

Treesa nodded. 'You're sure to. She's a big wife, dark hair, wears big gold hoop earrings. She's got her man and her two sons on strike. She works like a slave; she can lift the sacks about like feathers. And she's a wonder at getting stuff off the shops.'

Fran nodded. 'I know she is. I've seen her at it.'

Before Treesa could reply there was a loud crack, and then a clatter as Nee-wan shot out from the living-room and ran behind the dresser.

'God's mercy, what was that?' Bethel said. Nee-wan was pressed against the wall, eyes wide, his body racked by shivering.

They moved as one to the living-room door. 'Jeez,' Terry said.

A fire still burned in the grate but they could see it only dimly through the pall of smoke that hung in the air. As Fran watched, huge particles of dust began to settle on everything. 'I warned you,' Bethel said with grim satisfaction. 'You can't say I didn't warn you.'

While they cleared up, they had a heated discussion as to the cause of the explosion. Bethel blamed the unused chimney, Terry some impurity in the slack coal. 'It could've been a detonator,' Treesa said, but Terry laughed at the idea.

'We wouldn't be sitting here if it'd been a detonator, Treesa pet. We'd be sitting on clouds playing harps.'

Bethel did most of the clearing up, wielding the Hoover like a badge of office. Fran retired to the kitchen and put on the kettle again, and Treesa followed, the sleeping baby in her arms. 'It's amazing the way they'll sleep through things, isn't it?' Fran said.

'Even wars. As long as they're safe in their mothers' arms, nothing else matters.'

Treesa nodded. 'I know. It's the mothers that suffer. I feel sorry for the women in the support group, the ones that's got kids. They have to keep refusing them things . . . daft little things you'd take for granted, like an ice-cream or a penny bubbly. The kids don't understand. One woman cried today. She said, "My bairns look at me as though I begrudged them." I felt really sorry for her. And she's not the worst.'

Bethel had come back into the kitchen and was listening as Treesa continued.

'They were on about Mary Botcherby today. You know, she lives in Stafford Street? They say she's in a bad way. He's beside himself, but what can he do? He's always been a big union man.'

Bethel was shaking her head. 'I've been expecting this. She may be the first, she won't be the last. It's tick; they've got that much tick, no one could keep it up. Mind, I'll say one thing for Mary Botcherby – she never ticked on her grub. Some of them buy the week's groceries with a Provvy, and then they're paying for it for the next twenty weeks. But she had more sense than that. It was always cash on the nail for her week's shopping.'

Fran was remembering the scene in the corner shop not long after the strike had begun, when Mrs Botcherby had asked for credit for a few items of groceries. So that was why she had been so upset that night; the bastion of her financial affairs had been breached.

'I had a flat tyre on the way home,' Fran said as they drank more tea. 'I was trying to change it myself when a Panda car stopped. It was that boy whose mother lives in the wide back – he did it for me.'

Bethel cast a jaundiced look in Terry's direction. 'Aye, he's always been a good lad.'

Terry smiled. 'I'm not arguing, Sally. He is a good lad. He was one of our Brian's mates in school, and I've never heard a wrong word said about him. I know they've given his mam some stick, and I've told them it's wrong. But you can't blame them for having it in for the pollis, not after what's gone on on the pickets.

[124]

They join arms to hold you back and it looks as nice as nine-pence; and then, when there's nee cameras around and you're up close, they lift their knee.' He grunted. 'Just like that. And you're knackered for a week. They know all those little tricks.'

Fran could not believe that the entire police force was bent on disabling the striking miners, but there was no mistaking the sincerity in Terry's voice. Whether or not it had happened, he believed that it had.

When they had all gone she carried the evening paper through to the living-room and sat by the spitting fire. There was a terrible smell of soot but it was nice to see a flame. The front page carried pictures of the deterioration of Durham coal-faces. '*Recovery will take months*.' NACODS, the deputies' union, was poised to do a deal and avoid a strike; and 3,000 pickets had faced six rebel miners in Yorkshire and failed to turn them away.

The day before yesterday an angry crowd had besieged the police station in the next village to Belgate, howling allegations of police intimidation: but what about the intimidating effect of mass pickets? There had been road-blocks at Easington when the strike first broke and hundreds of men had pitted themselves against one returning miner. What were the police supposed to do? Cut off his brush and throw it to the waiting hounds? The word 'scab' had once meant the healing of a wound: now it was a missile to be hurled between former friends, with the police caught in the middle. Even in Belgate she could sense the tension when a police uniform appeared. The Sunderland MP had accused the police of a massive abuse of power and an erosion of civil liberties. But whose liberties?

There were the usual newspaper columns about men in court for stealing coal – but how could anyone expect them to sit and shiver in the shadow of stockpiled coal that seemed to mock their misery? Several times she had seen men scurrying by with coal, and once a cruising Panda had driven past and ignored the culprit. She minded them stealing coal a lot less than she minded the carnage in the woodland. Every time she saw them scavenging for wood she meant to protest, but their cold pinched faces stilled her tongue.

[125]

She put down the paper and turned on the telly. As she'd feared, the image of Arthur Scargill appeared. He was countering questions about men going back to work with his usual defence: 'There are more men out now than at the beginning of the strike.' As with most of his statements, it was based on truth but a distortion of that truth. The Belgate men and others like them had come out two weeks late on the promise of a ballot, so the numbers on strike had risen. But they had not come out because of fervour for the cause, as Scargill was suggesting; they had come out in the belief that by doing so they would get a ballot, and would then be able to vote for the strike to end.

It was a relief to climb into the car and drive away from Belgate. 'I will not think about the strike,' she said aloud as she passed the pit. The taste of soot was still on her tongue, in spite of cleaning her teeth, and enough was enough. They were eating Chinese tonight and she meant to enjoy it.

They chose a corner table and relaxed in each other's company. 'This is nice,' she said over coffee. 'Just sitting, not having to talk.'

Steve smiled. 'You're easily pleased.'

She put out a hand and touched his arm. 'I like being with you.'

Even in the shaded light of the restaurant she could see there was something sad about him tonight, an air of harassment. 'How's business?' she said. 'I know it can't be easy at the moment.'

He shrugged. 'Business never is easy. Beats me why there's always another mug ready to strike out on his own. But it's not that – it's Jean.'

Fran's heart sank. Steve's first wife was not her favourite topic of conversation.

'She knows about us. I suppose Julie let it out – Ian wouldn't say anything. He gets the brunt of it if she gets her temper up. Anyway, she's determined to play me up over the kids. She thinks they should spend every second Saturday with her, and they have to visit her mother on Sundays. She's trying to make it so difficult that I'll pack access in, but she'll have a long wait.'

Fran was puzzled. 'Why should she mind about us? She didn't . . .'

The words died on her lips. They were not flattering, but Steve finished for her. 'She didn't want me? Of course she didn't. Not while no one else did. But now you've come on the scene, it's different.'

They made an effort to change the conversation. 'What about Min?' he said. 'Is she still toeing the line?'

She regaled him with tales of Min's new role as Dennis's personal and private geisha. Steve laughed. 'It won't last. It's against her nature.'

Fran was not so sure. She looked at Dennis with new respect nowadays. He had handled his crisis very well indeed. She had always thought him weak, but she had been wrong. When the occasion demanded, he could be strong enough. Stronger than Harold – if Eve had taken a lover, Harold would have gone to pieces.

The thought of Eve taking a lover was so hilarious that she laughed out loud. 'Come on, share the joke,' Steve said, and she had to explain.

But in spite of the joke he still had a hang-dog look about him. She gathered up her jacket and bag. 'Let's go,' she said. She would take him home and comfort him in the only way she knew how.

15

Thursday, 15 November 1984

The classroom walls were covered with the trapping of Christmas, red-nosed reindeers and bloated Santas, three Marys and Josephs, and a dozen babies spilling out of straw-filled cribs.

Even the hamster's cage was topped with artificial holly and the ceiling lights cascaded tinsel. Fran looked down at the child's jotter once more. The heading '*Preparing for Christmas*', neatly written and underlined with more gusto than precision. A holly leaf was carefully crayoned in one corner with the statutory three berries underneath, but it was the words that held Fran's attention. '*We are not preparing for Christmas. There will be no Christmas till someone gets that slimy bastard Scargill off my dad's back.*'

She looked at the sea of down-bent heads. They were reading 'Charlie and the Chocolate Factory' and every face was rapt. She turned back to the essay: '*My dad has been on strike for thirty-two weeks. We go to my gran's on Sundays for a feed, and my mam has given the dog to some people. He was a good dog but she says he had to go. I want a BMX and Tracy wants a Sindy doll and some clothes, but my dad says when he goes back to work. I don't mind much but he does. He doesn't go out any more and my mam has stopped dying her hair. She says she feels old. Last Christmas was good. This one will be all right but we are not preparing much.*' She put '7/10' in the bottom right-hand corner and closed the jotter. If only she could write with so much power! If only she could show that essay to Scargill and Thatcher.

She wanted to tell Gwen about it in the staffroom, but Gwen was surrounded, and had tears of mirth in her eyes. 'So the kid was half-way out of the door when he turned back. "Here, miss, are you a student?" I said yes, and he thought a bit, and then he said, "I said you weren't. You look too old." I pushed him into the corner and I said, "I looked all right when I came in here this morning, but you lot would get anybody down."'

The bell signalled the end of coffee-break before Fran got Gwen to herself and by then it was too late, but the thought of that bleak appraisal of life in a striker's home stayed with Fran throughout the next lesson and up to the bell.

It was two weeks since the NCB had offered a bumper pay-packet to those who returned to work; £658, and no tax to pay. But still the Belgate men stayed firm. It was crazy really. They had voted against the strike in the first place, had been brought out by an untruth, and still they refused to cross a picket line. Not

[128]

even for £600. Terry had tried to explain it to her. 'They voted to stay in – a lodge ballot. So it was all right to go on working. Well, I didn't think it was, but that's by the way. Then they came out ... once they'd agreed to come *out*, they couldn't go back and cross a picket line. That would be blacklegging. You won't get a Durham miner blacklegging. They won't be bribed, not if they were offered £6,000.'

She had tried to express her puzzlement. 'But they were lied to, Terry.'

For the first time he had looked uncomfortable. 'It's not as simple as that, Mrs Drummond. They weren't exactly promised.'

She had referred to all the letters in the local paper from men who felt they had been betrayed, and he had taken refuge in incomprehension. 'Don't ask me, Mrs Drummond. I don't know what they're on about. I only know they came out under Rule 41, all straight and above board. And any road, even if Arthur has made mistakes, who else have we got to stick up for us? Tell me that. He said, "Come out," and I did!'

And he would stay out, she had no doubt about that. No matter what the privation, he would stand firm. There was the uncomfortable glow of a zealot in his eyes, and she both admired and feared it. He would stand firm while Belgate bled, while trees and fences went up in smoke, and men scrabbled in the earth of the mineral line for the makings of a fire. This morning she had seen the battle buses for the first time: single-deckers, every window covered with metal grilles. Behind the armoured windscreen the driver sat tense, his face obscured by a rapist's hood for fear of reprisals. There had been three men in the bus, that was all – fewer than the number of police accompanying them. She had felt a frisson of fear as she drove past. It was 1984, after all, and Winston Smith nearer than she had thought possible.

When she got home Treesa was already pouring tea. 'Eeh, Mrs Drummond, you're in for a laugh when you go in the room.'

A fire smouldered in the grate, duff was piled on to old wood. Nee-wan sat behind the settee, shivering uncontrollably, eyes wild. From time to time he peered cautiously round the edge of the furniture to check on this strange new addition to the home. A stick caught fire and cracked in a shower of sparks, causing the dog to twitch convulsively. 'He'll be a nervous wreck by the time things get back to normal,' Fran said, and sat at the kitchen table to drink her tea. The *Echo* headlines were stark. The leader of the back-to-work revolt at Wearmouth had had the windows of his home shot out. In spite of this discouragement, 139 more men in the North-east had gone in. The trickle back would continue, and with it all the misery of a divided coalfield. Every night there were lists of men in court for picket offences or stealing coal. Every family in the mining villages was becoming involved. Fran herself, although she had no direct connection with the pit, could think of nothing but the strike. But more and more her chief emotion was disbelief. How could a strike which the majority did not want drag on for nine months? She put aside the *Echo* and went upstairs to get ready.

She ran a wickedly hot bath. Now that the boiler was out of use she was using the immersion heater, which lurked in the airing cupboard, a voracious beast, gobbling up ohms or watts or whatever they called them. When the bill came in she would rue every moment spent in getting clean, but for now she was going to enjoy it. As she lay in the scented foam she thought about Steve. If they were married, he might be standing at the basin, shaving, making jibes. He might cross to the edge of the bath and flick the suds or scrub the unreachable places between her shoulder blades. If they were married, he might pull her dripping from the water and make love to her there and then on the curly carpet. 'I wish I were seeing Steve tonight.' Saying it aloud seemed to exorcise her longing, and she got on with preparing for an evening at Min's.

The one sure thing about tonight was that Margot would not be there! Since she had espoused the miners' cause, Margot had been put back on Min's list of no-longer-desirables. It had been strange to watch Min over the three weeks since she had arrived, tear-stained and distraught, on Fran's doorstep. She was as well-groomed as ever. She still made quips about Dennis, but once when she called him 'hopeless' her eyes had met Fran's and suddenly been filled with confusion. It made Fran feel powerful, being the only one who knew about the showdown. She was still curious about Dennis: there seemed to be a new set to his jaw, although he was as affable and apparently *laissez-faire* as ever. Did she just imagine the change, or had there always been a hint of steel beneath the sugar-coating? Just as Harold was marshmallow underneath, for all his blustering?

The suds were beginning to settle now. She hated that moment. In the bath you were safe, isolated from your troubles as though you had boarded a ship and waved good-bye to the shore. Once you stood up and lifted a foot over the rim you were back on the treadmill. She settled down in the water, determined to postpone reality for one more moment.

It was difficult to know who had come out on top in the Min/ Dennis situation. Dennis had appeared to dominate; on the other hand Min had got clean away with things. She had even kept her Capri. Fran realized she was grinning like an idiot and shut her mouth. The all-important Capri! It was true about cars being phallic symbols. Min enjoyed driving around in her fuschia pink penis, and would give up anything to keep it. So who were the weaker sex? Who finally won out?

On Saturday she had gone with Treesa to the support group. It was partly curiosity that took her there, partly a desire to help. Food was dwindling as shopkeepers felt the pinch. The local Co-op had set up a box by the door and people were tipping in one or two groceries as they left with their shopping, but it was never enough. Treesa's tales of families whose only meal of the day was at the church hall, and particularly of the plight of the single lads who had no income other than their picketing fees, had touched Fran's conscience. She had seen a boy going by with his meagre gift of food and felt her eyes fill. So on Saturday morning she had cleared out her tins cupboard and accompanied Treesa to the church hall. Remembering the gold-earrings woman she had been scared, but the faces that turned to her were welcoming. 'Come and look at this girls!' someone had shouted. 'Corn in Egypt.' They had oohed and aahed over tins of soup and packets

[131]

of suet. 'Let's get stuck in then, lasses,' a thin elderly woman said, and began to peel carrots.

Fran's intention had been to dump her gifts and run, but somehow she found herself dutifully chopping turnip. 'It's Irish stew,' her neighbour said, wiping away a tear. 'I don't know whether this bugger's grief or onions,' she went on, smiling at Fran. 'I'll be glad when I'm cooking for four again instead of feeding the five thousand.'

Fran nodded. 'It must be a strain.' She had a sudden feeling of sisterhood with the woman. It was not as she had imagined; these woman were ordinary wives and mothers, neither bold nor militant. Certainly not menacing as Gold Earrings had been. Perhaps the bold ones were sent out to forage; the gentler ones stayed home to stir the pots. As if the other woman had read her thoughts, she grinned. 'It's awful, isn't it . . . having to scrounge? It's not what we've been used to, but when it's a question of feeding your bairns you don't split hairs. I daren't go round cadging, so I'm on permanent onions. It's not as though I agreed with the strike, but we're all in it together now, aren't we? Whether we like it or not.' There was a pause, then she continued. 'I know who you are . . . and your little boy. I was sorry when you lost your man. He was no age. And it's good of you to help out.'

They looked at one another for a moment and then went back to the vegetables. Emotion was misting Fran's eyes, and she took out her hanky and blew her nose. 'It's the onions,' the other woman said. 'The bloody things get everywhere.'

When the stew was bubbling away in the huge open pans they sat round the table together, elbows on the board, discussing life in general and the strike in particular. 'It'll last into next year.' The speaker was relighting a cigarette stub no longer than her thumbnail.

'My God, Jenny, if you can't say something cheerful, say nowt.'

The smoker blew a defiant ring. 'I'm telling you! My man's never liked going down the hole. He's in his element now. He's got an old settee outside the pit gate, and he sits there declaring solidarity. If it's left to him, they'll be out till he's sixty-five.'

There was a roar of laughter. 'All the same, we've got to stick it out. If Maggie Thatcher beats the NUM she's got the working classes by the short and curlies.'

There was a murmur of agreement. 'I've told my man I'll cut his balls off if he goes back.' The speaker was young and plump and determined. '"I'll suffer," I've told him. "I'll give the bairns and do without meself." But if he scabs he'll come back to find the door shut.' The mood around the table was changing. Some chins were thrust out, other heads down-bent. The sound of the door clashing broke the spell.

'Treasure Trove!' Manky Margot advanced, her arms full of goodies. 'Take these, they're defrosting.' She recognized Fran. 'Oh good, you've come at last.' She leaned towards her. 'I've emptied Jean Goodison's freezer. "It's no good pontificating," I told her, "you have to be active." So she gave the lot.'

Relieved of her burdens, she put up her hands and tucked her lank hair behind her ears. Her sweater was brown. '*The colour of faeces*,' Fran thought and blushed at the very idea. Her CND badge was still in place but *Coal Not Dole* had been replaced by *I'm Supporting The Miners*. She turned towards the women, rolling up her sleeves. 'Right then, lead me to it.' As she walked towards the sink, the onion peeler lifted the frozen leg of lamb she was holding and brandished it at Margot's back. 'I'd like to,' she mouthed at Fran; and Fran, to her shame, had nodded agreement. Margot was a pain.

Since that first visit ten days ago, Fran had been back once, to deliver a sack of potatoes paid for by Gwen. 'Tell them I think they're mad but I like their guts,' Gwen had said when she handed over the money.

'I wouldn't dare,' Fran had answered.

Gwen nodded. 'Then say they came from St Jude. He's the patron saint of lost causes, isn't he?'

The bath water was stone cold now and Fran heaved herself to her feet. If Min or any of her cohorts rubbished the support groups tonight, she would defend them. After all, what else were girls' nights but middle-class support groups? Except that sisterhood only lasted until you went to the loo and it was your turn to be done over.

In the event, no one was really interested in the strike. There was a little gloating when Fran appeared, but it was soon over. 'There's 139 gone back today, Fran. Good old Maggie, she's going to win.' Fran smiled non-committally and they returned to their previous topic of conversation, the inquest on Diana Dors's husband. Half of them thought it romantic that he had died rather than live alone; the other half were sceptical. 'He'd lost his meal-ticket, hadn't he? So he lost his bottle. Heaps of people lose their partners, but they go on living.' They looked to Fran for confirmation. She had wanted to die after David's death, but life had re-asserted its hold.

'Can't we talk about something cheerful?' Eve said. God bless Eve, always pulling the irons out of the fire.

They ate from the usual groaning board, making the usual vows to diet tomorrow. Eve carried her plate to where Fran was sitting and perched on the arm of the chair. 'Everything all right?' Fran knew what Eve was after: she wanted information about Min's affair, but was too proud to ask.

'Fine,' she said ingenuously. 'How's the baby?'

But Eve was not to be deterred. 'He's blooming ... but that's not what I'm worried about.' Her voice dropped. 'What's Min up to? One minute she was flaunting that Hindson-Evans man, and then suddenly everything went dead. I can't get a word out of her. She just plays dumb when I hint and puts on a saintly expression.'

Fran made a show of wiping crumbs from her mouth while she worked out what to say. 'I'm sure it's over, Eve. In fact, I'm certain.' Eve was torn between desire to believe what Fran was saying and a fear that Fran was more in Min's confidence than she was herself. 'She didn't tell me,' Fran said hastily. 'I heard it from someone who works at the Royal. Hindson-Evans has a new girl-friend. A staff nurse in the theatre. Apparently it's quite serious this time.'

Satisfaction flitted across Eve's face, to be replaced by solicitude. 'Poor Min ... still, it was only to be expected.'

As Eve moved away, Fran glanced up to find Min's anxious

[134]

eyes on her. 'OK,' she mouthed, and had to repress a smile at the look of relief on her friend's face.

They ate and drank, then used up some of the surplus calories by dancing to a Wham LP. 'It was marvellous, Min,' Fran said as she made her escape.

'Drive carefully,' Min called as she climbed into the Mini. 'It worries me, the thought of you going back to that place. God knows what they'll get up to next.'

As though to belie Min's words, Belgate lay tranquil and silver in the moonlight without a sign of discord. Fran would have liked to pause in the car-park and drink in the sight of sea and sky, but it was after eleven and she knew Treesa could not sleep in an empty house. Remembering how scared she had been in the days after David's death, Fran always tried to be home before midnight.

Treesa was not alone when she entered the kitchen. Terry sat by the cold boiler, huddled in his donkey jacket, an Adidas grip at his feet. 'He's left home,' Treesa said, looking at Fran round-eyed. 'His dad's going in in the morning, and they've had a row.'

Fran looked at the boy's face, pinched now with misery. 'I can't stop with a scab, Mrs Drummond. He's betrayed the Union!'

Fran's heart sank at the boy's words. The strike was starting to crumble, but Terry refused to face it. In spite of the brave sentiments at the support group and Scargill's cockiness on TV, the dyke had been breached – only a few men as yet, but the return would snowball.

She unbuttoned her coat, fumbling for the right words. 'He doesn't see it that way, Terry. He thinks it was the Union who betrayed him. Can't you at least try to understand his feelings?'

The reply was swift. 'Scabs don't have feelings!'

Inside Fran something snapped. She was tired of trying to see both sides. 'For God's sake, it's your father you're talking about, not a total stranger. *He* has a right to work if he wants to, just as *you* have a right to strike.'

[135]

Terry got to his feet and reached for the grip. 'I won't argue, Mrs Drummond. You're entitled to your point of view.'

Treesa's eyes were beseeching. 'He's got nowhere fixed up, Mrs Drummond.'

Outside a fine rain was falling and the wind was from the east. 'You can stay here tonight, Terry. I can't let you freeze. But I won't be drawn in to a family quarrel. Your parents are my friends. You'll have to make other arrangements.' She saw his chin come up and hurried on. 'And don't give me any rubbish about pride. It's pride and arrogance that's responsible for all the trouble in this village. If you won't stay for your own sake, stay for Treesa's. She's got enough on her plate without worrying about you.'

Before she got into bed she pulled back the curtain and looked at the rain-soaked pavements. Where was it all going to end? Margot's badge had proclaimed *I'm Supporting The Miners* – but which miners? Those who had been forced into a strike against their will and who were trickling back day by day? Or the diehards like Terry, who would rather lie down in the gutter than share with a scab? Even when that scab was the man who had given him life.

16

Saturday, 1 December 1984

The sweaters were soft and luxurious and hideously expensive. She hesitated between beige and loden green, and decided the latter was more sensible for a man on his own. There were tiny Christmas trees at each end of the counter, and the till was covered in tinsel. While she waited to pay she thought about last Christmas, her first without David. She had wandered from shop to shop, rudderless, uncertain what to buy for Martin, turning her eyes from the sight of couples rapt with the magic of

Christmas. Now, a year on, she was buying a lambswool sweater for Steve.

A wave of longing for David washed over her. They had filled Martin's stocking together on Christmas Eve, one holding open the pillowcase, one putting in the parcels, laughing and whispering, standing at the foot of the bed to gloat over the child they had made together. She was roused from an ache of nostalgia by the sales-girl's 'Can I help you?' She put down the green sweater and turned away. 'Thank you, I haven't quite made up my mind.' Impossible to buy gifts for one man while you were remembering another!

She went up to the restaurant and bought herself a cup of coffee. There was still money about in Sunderland, in spite of the strike. The Wearmouth pit was huge, but its workers were only a small part of Sunderland's population. In Belgate the strike had killed Christmas. Streets that in times past had bristled with lighted trees in uncurtained windows were dark now, curtained to keep out the cold. But the cold got in just the same. That was the overwhelming impression now, as though winter had got into everyone's bones.

People who had never gone without a fire in their lives still sat by empty grates, as though by concentration they could restore a flame. 'I haven't been warm this year,' an old woman had told her yesterday in the street, and she had seen that the mis-shapen knuckles were blue. She sipped her coffee and tried to remember the summer. They must have been warm then. The summer had been grim but quiet, before the strike got its second wind. Scargill had promised that General Winter would defeat Mrs Thatcher, but it was his own troops who were succumbing and still he was marching on towards Moscow, oblivious of casualties. The faces of the strikers and their wives were desperate, but not as desperate as the faces of the tallymen who moved from house to house in search of payments they knew would not be forthcoming. The economy of Belgate was based on tick. Now the pendulum had slowed to a standstill.

She looked at her watch. Still half an hour before she was meeting Steve. A woman cleaning tables loomed into sight, and

Fran raised the empty cup to her lips. She never dared to occupy restaurant tables unless she could be seen to be there by right. She wondered if Steve was in the store already, guiding Julie around the toy department, and wondered once again what would happen at Christmas. He hadn't mentioned it yet, and she didn't like to ask. The attendant began to clear the next table, throwing half-eaten food into a plastic container and stacking plates. Across the world in Ethiopia people were dying of hunger, and here the means of their salvation was shovelled into swill. Fran gathered up her bags and rose to her feet. If she sat here any longer she would get the blues, and she wanted to be in a good mood when she met Ian and Julie.

She bought the sweater and some new lights for the tree, and quelled her rising panic over money. There was only one way to cope with Christmas: get what you needed and worry about it later. If you once paused to cost it out, you would wind up carving an Oxo cube. In each department the clocks ticked remorselessly towards four o'clock. She thought of Laurence Olivier urging 'Once more unto the breach', and made her way to the rendezvous. Last year Julie had been a small dark-haired girl in a Red Riding Hood coat and Fair Isle knee-socks. Today she wore cord jeans and a fur-trimmed jacket, but the small, closed face was the same. Last year she had ignored Frances. Today she muttered a sulky 'Hello' and tugged at her father's arm. Each time they had met in the last twelve months, Fran had made an effort. It couldn't be easy to leave your mother behind and meet your father's girl-friend. But there was something faintly insolent in the child's attitude that made forbearance hard. The boy was different.

'No Martin?' he said. There were small pustules on his brow and a faint moustache along his upper lip.

Fran smiled. 'He's gone off with Mike Malone to look for firewood. They're going to make a fortune in one afternoon.' He had always been kind to Martin and she was grateful. 'How are the A-levels?' He fell into step beside her and she nodded sympathetically as he recounted his troubles.

They paused in the rainwear department. 'What about Santa

Claus?' Steve asked hopefully.

Julie's nostrils flared. 'No way!' Last year she had been a child afraid of the bearded figure; today she was a woman, contemptuous of the very idea. It was too swift a transition. She turned to her father and administered the *coup de grâce*. 'It's a proper con, mam says. They only give you rubbish.'

As they sat in the restaurant, Fran toyed with haddock and chips and thought about the future. If she and Steve were married, Julie would be her step-daughter. Access days would be statutory, even access weekends. The fish turned to wormwood in her mouth, and she chewed frantically. Suddenly she caught Ian's eyes. He was looking at her sympathetically, as though he knew what she was thinking. If she married his father, there would be Ian too, so it wouldn't be too bad.

She was about to ask his plans for Christmas when she realized what a mine-field that would be. Would he expect to spend it with his father, or accept that his father's place was now with her? At seventeen could you relinquish your father to another home, another family's Christmas? She was glad when the meal was over and they made their way from the store. 'See you tonight,' Steve murmured, eyes bright with fear that she might expect a kiss in front of Julie. She curbed an unreasoning impulse to clasp him around the neck, and made her dutiful good-byes.

She called at Bethel's, on the way home, to hide the gifts she had bought for Martin. 'I like him to be surprised,' she told Walter, who was drinking tea by Bethel's one-bar fire.

'Well, he won't find out from me,' Bethel said, shutting the cupboard door on the gifts to emphasize her point. 'But I doubt you'll keep quiet.'

Fran opened her mouth to protest but Bethel had moved on to higher things.

'The money's pouring in for that taxi-man's bairns.' She pushed a mug of tea towards Fran. 'Pit folks sending in out of shame, I shouldn't wonder.'

Fran looked at Walter but he was uncharacteristically silent. The day before, a man driving miners to work had been killed when a concrete block crashed through the window of his taxi. 'They've come down to murder,' Bethel said, remorseless. 'The miner used to carry his head high but now ...' She caught Fran's apprehensive glance at Walter. 'Oh, he'll say nowt. Ask him about Libya ... watch him squirm!'

Walter's mug thudded to the table and the wheels of his chair spun for the door. Fran could bear no more. 'Walter, please ... she's only teasing. I know she shouldn't, but don't fall out!'

He turned at the door. 'I don't have to stay here and listen to rubbish, and neither do you. Hadaway to your own home and see to your bairn. You'll get nothing out of that one. She's far ower bitter.'

Bethel's reply was triumphant. 'I've stung you this time, Walter, haven't I? Your precious NUM's gone cap in hand to Gadaffy ... that's what you cannot stomach.'

To Fran's horror she saw Walter's lip tremble. 'No, I can't stomach taking cash from them as shot down a nice young girl, Sally Bethel. But think shame of yourself for rubbing my nose in it. It's bad enough to hear Union men saying, "We'll take cash from anyone." It's bad enough to see the Union I had pride in prostitute itself for money, but to have a friend ram it down me throat ... that's too much.'

When he was gone Fran felt her face going stiff. She was angry with Bethel and she would have to say so, but she didn't know how. It was Bethel who broke the silence in uncharacteristically meek tones. 'Aye, I suppose I went a bit far.' Fran tried to look reproachful, and Bethel bristled. 'But was it or wasn't it the truth? They're messing in the gutter now, and we might as well all admit it. Canny lads like Fenwick being tormented night and day ... no, it's time to stop excusing it. This is not a pit strike; the bugger's political, and that's wrong! We'll shift Thatcher through the ballot box. No other way!'

As Fran parked the car in the back street she resolved not to think about the strike any more that night. She wouldn't read the *Echo*, not even if she got withdrawal symptoms. She was contemplating a hot bath and a blow-wave when Martin met her in the kitchen doorway, eyes bright. 'Mrs Malone's here.'

Fran motioned him to precede her. 'All right then, let me get in. It's cold out here.' They eyes met and he grinned. 'Yes,' Fran said dryly. 'And it's cold in here. I hope you took Mrs Malone in to the fire'.

The big, red-haired woman was sitting by the fire, her grandchild on her knee. 'By, he's lovely, isn't he? The image of his dad.' Treesa was sitting proudly on the other side of the fire, enjoying praise of her son.

'Have you had some tea?' Fran asked.

Treesa nodded. 'It's not been made long. I could top it up. Would you like a cup?'

Fran was about to refuse, having had about as much tea as she could drink, when she saw Mrs Malone's face. There was a plea in the blue eyes. 'OK,' she said. 'Yes, I'd like a cup.'

As soon as Treesa had carried away the teapot, Mrs Malone moved forward. 'I don't want her to hear, Mrs Drummond. She's that thick with our Terry, she's sure to tell him and then he'll turn awkward. I want you to speak to him, Mrs Drummond. He'll listen to you. It's killing his father. Killing him. He lost one son to the pit, now he's losing another. I'm not sure this isn't worse, seeing a lad you've brought up walk past you in the street.'

The baby on her lap stirred, disturbed by the vehemence of her tone. 'There now, pet, hush a minute for your nana. It's breaking my man, I'll tell you that for nothing. He's stood up to a lot in his time, but this'll finish him. Him a scab, him as stood by the Union right and wrong for years! I've seen him cry ... and I'll never forgive Scargill for that. You know why he went back – because they tricked him out. Betrayal, that's what he calls it. I don't know the ins and outs, I cook and clean, I'm not political ... I don't blame Scargill any more than Thatcher. But they're trying to murder this coalfield between them, I do know that.'

There were sounds of Treesa's return from the kitchen and she drew back. 'Mind on what I said ... don't let him know it was me that asked – but do what you can.'

There was no time for a bath after Mrs Malone's departure, so

Fran picked up the evening paper after all. Scargill was in the High Court fighting over NUM assets. Nothing new there! She turned to the letters page for her daily fix. As usual the letters all had pseudonyms, derived from the same fear that caused men to appear on local TV with their backs to the camera. Shades of Big Brother! One writer wanted the NCB to invoke the law. Another, signing herself 'Fed-up Miner's Wife', wanted to know where cash donated to miners' families was going, because she wasn't getting any of it. 'Plain Common Sense' wanted Maggie Thatcher to '*Climb down and help this country*,' and 'Worried Mother' vowed that if the council helped the miners at Christmas she would never vote labour again. '*My husband has been out of work for four years, and we have had nothing.*'

As she folded the paper Fran reflected that the strike was turning the out-of-work against the miners, and that was a pity. A recent article had asked sympathy for the pregnant wife of a striking miner, but at least she had a wage to look forward to at the end of the strike. For the out-of-work there was nothing.

She met Steve in the Saracen. He was making jokes, fussing over her drink, but she could feel the unease in him. It reminded her of dates with Edward a year ago – an attentive escort who was nevertheless on hot bricks. It was not a pleasant feeling.

She sensed his relief when she mentioned the strike. 'How's your support group going, or have you chickened out?' She told him about her last flying visit. 'I took some potatoes, and they were pleased. But that big woman was there ... the one with the hoop earrings ... she scares me. It's as though she's ready to explode all the time.'

He smiled. 'Who says women are the weaker sex?'

'You don't think it'll end before Christmas?' Fran knew the answer even as she asked the question.

'No chance. They're making their preparations for a striking Christmas – toys from France, turkeys from Germany. All your show-biz do-gooders rallying round to help the miners and none of them with a blind idea of what the miners really think ... the real miners. The ones that go down the hole instead of attending Union meetings.'

[142]

'Things'll have to be different when all this is over,' Fran said. 'The rank and file'll have to have more say. And I think they will. They've learned their lesson.'

Steve shook a doubtful head. 'They'll forget the pain. They'll start to earn again, and they'll forget.'

'I think you're wrong,' Fran said. 'It's gone too deep. Families split, marriages cracking ... they'll remember, all right.'

They were on to the coffee now and suddenly tension was there again. 'Look, Fran, there's something I must get straight...'

He was not going to be with her at Christmas. Jean had invited him to stay over the holiday to be with the children. 'I've said yes ... you know how much it'll mean to Julie. Besides, Jean would only take it out of Ian if I said no. But I'll make it up to you at New Year. You know who I want to be with, don't you?'

Fran hung on desperately to her dignity. It would be all right as long as she didn't cry. 'Of course you must go. I wouldn't want to be separated from Martin at Christmas. I understand.'

Driving home she felt anger wash over her. Damn Jean! Damn Julie! Damn Steve, for that matter! What about her Christmas? And Martin, with no man around? How bloody dare he drop her at Christmas and run back to his wife? His ex-wife, for whom he seldom had a good word? She knew she was being unfair, but she couldn't help it. She understood the anger: it was the emotion you substituted for other deeper emotions that could not be borne. A return to the primitive, a beating of the chest at the absolute bloodiness of life. It wasn't as though she was madly in love with Steve. As Belgate came into view she tried to analyse her feelings for him, but it was difficult to know where love began and fear of a vacuum ended.

She moved into a lower gear and into her own back street. She had brought the car to a standstill when she saw the masked figure, all dark except for the white patch that contained his eyes. And then another and another, coming over a backyard wall further down the street.

When at last she plucked up courage to get out of the car, the back street was empty. Useless to tell herself that she had imagined them – they had been real and sinister.

When she got in she would dial 999. But even as she thought it, she knew she would not.

17

Christmas Eve 1984

'Will it do?' Treesa's face was anxious. The dress, which had fitted her before the baby, now bulged at every seam, riding up over her stomach.

Before Fran could speak Bethel sniffed. 'You want some sugar on your ankles!'

Treesa's face was blank. 'Sugar on me ankles?'

Bethel smiled as the well-sprung trap closed. 'To see if you can 'tice that skirt down a bit!'

Fran laughed nervously but Treesa's eyes filled. 'I knew it was too short! Well, that's it, I just can't go.'

It took five minutes to calm Treesa down. 'Honestly, Bethel,' Fran said, when Treesa had gone back upstairs. 'Honestly ... she hasn't been across the doors for a year. Now Terry's persuaded her to spend one night at the club – it took him weeks, and he can ill afford it – and you've done your level best to ruin everything. You're getting worse.'

Bethel looked back, unrepentant, cheeks rosy beneath the grey hair. 'If she's that easy put off, she's better stopping at home.' She saw Fran's lips forming an angry retort and hurried on. 'Any road, I didn't come round here to argy-bargy over Treesa Carruthers. I came for two reasons. One – are you going out with that feller of yours tonight? I need to know if I'm wanted, I can't drop everything. And second, what time do you want Walter round here tomorrow? I'll be coming in early to do the veg, but we don't want him here criticizing.' She paused for breath, and then delivered a final thrust. 'And to go back to Treesa for a moment, I wouldn't be encouraging anything between her and that lad if I was you. He's not like their Brian – *he* did have a bit about him ... the only one of that family that wasn't barmy. This one's a proper little communist. He's left of Mao Tse-Tung, if you ask me.'

Fran stood up. 'I'm not going to rise to the bait, Bethel, not on Christmas Eve. You know how I feel about the Malones. I'm going to put the kettle on and we'll have a nice cup of tea.' She ignored Bethel's allegations that she would be waterlogged from tea-drinking if she came round here much more, and brewed the tea. She didn't refer to not going out with Steve later on, and with surprising tact Bethel did not repeat her question. Instead she brought up the matter of Christmas toys.

'They've all been gloating over what they were going to get from the miners in France. Toys? You'd think it was double-decker buses they were expecting, not Dinky cars. Any road, there's only a few stocking-fillers come, by all accounts. I met one lass this morning, crying. Her man's COSA – good enough to strike with the NUM but not good enough to get the toys. They're for NUM only. Not that she's missing much – Ellis's wife went for her four bairns, and came home with two plastic skittles for the little 'un. She was nearly hairless when I saw her. Serves you right for counting your chickens, I told her.'

Fran groaned. 'Honestly Bethel, talk about a Job's comforter.'

Bethel's eyes flashed. 'I've got no comfort for this sackless lot. They want to get back to work before there's no work left to go back to. There's faces collapsing right, left and centre. I've told Walter – Scargill'll close more pits than MacGregor could. Mind, I've got no room for that American bugger; he's less use than a one legged man in an arse-kicking contest, if you'll excuse the language. But this business of begging here and scrounging there ... they're out in Durham market place with tins, bold as brass. My man won't be turning in his grave, he'll be spinning. Money from that mad Arab ... all right to pal up with murderers, but they'll cross the street if they see Fenwick doing his bit shopping. And there's Botcherby trying to put a good face on it while his wife goes round the bend and his poor little bairn gets

[145]

old afore her time. If that's pride, if that's loyalty, I think he's giving it to the wrong ones.

'And that's not all! You've got daft wives with bairns in push-chairs marching on the Electricity Board protesting at being cut off for non-payment. It's not fair, they say. And while they're protesting, their men's dancing round the power stations trying to get us *all* cut off, old-age pensioners and everybody. "Make your mind up," I told one. "Do you want to freeze, or don't you." Old people there, never done any harm to anybody – they've cut off their concessionary coal, or if they get it it's full of stone. They're sitting shivering over one-bar fires, and the strikers are even trying to stop those. "It's not Mrs Thatcher you're punish-ing," I've told them. "It's your own kith and kin." But they don't listen.'

Fran tried to point out that Mrs Thatcher had cut £1 off heat-ing allowances and slashed regional aid, but Bethel was deaf to reason. 'There's Alfreton pit collapsing for want of safety work. You know why? One girl went in to type and the safety men downed tools: "We're not playing if she's playing!" Talk about bairns? I told Walter, and he says the lass should've known better ... the lass should! He's getting worse!'

She was still on her soap-box when Fran escaped to the shop for some last-minute purchases. Normally at this time the shop was crowded both sides of the counter. Last Christmas Eve she had stood in rank to wait her turn. Now the shopkeeper coped alone and the only other customer was Mrs Malone. Fran's heart sank. She had tried to persuade Terry to go back home but had come up against a stone wall. '*I cannot, Mrs Drummond. It's not that I wouldn't ... but how can I ask the lads not to scab if I sit down at the table with a scab meself?*' When Fran had relayed a version of his answer to his mother, she had put down her head on her kit-chen table and cried. Tonight she gave Fran a wan smile. 'Eeh, it's not like Christmas Eve, is it? There's nobody in the streets. You'd think it was the middle of the night.'

The shopkeeper joined in. 'It's the daft little things you miss – that's what they tell me. The nuts and tangerines and the big fire, getting your hair done, even wrapping paper. There was a woman in here last week cried over the wrapping paper. "I've got nowt to wrap up," she said, "but I still hanker for a nice bit paper and string."'

As Fran walked home she was remembering the Sunderland vicar who had warned that miners' marriages were on the brink of disaster. That had been weeks ago. This Christmas would make them or break them, but none would escape its effect.

She made the stuffings when she got home: sausagemeat for the neck, and sage and onion for the inside. The trifle base was already in the fridge, the roast potatoes par-boiled and coated with butter to preserve them. She deserved a rest! She carried the *Echo* through to the spluttering fire and curled up in a chair to get out of the draught.

According to the paper, an uneasy peace had settled on the coalfield since the pits closed last Friday, and there would be no picketing of safety men over Christmas. MacGregor had gone to the States for a family Christmas there, and the thought of his departure cheered Fran enormously until she read that Arthur Scargill would be having a working holiday. 'Oh dear,' she thought, and went back to the kitchen.

Martin was at the fridge, filling two glasses with milk. Mike sat at the kitchen table. 'You look miserable,' Fran said.

His usually cheerful face was glum. 'I'm all right.'

Martin closed the fridge door with his elbow and carried the two glasses to the table. 'No, you're not.' Mike's brows came down in warning but Martin was not to be deterred. 'He wants their Terry home for Christmas, but he's stopping at his lodgings.' Mike's eyes were on the glass of milk but he did not drink. 'Go on,' Martin said, 'tell her. She knows already. You can't keep a secret from someone who knows already.'

Suddenly Mike was out of the chair and round the table. 'Shurrup,' he said, between clenched teeth. His fist caught Martin in the chest and sent the milk flying. Mike looked at Fran, eyes half-afraid, half-wild. 'I don't care,' he said, and then again, 'I don't care!'

When the kitchen door slammed behind him, Fran fetched the dishcloth and mopped up the milk. Martin rinsed the glasses

[147]

in the sink and stacked them on the drainer. She wondered if she should speak, but wasn't sure what to say, and it was a relief when the phone jangled in the hall and called her away.

'I'm off now,' Steve said. 'Girded up for the ordeal.' She knew what he was trying to do – assure her that it was the children he was going to see and not Jean.

'It won't be so bad,' she said, wishing her voice carried more conviction.

'Thanks for the parcel,' he said. 'It feels nice. Don't open yours till tomorrow.' There was a pause and then, 'I love you, Fran. You know that.'

She made tea and carried a cup up to Treesa. 'Don't panic,' she said. 'Just drink your tea and then we'll fix things up. I've got heaps of things, and I'm bigger than you.'

Treesa slurped her tea and sniffed. 'Nobody's bigger than me. I feel like a house end.'

Fran nodded towards the crib. 'He was worth it, wasn't he?' The baby slept serenely, unaware of tensions within and without the house that was his home.

Treesa smiled. 'Yes. Well worth it.' She blew her nose on a tissue. 'I'm sorry to be going on like this, but it's been a bad week.'

Fran nodded. 'I know.' The day before yesterday had been the anniversary of Brian's death in the pit. Treesa had carried the baby to Mass and returned dry-eyed and composed, making Fran ashamed of her own reddened eyes. Now she sat down on the edge of the bed. 'Things will get better, you'll see. They'll sort out your compensation soon; the strike will end eventually ... it has to. And then things can get back to normal.'

Treesa nodded and was about to smile when a thought struck her. 'You won't want us out of here, will you? When the money comes? Not straight away? That's why I've never grumbled about it taking so long to prove about Christopher being Brian's bairn, and having a right to claim, and everything. Because I was happy stopping here.'

Fran reached out and covered Treesa's hand with her own. 'You and Christopher belong here. For as long as you want to stay.'

One day, if things went right, Treesa would have a home of her own and a man to love her, but this was not the time to mention it. As if on cue the baby stirred and woke, and they could crowd round his crib to admire. Sometimes, Fran thought as she went downstairs, sometimes it seemed children were the only worthwhile thing in life. The only thing that didn't cause you pain. Then she remembered the Malones, and the pain caused there by son to parents. So there was no escape after all, no area of life which guaranteed you peace.

It was hard to imagine Terry as a militant when he knocked at the door and entered the kitchen. His hair had been trimmed of its wildness and he wore a collar and tie. She couldn't resist a comment. 'You look smart.'

The rosy cheeks grew rosier. 'I thought I'd make an effort, seeing as it's Christmas. One of the women at the support group, she used to be in a big hairdresser's. She's doing cuts. She does a canny job, doesn't she ... 50p for a married man and 25p for lads.' He grinned. 'Another good reason for not getting wed.' He looked down at his clothes. 'I got the shirt and jacket from the nearly-new last Wednesday, and the tie's me mate's. I'm lodging with his mam. She said put it on.' Suddenly there was a silence between them. Mention of his new lodgings was a reminder of the home he had left, and of Fran's efforts at persuasion on his mother's behalf.

As she licked her lips to try again, he spoke hurriedly, as if to stem embarrassment for them both. 'Is Treesa ready? We'll have to get down the club or we'll not get seats.'

Fran was not so easily put off. 'Are you going to call on your parents over the holidays? You can say it's none of my business and you'd be right. But the strike's over now, surely you can see that? Why prolong the bitterness? I feel so sorry for your mother, losing Brian and now you. And think of your father...'

He cut across her words. 'He didn't think of me did he, before he betrayed the Union? I've taken some stick because of him. I'll never forgive him. Hard? I know it's been hard – hard for everyone. But we've stuck it out. We will stick it out, Mrs Drummond, don't get any wrong ideas. The rats can scuttle back, but the men'll stop out till Doomsday if they have to. Look at Billy Botcherly – *there's* a bloke to be sorry for, if you like. A wife bad with her nerves, and everything. But he doesn't crack! He's on the rack, that man, but he doesn't scab! My dad's always had good money; he could've stuck it out ... so I'll never forgive him, Christmas or no Christmas.'

Fran felt bound to defend Mr Malone. 'He hasn't gone back for the hardship, Terry, or the money. He's gone back because of what he sees as an injustice. He wasn't given a say; they've even denied the men meetings. There are others who feel the same, Fenwick for one. It's an NUM rule that you ballot on a strike, isn't it?'

His nod was contemptuous. 'Yes, let's have the old chestnut trotted out again. As for Fenwick, he's made his bed. I didn't agree with his pigeons being brought into it, but that wasn't the Union, that was hot-heads. There's been attacks on Union men's homes, don't forget that! It's not just violence by our side. Everything that's been done in this strike's been strictly according to the constitution. Arthur's a good Union man, he plays it straight. Everything he's done's had the backing of the executives. And them as go against the decisions of the executives are scabs.'

Fran's spirit failed in the face of such intransigence. Terry was marching to his own drum, and nothing and nobody would change him. He had scrabbled for duff to earn the money for tonight's outing – pointless to spoil it with an argument, especially one that could not be won ... 'I'll go up and see if Treesa's ready,' she said, and left the room.

She found Treesa sitting on the edge of the bed, one hand on the crib where her baby slept. She was dressed in her slip, covered by a wool cardigan. 'I cannat go, Mrs Drummond. I cannat get into me dress ... an' anyway, even if I could, I can't face it. Everyone'll be thinking about Brian. I know it, I can see it on their faces. They don't understand about Terry and me ...' Suddenly, she looked up. 'You know there's no funny business, don't you?'

Fran offered up a swift prayer for guidance and sat down on the bed. 'Yes, I know exactly how things are between you and Terry, Treesa. I know how you felt about Brian. But I also know Terry's made sacrifices for tonight. You know he's had nothing but the money he's got for picketing, and that's hardly enough to keep body and soul together. He got the money for tonight by selling duff from the mineral line. He did it so you could have a good time, to take your mind off your troubles. If you don't go, all that'll be for nothing.'

Treesa made no reply but she ceased to rock the crib and folded her arms across her chest. 'Sometimes,' Fran said slowly, 'sometimes women have to do things they don't want to do. Not because they're weaker than men, but because they're stronger.' Suddenly she was back in Steve's flat a year ago, hiding in his bathroom because she was afraid, emerging at last because he had such need of her. 'I'm not asking you to enjoy tonight, Treesa ... although I think you might ... I'm asking you to go for Terry's sake – and Brian's. Do what you can to heal the break with the Malones. Maybe not tonight, but when you can.'

Treesa sighed and nodded. 'I know.'

As Fran scurried in search of suitable dresses for Treesa, she vowed to afford herself a shield one day and use '*I know*' as her motto.

Twenty minutes later she stood in the doorway watching them leave, giggling a little to cover their awkwardness but with at least a touch of anticipation. Treesa looked good in the jade blouse, the black wraparound skirt and her black mohair cardigan. When Fran shut the door she felt the first stirrings of Christmas.

Eve rang at seven to make sure she hadn't changed her mind about staying in Belgate for Christmas. Min rang at seven-thirty to point out what she was missing. 'I'd have thought you'd be glad to get Martin out of that hell-hole. God knows what they're plotting as a holiday diversion – blowing up the railway line or rifling the Co-op store. We're having goose ... turkey's so plebby now. I've really excelled myself, and it's not too late to say yes.'

She assured Min her answer was still no, and put down the

phone. She lit the tree and put out the centre light before Martin brought in his cocoa. They sat either side of the fire, strangely content, discussing the exact moment they would give Mike Malone his gift. She had first suggested delivering it to his mother for inclusion in his stocking and then had thought better of it: Belgate stockings would be thin this year, or even non-existent. She had gone to town on Mike's gift at Martin's insistence. Better avoid comparison with what his parents would manage. Mr Malone was back at work but they were still deeply in debt. So the boxing gloves and punchbag were wrapped in all their knobbly glory and hidden in the front room. 'When he comes round tomorrow,' Martin said, wriggling with pleasure at the very idea, 'when he comes round, we'll push him in there and ... wow ... I can see his face!'

After he had gone to bed, uncomplaining in his haste to bring on the morning, Fran was suddenly lonely. She went in to check on the sleeping baby and pulled aside the curtain to look on the frosted street. It was quiet and strangely peaceful, as though the holiday had brought about a hiatus in the strike. A truce, so that you almost expected to hear 'Silent Night' and see opposing troops come out from their trenches to fraternize. If only she could have moved Terry Malone. The thought of his relentless young face drove her down to the kitchen in search of coffee and a tot of the Drambuie Gwen had given her and which she had been saving for New Year.

She made up the fire, sorting carefully through the dust for pieces that were not slate. Slate cracked when heated and ricocheted round the room, reducing Nee-wan to a jelly. 'Good dog,' she said when he settled behind her chair. He was the only companion she had, so better make the most of him.

Her textbooks looked at her reproachfully from across the room, but she was not in the mood for work tonight. Not on Christmas Eve. A group was on the TV, two boys, two girls, as bland and wholesome as corn cobs wrapped in tinsel. '*Love, love, love,*' they sang, and were followed by a comedian who spewed out hate. Most jokes were barbed, if you thought about it. Other people's discomfiture was funny: 'It didn't happen to me, goody-

goody gum-drop.' So you could afford to laugh. Steve had been funny tonight – distant and strained. 'I love you,' he had said before he rang off. He always said that, but tonight it had been ... a shibboleth. And where on earth had she got that word from? She reached for the dictionary. '*Shibboleth, a party catch-word.*' Appropriate or inappropriate? She couldn't decide.

She was suddenly horribly depressed, worse even than last year. In Belgate they were thronging the clubs for one good night out. In Sunderland, Eve would be putting the final touches to her feast, filling stockings, standing with Harold to gloat over the new baby. She poured herself another Drambuie and kicked off her shoes. A new and uncomfortable thought was pricking at the back of her mind and must not be allowed to emerge.

A quarter of the way down the Drambuie she accepted defeat and brought the unbearable into view. In Sunderland now Steve would be sitting with Jean, Julie asleep in the bedroom above, Ian off somewhere with his friends. Perhaps he had made a lasagne, put a candle in a glass. Perhaps Jean would turn to him just like she, Fran, did and he would draw her to her feet and up the stairs to bed. She had a sudden mad impulse to ring Jean's house and put the cat among the pigeons, even going as far as looking up the number. And all the while a voice in her head reminded her of her doubts. Did she love Steve? Would she marry him if he asked her? Or was Nature simply abhorring a vacuum and so causing her to suffer like this?

In the end she put away the phone book and went upstairs to wash her face. Christmas, Christmas, you longed for it from afar and when it arrived it was often more than you could bear.

The baby was still asleep, a fist to his chin. As she watched, his brow wrinkled and then cleared and his mouth moved in a quick smile. It was only wind but it cheered her enormously. There was something about babies that was balm. In all the arguments over Warnock, no one could deny that. She wanted to pick him up and hold him but knew she must not. She contented herself with a touch to his cheek. 'Happy Christmas, Christopher,' she said and tip-toed to the door.

When she was ready for bed she collected Martin's gifts from behind the chair where Bethel had hidden them earlier and carried them upstairs, listening through the crack of the door to make sure he was asleep. She was half-way across the room when he spoke. 'You can put the light on, mam. I'm not asleep.'

She put down the parcels and put on the light. He was propped on one arm and he patted the bed. 'Sit down for a minute. I promise not to look.' He grinned. 'That is, if there's anything to look at.'

She pursed her lips. 'Oh, there's the odd thing. Nothing much.'

There was silence for a moment, and then he spoke. 'I remember you and dad doing it. I used to pretend to be asleep, but I never was. You used to giggle and whisper, and then he'd give you a kiss.'

She felt tears fill her eyes but made no move to brush them away. 'Yes, dad always enjoyed Christmas Eve.'

He changed elbows. 'I've been thinking about things.'

She waited. 'Tomorrow, could we send something to Ethiopia? A cheque, because the Post Office's shut.'

She nodded. 'That's a good idea.'

He looked relieved. 'I'll pay my half.'

She nodded again. He looked away and she wondered what was coming next. 'I'm sick of the strike,' he said. 'At first ...' Now he was looking sheepish. 'At first I thought it was fun. You know, exciting. Always someone fighting, and things. But now it isn't funny any more. Mike fights with everyone all the time, and sometimes ... well, it's just not nice any more.'

She smoothed the sheet and settled him down. 'It can't last much longer, darling. One way or another it has to be over soon.'

In her own bedroom she prayed for Belgate, wondering as she asked favours if the God who had allowed the strike to start had the power or the inclination to bring it to an end.

18

Tuesday, 5 January 1985

Down below her, the tiny figures moved with precision, enacting a familiar ritual. She had watched it often during the holidays, and she knew the pattern. In the clifftop car-park, a few hundred yards from the pit, the battle-buses were waiting, with metal-meshed windows and masked drivers. Clustered near by was a gaggle of blue police vans, their occupants outside, jumping and clapping to escape the cold. Sometimes they kicked a ball around, scoring between imaginary goalposts and cheering superior moves. Then the convoy would drive into view, blue flashing lights on the vans, strained faces behind the wheels of the ordinary buses that were considered safe as long as they were away from the pit. In summer the car-park lay between fields yellow with wheat, dappled cows in green pastures, a sea striped blue and sunlit. Now the landscape was barren, striking in sympathy.

The normal buses disgorged working miners, tiny men in parkas and woolly hats, bait boxes under their arms, looking neither right nor left till they reached the safety of the armoured buses. A quarter of a mile away, three or four hundred men were waiting at the pit gates to chant and jeer and jostle and bang impotently on the battle-bus sides. At first Fran had held her breath, expecting a raid by pickets on the car-park, but none came. The battle-buses would leave the car-park unmolested, drive a few hundred yards, and enter the pit in a hail of stones and abuse. The empty shuttle buses would drive out of the car-park and vanish; the police would laugh and joke and climb into their blue vans; leaving the car-park again deserted, with only the distant ugly clamour to prove an exchange had ever taken place.

Some men had refused the shelter of the buses, preferring to walk in, heads erect, eyes fixed on nothing in particular as though oblivious of the shouts of 'scab', the blows, the spittle that flew through the air to land on shoulders and chests and wincing, unprotected cheeks. Fran could never decide whether they were extra-brave or merely foolhardy. Most of the men rode safe in the armoured buses, and moved obediently through the exchange in the car-park like marionettes.

Today was routine. From the shelter of the trees Fran watched, wondering how much it was all costing, wondering how grown men could participate in such a charade. The whole coalfield was moving obediently through some ghastly minuet, no one quite sure whose music they were dancing to, but dancing all the same. Striking miners chanted at the pit gates, working miners embarked and disembarked. Police glided here and there, forming and reforming with expertise. These were the police who had collected for the strikers' children at Christmas. Now, in a glad New Year, they were facing those same strikers on the battlefield and would mount a baton charge if they had to. If everyone stood up and said, 'Enough,' it would be over – but no one did. Only MacGregor and Scargill spoke, and theirs was a barren language. Yesterday she had seen Angela Botcherby in the corner shop, spending the family purse with the gravity of a pensioner.

When the car-park was empty, Fran retraced her steps into the wood. Next week she would be back at college, and walks with Nee-wan a luxury, so she meant to spin out today. To right and left, raw stumps gleamed white amid blackened outer trunks. Even the bridge across the beck was gone now, chopped down in the night and spirited away like the park benches. The Union was distributing logs to pensioners and no one could begrudge them, for old people felt the cold more keenly. She felt warm inside her 'sheep' and full of resolutions. She liked new years, they reminded her of brand-new exercise books. She walked on, enjoying the crackle of winter twigs beneath her feet, the sparkle of spider's webs in crevices hoary with frost. She must persuade Martin to come out with her sometimes. He was missing so much beauty. She was ready to whistle up Nee-wan and turn for home when she came across the clearing. It had been a natural

[156]

space in the wood, a circle of grass. Now it was scorched and blackened, with here and there pieces of broken glass.

She stood, stupid, thinking of Martians and extra-terrestrial fireballs, until a more mundane but equally horrifying explanation dawned. Someone had been throwing petrol bombs! She felt a sudden desire to laugh. This was Belgate; this was an English wood. This was an idiot making a mushroom cloud out of a molehill. Except that before Christmas a bus full of working miners had been attacked with petrol bombs on its way to the pit.

Nee-wan was digging furiously in the ash. Fearful of cut paws, she snatched him up and carried him to safety.

Lunching with Martin, she struggled not to tell of her discovery. He was too young for such a disclosure; he was sensible and steady, but even sensible children experimented sometimes. Better not put ideas into his mind. 'Bethel and Walter are coming to tea,' she said.

He grinned. 'That'll put you in a good mood, then; I'll be all right for a loan.'

She smiled, a little taken aback at his perception. 'How do you know it puts me in a good mood.'

He tapped the side of his nose to suggest wisdom. Suddenly his eyes gleamed. 'Do you want to hear a song?'

The tune was 'What shall we do with the drunken sailor?' The words were new:

'What shall we do with Maggie Thatcher?
What shall we do with Maggie Thatcher?
What shall we do with Maggie Thatcher, early in the morning?
Burn, burn, burn the bastard,
Burn, burn, burn the bastard,
Burn, burn, burn the bastard, early in the morning.'

She let him finish and gave him a lecture on democracy, but she knew her words were falling on deaf ears.

She was washing up when Terry arrived. 'Where d'you want

[157]

it?' The paper sack was filled to the brim with duff and exuding dust from every seam. She made a place for it behind the pantry door and thanked him. As usual he refused payment. 'Not from you, Mrs Drummond. Besides, it's for Treesa and the bairn as well.'

Fran closed her purse. 'Well, it's very kind of you. And I hope you're being careful, Terry. That bank's completely overhung now. It must be dangerous. The *Echo*'s on about it nearly every night. There's been people killed in other parts of the country.'

He shook his head in derision. 'They weren't miners, Mrs Drummond. That's the difference. Don't you fret yoursel', I know what I'm doing. And I never go in without me marrer there. There's nee danger if you're careful.'

Fran gave way. 'Well, if you're sure ...' They were so confident, the Malones – so certain and optimistic. Was it their Catholic faith or their Irish blood? She could never be sure.

She sat down to do an hour's work on her holiday tasks. She was reading Piaget but the words just wouldn't penetrate her brain. Eventually she put her books aside and started preparations for tea.

'I hope you don't get him on about the strike,' Bethel said when she arrived. She had put on her crimplene dress in honour of the tea party, but scorned under-pinnings so that her bosom heaved right and left in glorious abandon.

Fran nodded. 'I know. Everybody's sick of it.' She had wanted to confide in them about the petrol bombs, but perhaps it was best to keep quiet. They might advise her to dial 999 and she wasn't sure how she would react to that. Anyway, the police had ways of knowing things, so it wasn't really up to her to be a nark. She was pondering the concepts of honour and informing, when Walter arrived, abusing the steps and Bethel in the usual equal proportions. 'It's the last time I'm coming here. Of all the God-forsaken ways to get into a house. He was a step-fanatic, the feller that built this. It wants bulldozing.'

Fran felt herself relax as she always did in Walter's presence. He was such fun!

As they settled down, complaining about the fire, she mentioned her visit to the blast. 'I've been meaning to tell you for ages. It was like walking on the moon. Bare and desolate, nothing growing. I felt frightened.'

Walter positively glowed. 'Frightened? Frightened! That's a townee for you; nee guts. You should've seen the blast before the war. People lived in the caves down there ... they'd have frightened you, all right! Loppy Dick with his staring eyes and his woman, Blast Martha ... and Sandshoe Sammy. Characters, that's what they were.'

Fran knew better than to interrupt. She merely widened her eyes.

'They turfed them out about 1937, but they kept on going back. They liked living like that, free to come and go. They didn't want council houses ... or they didn't want rent books, more like. The military went in while the war was on, blew the place up. Aye, they'll not be content till we're all homogenized. He was crawling with lops, old Dick, a bit of sacking round his shoulders, hair like a raggedy mat. I mind on he used to stand and rub his back against the corner walls, just to stop the itch. He came from a good family, you know. Richard Thomas was his name. Proper gentleman ... but filthy.'

Fran was intrigued. 'How did he live?'

'Door to door. Bit of tea here, bit of sugar there, sixpence here or a box of matches. He managed. Then there was Ganny Airship. She lived alongside the Bottleworks, long skirts, always saying she was going away in a flying ship. By, she was a character. They won't stand for that nowadays. We've all got to fit the mould.'

The thought of Walter fitting a mould was so hilarious that Bethel and Fran burst into laughter. 'Aye, laugh away, hinnies. But you mark my words.'

Bethel leaned over and dropped her voice. 'I told you to get Walter on about the blast.' There was a note of pride in her voice.

'I must give you back your copy of *Peter Lee*,' Fran said. Walter had loaned her Lord Lawson's biography of the miners' leader at Christmas, and she had read it twice. 'I liked it. He was everything you said he was. And there was one bit ... someone had underlined it ...'

Walter closed his eyes and began to recite. '*Not only men but nations must realize that the human family is thus so linked together that we must work together in a co-operative spirit if civilization is to endure.*'

Fran nodded. 'You know it by heart.'

Walter sighed. 'Aye, he was a great man, all right. God only knows what he'd make of this lot.'

Bethel groaned. 'Don't start. Think of your blood pressure.'

But it was too late. Walter was into his stride. 'They've only got themselves to blame. If they'd stuck by the rule book there'd've been none of this. They've buggered the Union. A hundred years of striving thrown away on one man's bloody vanity. It makes you weep.'

Fran daren't look at Bethel who would be gloating over Walter's apparent change of heart, but she couldn't resist a question. 'Why don't they go back then? They didn't want the strike; they only came out because they were promised a ballot. So when that promise was broken, why didn't they go back, together, in a block?'

Walter spread his hands over the tartan rug that covered his knees. 'It's not that simple, bonny lass. They had a lodge meeting and they voted to stay in. So they could cross the picket lines at the start because they'd made a joint decision. Then they met again, and they swallowed a lot of pap and voted to come out. Once they were out they couldn't go back in because it would mean crossing a picket line. And that would be scabbing, and scabbing is something a miner does not do. Do you understand?'

Fran shook her head. 'No, not really. Why don't they have another meeting and vote to go back in?'

He smiled. 'Because the Union never lets the dog see the rabbit. And if they did get a meeting, it'd be a show of hands and you'd have the militants down the front counting ... but really marking down anyone who crossed them. It'd take a brave man to stand up to that lot.' He leaned towards Fran. 'I'm talking about your boy-friend, young Malone. Butter wouldn't melt when he's in here, but you see him out there making his mouth go. That's a

[160]

different story!'

Bethel set down her cup with a clatter. 'I'm glad someone else is telling her. Gullible, that's her trouble. But mark my words, there'll be bloodshed here before we're finished. Look at Botcherby's lass ... she'll never be right again.'

Fran felt it was time she made a contribution. 'Has she always had trouble with her nerves?'

Bethel's snort of contempt was instant. 'Nerves? It's not nerves that ails her, it's stark bloody fear of the club woman.'

Fran knew about clubs, the slip of paper that entitled you to buy goods in the stores of Sunderland and for which you paid week after week. Bethel was continuing. 'She's not the only one – they're battening on each other now. Them as has money's saying, "Take a ten pound club out and I'll give you five for it." They're that mad to get a bit cash, they do it. The five pounds is gone in a flash, and they have ten to pay back – more with the interest. There's some of them so far in now they'll be lucky to be left with what they stand up in.'

Walter had fallen to musing, anger gone. 'We dreamed about nationalization you know. Before the war there was a miners' MP tried to put a bill through. We thought it'd be a piece of cake once we were the masters ... but the first fifteen years after nationalization were my worst in the pit and no mistake. We put up with it because we believed in the dream. We thought if we got rid of the slag-heaps we'd have a green and pleasant land. But we've got coal they can't sell, piled higher than the slag-heaps ever were. Now you've got too many chiefs, and what Indians there is is barmy. When a pit's done, it's done – it doesn't have to be exhausted. I mind on when there was coal there, tons upon tons of it, laughing at you from behind a fault ... and you had to let it go. Now they've had near enough a year of neglect. If I was still a pitman I'd be witless with fright to go down again and sort those faces out. There'll be more than a few too dangerous to work. It'd never have happened in Attlee's time. He'd've sorted it.'

Fran nodded. 'What about Kinnock?' Walter's face lit up with delight. 'Our Neil? He needs a cure for fence-sitter's arse, that one. Never send a boy to do a man's job. Not that he's not a sight better than Thatcher. She'd curdle milk.' He sighed. 'Aye, it's a sad day for the miners.' His fingers touched the rug over his knees, as he began to hum and then sing:

'The flour barrel is empty now, their true and trusted friend,
Which makes the miners wish today the strike was at an end.
The pulley wheels have ceased to move which went so swift
    around,
The horses and the ponies too are brought from under-
    ground.'

He looked up as he ceased to sing. 'That was written in the Durham lock-out in 1892 but it's still true today.'

Treesa came into the kitchen, the baby in her arms. 'Aye, it's not a bad little bairn,' Walter said when Christopher was presented for inspection. 'Let's hope it takes after its mother's side when it's grown.'

Fran saw Treesa's brow cloud and rushed to repair fences. 'He's like his daddy, and we love him for it.'

Walter's grin was evil. 'His dad was all right, it's his uncle that's causing all the trouble.'

Fran looked apprehensively at Treesa, but the young girl stayed calm. 'You can witter on as much as you like, Walter, but you won't change my opinion of Terry. I don't agree with every-thing he says or does, but he's all right. And it's not just miners causing trouble – there's a few policemen got something to answer for, not that they'll ever have to.'

The best thing about Walter, Fran reflected, was that you never knew which way he was going to jump. 'Aye, you're right there,' he said, as meek as a lamb.

While she washed up she thought about the evening ahead. She wanted to enjoy tonight, make Steve enjoy it too. If he wanted her to go back to the flat, she would go. She pictured him in her mind's eye, smiling, drawing her towards him, his lips tracing mouth, throat, breast, belly ... they had not made love since before the New Year. Which meant they had not made love this year. Which was a long time. At New Year they had both been tired and more than a little drunk, and since then he had been worried about business. 'It's only money,' she had teased, and had seen his irritation. It was more than money to a man; it was prestige and virility and being able to look your neighbour in the eye in the pub.

They met in the Saracen, Steve rising from the fog of smoke to wave a welcome. 'It's packed tonight,' she said, squeezing in beside him. They were sharing a table with three young men, heads together, faces turned away from strangers. While Steve was getting her a drink she realized they were miners and for the strike. They sipped their halves of Exhibition carefully, spinning them out, and she strained her ears to catch their conversation. 'I don't hold with that, Jimmy. Not the position he's in.' One was advocating some sort of mayhem, another disagreeing. The third stared into space, obviously weighing the matter.

'Look at it like this, Jimmy,' the second one said. 'He's a one-parent family through no fault of his own. So he gets social for the kids but they keep fifteen quid off, which leaves nowt. Well, as good as nowt. Now in my book the Union's got two choices: tell him to stop out and pay for his bairns, or let him go through. You can't say stop out and let your bairns starve. Them kids has no mother.'

The first man shook his head. 'You let one through, they'll all be at it. It's hard, of course it's hard, but this is a bloody war we're fighting!'

The third one finished cogitating and put down his empty glass. 'I'd go in if it was my bairns,' he said and wiped the last wisp of froth from his lip.

As Steve slipped into the seat beside her, the three rose to their feet. 'It's a bad do when you've got to make do with a half,' one of them said, laughing.

The third man slapped him on the shoulder as they moved away. 'You should thank Arthur for getting rid of your beer-belly for you.'

His friend laughed and hitched up his slackened jeans. 'It's a good job I can thank the bugger for something.'

When they had gone Steve grinned. 'Bloody but unbowed?'

Fran nodded and moved closer. 'Tell me what's been happening to you. I'm sick of the strike.'

There was only one thing she wanted to do, go home with him and climb into his bed, but first she must play out the charade of drinking and talking like civilized people. She put out a finger and traced the tendons of his hands. She liked his hands, lean and brown with the wrist-bone somehow vulnerable where it protruded from his slightly fraying cuff. 'Let's get out of here,' she said when desire overcame discretion. 'It's ages since we had time to ourselves.'

The wind was bitter and whipped her hair into her eyes. She reached for his hand and urged him to run for the car. Some lines of poetry came into her mind, remnants of a long-dead literature class ... '*to bundle time away that the night come*'. She would have liked to share the poem with him but two things stopped her. He was always embarrassed if she launched into a literary discussion, saying, 'that's too deep for me' – and she still did not feel safe enough with him to admit she wanted him to take her to bed.

Instead she stayed silent as the car threaded the Sunderland streets and drew up outside his flat. 'Do you want a drink?' he said, switching on lights and struggling out of his coat. If she waited, the moment would be past. They would drink and talk, and the clock would move round too fast. She let her coat drop to the floor and reached for him.

As she moved against him she felt his body respond, and a flicker of triumph ran through her. 'I love you,' she said against his ear, half whispering, half licking his so-desirable flesh.

'Oh Fran,' he said and then again, 'Oh Fran.'

They moved into the bedroom, she stumbling out of shoes, he trying to hold them both upright. Some innate modesty made them turn away to undress and then they were between the cold sheets and reaching and turning.

She knew almost at once that he could not make love to her. He was going through the motions but she had a distinct sense

[164]

that his mind was elsewhere and that elsewhere was not a pleasant place. 'What's the matter?' she said at last, sliding her arms around him to show him that all was well. If they could lie there for a moment, if he could relax, everything would come right. But he was pulling away from her, sliding from beneath the clothes to sit on the edge of the bed, head in hands. 'If you can't, it doesn't matter. You know it doesn't matter...'

He cut through her words. 'It's not that ... well, it's not just that. I've been trying to tell you for weeks now. I'm going back to Jean.'

As she drove through the bleak winter night, her tears were tears of indignation not tears of loss. He had known for weeks and had not spoken. He had allowed her to attempt a ridiculous, humiliating seduction, and still he had not spoken. The thought of being naked in the bed with him made her feel unclean – because there had been three of them in the bed; Jean had been lying between them, watching them behave like fools.

She tried to rationalize her feelings. She had always known he was weak; that had been half the attraction, his need of her. So why did it matter so much that he had proved what she had known in her heart all along? Perhaps only women were brave? Perhaps she should not be crying after all.

19

Saturday, 2 February 1985

She felt a sense of release as she breasted the bank and saw the Palace Green laid out before her, shimmering still with frost at ten in the morning. She had tried in the last few weeks to keep busy and look happy, but Bethel was hard to fool. 'So it's off then, the big romance?' It was a statement rather than a question and only required a shrug in reply. 'Aye, well, there's better fish in the sea than ever came out of it.' And then, when that failed to elicit an instant, glowing response, 'For God's sake get yersel' off this week-end; buy something you can't afford and cheer up. I'll mind the bairn. There's that many long faces round here nowadays, it gets a body down.'

Obediently Fran had arranged a trip to Durham, done her grocery shopping in advance and left the day free for sybaritic pursuits. Except that there was nothing she wanted to buy, nothing she wanted to do. As she neared the door of the Cathedral she prayed as she had done for the last few nights, *'Please God, give me a quiet mind.'* It wasn't much to ask, just freedom from the thoughts that had racketed round her head since that night with Steve ... shame, indignation, a sense of loss. And if she was truthful, a feeling of relief. He had dumped her – that was the harsh truth! And in dumping her he had relieved her of the necessity of making any sort of commitment. She was back in mid-stream, treading water and well away from rocks or rapids. Except that she wanted to be loved; she even indulged in fantasies where figures of authority, uniformed and in command, made love to her with unofficial fervour.

She slipped into a pew and fixed her eyes on the rose window, hoping to exorcise her randy thoughts; but the image of her phantom lover remained in her mind. She closed her eyes and buried her face in her hands, seeking to fill her head with prayers. It was useless. She stood up and moved into the aisle. A year ago, in the aftermath of David's death, she had come here with Martin and prayed for God to ease her path. Instead he had piled difficulties in her way. True, she had overcome them but the going had been tough. Now she was tired of struggling.

She found herself in front of the Miners' Memorial, a masterpiece of carving, with tiny, distorted miners guarded by fat cupids garlanded with vines. *'Remember before God the Durham Miners who have given their lives in the pits of this country.'* If the strike came to an end with an honourable settlement, she might cheer up. There was no fun in Belgate now, a war-torn town in a ravaged countryside. Yesterday she had seen a dog, ribs sticking through its skin, scavenging dustbins as they stood in the back street for collection. And Scargill and MacGregor, urbane and smiling, continued to preside over a civil war that was cracking communities throughout the country.

She put a pound note in the collecting box before she left, to pay for lack of reverence in her thoughts. She had hoped to find peace in the Cathedral and found only stone.

She was half-way down Silver Street when she heard the shout – 'Hold on, Stirling Moss!' The last time she was here she had met Steve in the Market Square and her knees had threatened to give way at the sight of him. This time it was Min with Dennis in tow, loaded with dress bags. 'Where are you off in such a hurry? I saw you from the boutique window, and we raced out but you were gone. Anyway, we've found you now! Where's Martin?' Min's eyes were bright with curiosity, and not about Martin. 'Is he here ... Robert Redford?'

It was time for a statement. 'Martin's at home and I don't see Steve any more. He's gone back to his wife.'

Min's eyes flashed 'I told you so,' in Dennis's direction, but he was rearranging his parcels to free an arm.

'We're going for a drink,' he said when he'd succeeded. 'You look as though you need cheering up, Fran, and I've got a mouth like a birdcage.'

They settled in the Market Tavern, hemmed in by market traders come in to escape the chill. Fran smiled at Dennis. 'Long time no see.' As the words left her mouth, she regretted them. The last time she had seen him, apart from fleeting glimpses, they had been discussing his wife's adultery. How unkind of her to remind him! She raised guilty eyes and found him smiling.

'Cheer up, Fran. What can I get you?'

When he had shouldered his way to the bar, Min moved closer. 'Are you upset? About the car man, I mean? He wasn't your type, Fran. He was nice ... sexy, even, if you like them thin and intense. But he'd never have been another David.'

Fran licked her lips. Min, Min, insensitive bloody Min. 'I didn't want another David ... you won't replace someone just like that. Steve was – is – a good friend. It was never more than

[167]

friendship.'

Min made a face to show tolerant disbelief. 'Don't take my head off, I only asked! You know I care about you. If you knew how many times Dennis says he wishes you were out of Belgate ... he thinks the whole place will erupt before long. Someone at Ladies' Circle was saying they're all being sent for training with the IRA...'

Fran threw back her head and laughed. 'Sometimes, Min, you are so *ridiculous*...'

The nice thing about Min was that she took insults on the chin. Her face drooped, and then brightened. 'Well, as long as I've made you laugh...'

Dennis walked back with her to the car-park to deposit the parcels and return for more. 'Take care, Franny,' he said as she was about to climb into the Mini. On an impulse she straightened up and kissed his cheek. 'And you,' she said warmly. 'Don't change, Dennis. I like you as you are.'

She drove out of the car-park and took the Belgate road before she let the tears come. She didn't know why she was crying, but she knew it was right that she should. When the tears ceased, she pulled into a lay-by and dried her eyes. She felt cleaned out, rested. As she put the car into gear again, she thought that perhaps God did exist after all. She had gone to the Cathedral to beg for a quiet mind and, in the most roundabout of ways, she had found it. Remembering the mad money still unspent, she went into the fish and chip shop before she reached home and bought cod and chips for everyone.

They had finished eating and were sitting companionably, elbows on table, when the kitchen door opened. 'It's only me!' Margot was wearing a Friends of the Earth sweatshirt under her duffle, which provoked Fran to think uncharitably of Nature in general and the Earth in particular. Margot was a walking mass of allegiances, nothing more. Pull out the front of her jumper and there would be a junction box with wires and a voice box that went on whirring 'Demonstrate!' long after the robot that housed it had shuddered to a halt.

By way of penitence for her thoughts, she gave Margot her chair and watered the pot. 'Lovely,' Margot said, clasping the mug around its middle in what she probably hoped was true working-class fashion, '*Stop nit-picking*,' Fran told herself sternly, and pulled up another chair.

Margot was wearing her 'I've-done-my-little-bit-for-the-miners' look. Something was coming. 'We're having a woman's rally next month. And a vigil. The whole department's giving support, and there'll be token attendances from all over the region. Some of the women from the support group may come, but I've told them it's optional. The whole point is to show that *non-mining* women are in this struggle with them, shoulder to shoulder. We're planning a token ... something quite massive for each month; the rally and the vigil for March, and a Day of Hunger for April...'

She never got around to May. Bethel had risen to her feet and appeared to be steaming at the nostrils. 'A day of hunger for April? Well, now, that's nice. There's been hunger around here for twelve months in case you've missed it. And how many bellies will you fill with your token-this and token-that? I'll tell you – none! You lot'll watch this strike drag on week after week because it suits your purpose. I'd even go so far to say you're wetting yoursel' in case someone solves it. Get away to hell out of it, before I forget I'm a lady and bash the life out of you.'

Fran accompanied a flushed Margot to her car. 'I'm not going to take umbrage, Fran. Poor thing, it's her age. I'd have a word with the doctor, if I were you. I can give you the address of the Alzheimer's Society ...' Seeing Fran's blank expression, she explained. 'Alzheimer's ... it's just the trade name for senile dementia ... the silent epidemic?' She looked at Fran expectantly.

'I don't know about epidemics, Margot, but I do know Bethel isn't senile. OK, she may have been a bit outspoken ... rude, even ... but there's nothing the matter with her brain.'

Margot unlocked the door of her car and turned with a tolerant smile. 'Well, let's hope you're right ... but give me a ring if you need advice.'

For 'if' read 'when', Fran thought, and loathed herself for waving good-bye to the retreating Volkswagen.

To banish the last lingering trace of Margot's visit Fran whistled up the dog and went for a walk. The days were drawing out now, but still the daylight would not last for much longer. She made for the allotments because they were within easy reach and because their very haphazardness was a comfort. Old sinks and galvanized buckets and blunted spades were thrown aside there, and within days had become part of the landscape, their edges gentled by grass, their colours muted by wind and rain. There was a new addition since her last visit, a hand-printed notice pinned to a gate: 'THIS PLOT BELONGS TO A STRIKING MINER.' There had been bitter tales of winter produce that vanished in the night, and this was the result. She peered over the fence to see if the notice had been obeyed, but the earth was barren, whatever had grown there gone.

She came out at the other end of the path and walked down the alley that led to the main street. The wooden fence that bounded the path had almost disappeared; only the concrete plinths remained, the rusted hoops that had held the posts dangling empty. When the brick wall began it was daubed with graffiti: '*Kill the Pigs*' and '*Scabs are Shits*' and everywhere the plaintive '*Coal not Dole*'. Even the war memorial had not escaped. When she reached it she saw that beneath the dates 1914–18 and 1939–45 someone had added '*1984–5 The People's War*' in white spray-paint.

She put Nee-wan back on the lead for fear of traffic and turned into Stafford Street. The problem was, who were the people? As far as she could see Britain was turning into a mass of pressure groups, all of them maintaining that they spoke for 'the people'. But she doubted very much if any of these self-appointed spokespersons had much in common with the British people. She was searching her mind for something she had read once about the voice of England that 'has not spoken yet,' when Nee-wan whined and pulled on his lead. She turned and saw Terry Malone behind her. He bent to fondle the dog and then fell into step beside her.

'Have you seen Treesa today?' she asked.

He shook his head. 'No, I was just coming round now.'

Fran grinned. 'You're lucky you weren't in an hour ago!' She told him about Bethel's treatment of Margot, expecting him to laugh, but his face clouded.

'That's half the trouble with the strike, Mrs Drummond – outsiders sticking their fingers in. I don't mean you, you belong here; but the likes of her ... what's *she* doing coming over here every day? She's just a laughing-stock to the men. They call her Tokyo Rose because she's always spouting propaganda. OK, she's only a joke. But you get all sorts on the pickets. They wouldn't know a pit from a pot-hole, but they're in there, causing trouble – and then we get the blame for it. It's the same with the pollis, they come from everywhere but here. If we'd been left, just local lads on the pickets, local bobbies on the police lines, you wouldn't've had half the trouble. Not a half of it. And...'

Fran was never to hear what else he had to say. She was still glowing from his description of her as 'belonging' to Belgate when she saw his words freeze on his lips and his eyes widen. She followed his gaze and saw the cause of his consternation. Mrs Botcherby had emerged from her front door, head erect, arms at sides. She was naked except for her fur-trimmed slippers that slopped absurdly on the ends of her spindle legs. Fran stood looking at her, thinking of Norman Mailer and something he had written about naked men and women moving forward into gas chambers. '*Here a titty and there a twat ...*' Mrs Botcherby's tiny breasts sagged pathetically, there were silver stretch-marks on her abdomen and her pubic hair was black, tinged with grey. Long after Terry had shrouded her in his parka and was shepherding her back into the house, an image of her nakedness remained in Fran's mind. In a frozen chicken factory the live chickens were hung from wires and rotated so that someone could slit their throats. They had tied Mrs Botcherby and hung her on the wires, but no one had had the courage to administer the *coup de grâce*.

[171]

20

Monday, 4 February 1985

It was a relief when light began to filter through the curtains. She had slept fitfully, never more than twenty minutes at a time, waking always in a fever of anxiety over a dream. In one she had been terribly conscious of having sweaty feet; people had moved away from her and she had been ashamed. In another she had tried to crawl through a gap between two stones. On the other side was freedom and pure air, but the gap narrowed as she struggled through, so that she woke scrabbling at the duvet to escape.

She looked at the clock. Ten to seven. If the rumour was true, Terry Malone would be nearing the pit gates now. She couldn't believe it, but Bethel vowed it was fact and Mike, when tactfully probed, had not denied it. She snuggled down to escape the chill and pondered her dreams. What had caused them? In her waking moments she had thought almost continuously of Terry Malone and sometimes of shortage of money. She had wondered briefly if Steve was curled round Jean in sleep or if they were occupying distant edges of the mattress, but she had put such thoughts resolutely aside. Whatever she was going to lose sleep over, it wouldn't be a man.

At five to seven she jumped out of bed and snatched for her dressing gown. Outside the world was ice-bound. Two birds hunched morosely on the frozen telephone wires and there were frost patterns inside the window panes. She wondered if Treesa had taken the baby into her bed and hoped she had. He was nearly seven months now, too big to smother but too small to resist hypothermia. Downstairs she put on the oven to warm the kitchen and began Martin's breakfast. 'Have you heard anything?' he asked as he came into the kitchen.

She shook her head. 'Not yet.' The radio was spilling news,

but there would be no figures for a return to work for another hour or more. And then they would not mention Terry Malone. They would not know of his existence.

She couldn't believe Terry would go back, not even after the trauma of Saturday. They had bundled Mrs Botcherby into the house and Terry had sprinted for the phone box. Fran had stayed until Botcherby arrived, carrying a sliced loaf and a bottle of sterilized milk. He had listened in silence, then mounted the stairs to check on his wife. Angela sat on the settee while all this went on, methodically buttoning and unbuttoning her cardigan, not saying a word and – more significantly – asking no questions.

When Botcherby came downstairs, Fran had sensed he wanted her to go but was too polite to say so. 'It's the pressure,' he said as he saw her to the door. 'Pressure, pressure, always more pressure. She couldn't stand not being able to pay her way.' Now Mrs Botcherby was in hospital and Belgate seethed with rumours, the chief one being that Botcherby was returning to work and so was Terry Malone. Could one incident change a deep-held conviction? She had seen pain on Terry's face on Saturday, and pity – but no sign of wavering.

Martin was snap-crackle-popping with gusto, the milk leaving a white moustache on his upper lip. In some Belgate homes this morning there would be no breakfast. And yet, for the most part, they stood firm. They had not wanted the strike, they had fought against it; but now, after eleven months of deprivation, they still stood firm. It was an enigma, but a marvellous one. They had stuck together and survived with only a handful of casualties. But if Terry went back today, she had a feeling the dyke would break.

Martin was finished now, scraping his chair back from the table. 'I might know before you,' he said. 'I might find out off Mike.'

'From Mike,' Fran corrected.

He nodded irritably. 'I know, I know. But if he goes back, will it be right?'

Fran shook her head. 'I've told you, I don't know. If a man has a right to strike, he surely has a right to work. The trouble is they all think they're right, the strikers *and* the workers. They're both

[173]

convinced.'

'So they do things like fighting, because it's in a good cause?'

Fran nodded. 'They think it's in a good cause ... but that doesn't make everything they do right ...' Her voice trailed away. How could you explain civil disobedience to a ten-year-old? Even when that ten-year-old was determined to have an answer?

'Well, what would make you do things like that?'

Suddenly it was easy! 'I'd only fight if they tried to stop me voting. That's the most important thing. If you can vote, you can change things. And don't you forget that!'

She felt quite light-headed with wisdom until she remembered that nowadays there was hardly anybody worth voting for.

She got Nee-wan on his lead and set Martin to school. The streets seemed oddly empty, the houses eyeless and closed. 'It feels like war-time', she thought. Any moment resistance fighters would spring out from a back street and tanks rumble round the Half Moon corner. And then a film crew would materialize and shout 'Cut!' It was all unreal. It was too early for shoppers, but the single woman she passed, hurrying to the corner shop in carpet slippers, was raking in her purse as she went. She looked up as Fran drew level. 'It's a bugger, isn't it?' she said.

Fran was opening the back door when the man hailed her. He was wheeling an ancient bicycle with a sack strapped to the saddle. 'Want some coal, lady? Proper coal, no rubbish?' He looked cheerful inside the shabby parka. *Coal not Dole* was pinned to his chest. She wondered where he had got 'proper' coal, and the question showed in her face. 'Fell off a lorry,' he said. 'And you can't turn down a chance like that nowadays, can you?' So it was stolen ... from the pit-heap probably.

'No thank you,' Fran said politely. 'I wouldn't dare.'

He grinned. 'Who's to know, missus? The evidence goes up in smoke.'

She shook her head. 'No, sorry. I'm too scared.'

He shrugged and began to walk away. Her conscience pricked. What if he was on strike and needed the money? 'Never mind,' she called out, 'the strike'll be over soon.'

[174]

His face, when he turned, showed consternation. 'I hope not, missus. I'm working up a canny little business here.'

She had to wait until ten o'clock to hear what had happened. She sat down to work on her essay but the radio kept diverting her. At nine o'clock they predicted a record return in the North-east – well over 800 'new faces'. But of the most important face of all there was, predictably, no mention. When Bethel arrived she insisted on putting on the kettle and removing her hat, coat and scarf before she was willing to talk. 'Come on,' Fran urged. 'Just tell me ... did he go in?'

Bethel took out her cigarettes and lit up. 'He did and he didn't.' She was being deliberately perverse but urging would have a reverse effect. Fran sat back and waited.

'I got it off Mary Whiteside, who went down with her man to make sure he got in all right. She says they were shouting and brawling, and them at the back were throwing rocks ... only half the time they were hitting their own men, not the pollis. The buses went in, and then half the pickets ran round the back because some men were getting in over the fence behind the washery. And then Botcherby comes round the corner with Malone's lad beside him, and Mary says it all went quiet. Botcherby's face was a study, she thinks he was drugged; and Terry Malone had a funny little smile on his face. Then someone at the back shouted 'Scab!' and they surged forward, and then Ella Bishop ... you know, the big wife with the gold hoops? ... she got on Botcherby's other side and fended them off.' Bethel paused and drew on her cigarette. Something good was coming! 'And then ... they got up to the gate, and Botcherby went through, and young Malone turned round and walked back. Without a word. Not a look to right or left. Mary says they might've known he wasn't going in because he had nee bait and nee towel, but nobody twigged.'

'So he just went along to make sure Botcherby got in safely?'

Bethel nodded. 'I think he was mad not to go in hisself but ... well ...' She gave a leer that might have been a grin. 'I'll say nowt more, or you'll be going on and on about all the Malones being angels. Funny angels, that's all I can say.'

Before they could further discuss the Malone family, Treesa appeared in the doorway, the baby in her arms. 'It's all right,' Fran said. 'Botcherby went in all right, but Terry didn't.'

Treesa sighed. 'Thank God for that. I couldn't stand any more trouble at the moment. I don't think the bairn's very well. He's been wingey all night, and I've just got him off.'

Bethel and Fran moved nearer. 'Poor bairn,' Bethel said soothingly. 'Well, he looks peaceful enough now.'

Fran touched his brow. 'He's rather warm.' The baby's face quivered with a spasm of wind, and all three women smiled. 'It makes you wonder how anyone could hurt them, doesn't it?' Fran said.

Treesa shook her head. 'They were talking at the group yesterday about a lass in the wide back street. She's got two bairns under five and she fell again, so she's had an abortion.' Her face was full of Catholic conscience. 'I know it's bad times, but there was no need for that.'

Bethel's face sharpened. 'Don't go criticizing other people, miss. Unless you're a fly on the wall, you don't know all the ins and outs.'

Fran saw Treesa's chin come up and hurried to smooth things over. 'Come and have a cup of tea.'

Treesa shook her head. 'I've got to get down there and get the dinners on. I came to see if you'd watch the bairn down here, seeing he's off colour.'

Fran looked at the blank sheets of essay paper. The relevance of Montessori to the present-day teaching situation could wait another day. 'Better than that,' she said. 'You stay with the baby and I'll go in your place.'

She walked to the church hall, glad of the time to pluck up her courage. It was always a bit of an ordeal to walk into the support group. She was still an outsider among women who had grown up together and were bound together now by a fierce belief in what they were doing. In some ways they seemed more fervent than their men. *'I've told my man he can go back in,'* one had said

[176]

last time, '*but I'll have had the door locks changed when he gets back.*' If it was true that northern men had dominated northern women in the past, the wheel had certainly turned full circle.

As she reached the end of the street she heard a rhythmic thudding. In a front garden stood a beautiful Victorian sideboard, intact down to the original brass drawer-fitting. A man and a woman were laying into it from either side, raising their axes shoulder high in their haste to shatter the ancient wood. Fran wanted to protest, but it was too late. The axes had gouged through layers of age and veneer, and the raw wood was exposed. As she drew level the woman looked up. 'It's a nice state of affairs when you're chopping up your home to keep warm. Still . . .' She gestured at the man, '. . . he's in his element 'cos it came from my side an' he's never liked it.' The man grinned and redoubled his efforts as Fran moved on.

In the event the support group was less of a strain then she had feared. Today the women were mostly silent, chopping and stirring with a tense dedication. 'Aye, lasses, let's give them a good meal,' the gold-earrings woman said. 'Cheer their little cotton socks.'

The woman next to Fran sighed. 'Poor Ella. She won't admit it's over bar the shouting.'

Fran turned off the tap and pulled the plug. 'Do you think it's over?'

The woman leaned closer so as not to be overheard. 'I bloody well hope so.'

Their work done, they carried mugs of tea to a quiet corner. Fran had seen the woman before, working around the kitchen. Now she saw that she was no more than thirty, her brown hair covered by a cotton scarf, her eyes ringed with black pencil. 'I thought they were right to come out; I still think so. But they've had it now. The sooner they go back, the better. Mind, there'll be scores to settle – I won't forget some people. And the pollis! I've brought my bairns up to respect them, but never again.'

Fran looked at her enquiringly. 'What changed your mind?'

The woman's face darkened. 'They've enjoyed this. Not just bashing the men – that was fair enough, to give as good as they got. But the way they've treated the women on the pickets is disgraceful. If they could give you a dig they did. That's what's bitten into my man – seeing me pushed around.'

Fran had never been on a picket line but she had seen the jostling, swaying masses on TV. Who could decide who had injured whom in such a mêlée? And after all, if there had been no pickets there would have been no policemen. She was wondering whether or not to defend the police when the woman groaned. 'Oh my God, where's the fall-out shelter?'

Fran turned and saw Margot in the doorway, swathed in what looked suspiciously like a horse-blanket and handing out goodies right and left. 'She gets right up my nose,' the woman said. 'She doesn't care about us, she just wants to be able to say she's on the side of the workers. It makes you sick. You know what the men call her?'

Fran nodded. 'Tokyo Rose.' She shrank down in her seat and prayed Margot would not notice her and claim kinship.

She managed to avoid Margot as the diners thronged through the doors and took their seats. Then it was all systems go as plates were filled, delivered, cleared, retrieved, scraped, stacked and washed. 'By God, that was good,' a man said, giving a vigorous belch.

'You know what it was, marrer?' his neighbour said. 'Kit-e-Kat stew.'

The man belched again. 'I was that hungered, it could've been pussy-cat stew. It all goes down.'

Fran smiled but she looked at the children, eating wordlessly, eyes raised above spoons to look around. What must they make of this?

As the room cleared, Margot bore down on her. 'Hello, Fran. Doing your bit, I see.'

They left together, Margot insisting on giving her a lift. 'I'd ask you in, Margot, but I simply must work on my essay. I only left it to help out Treesa.'

They were passing the bridge near the Co-op when they saw the man running up from the mineral line. His hands waved in the air and his mouth hung open in an anguished O. 'There's something wrong,' Margot said and slammed on her brakes.

Fran was first out of the car. 'He's down ... there's a ton of earth on top of him ... I've tried ... hopeless ...' He went off at a shambling run to get help. There was a low stone parapet to the bridge and Fran leaned over. The overhung bank had fallen, that much was plain. But all that could be seen of the trapped man was a pair of jeans and track shoes, both holed in the centre of the sole.

'It's no good, Fran.' Margot was behind her, her voice sombre, but Fran was already climbing the parapet, her feet feeling for the bank below.

She started to dig, clutching at clods of damp earth, feeling the sharp edges of rock and shale but sensing no pain. Her nails were breaking but she clawed away, weeping as more earth tumbled down for every piece she removed. And then someone was shouldering her aside. 'Howay pet, this is men's work.' He was heaving, digging, making way.

She looked up and saw two policemen scrambling down the bank. One shot his watch from his cuff. 'How long?' he said to her and when she did not answer ... 'How long has he been under, missus? Pull yourself together!'

Fran drew breath. 'A minute. Perhaps a little longer.' His eyes dropped to his watch and he began to count. His mate had joined the digging, pausing only to snatch off his helmet and hurl it aside. It was not until they had scraped enough away to pull on the legs that Fran saw the blue parka and the striped T-shirt beneath, and knew it was Terry Malone.

The policeman's voice intoned, 'One minute forty ... forty-five ... fifty ... fifty-five ... two minutes...' But Fran was back in her own kitchen more than a year ago. What had Brian Malone said then? *Our Terry would die for Arthur Scargill.*' His face was the colour of storm clouds, the lips blue. The miner who had begun the digging moved back, defeated, but the policeman put his fingers into the dead mouth and pulled forward the tongue. 'Never mind counting, Ted ... it's past that.' As his mate moved forward he drew breath and bent to the open mouth, sealing the nose with his fingers. 'Ready?'

The other placed his hands, wrists inward, on the striped and lifeless chest. 'Ready.'

As they blew and pressed alternately, Fran glanced up at the bridge. Margot stood there, a crowd around her, arms folded across her chest. Fran looked back at the body and the two figures bearing down on it. Someone would have to tell them to stop. It wasn't seemly. She would have to tell them it was too late. Why was it always her? The two policemen were Terry's age; in another place, another time, they might have been his friends.

'Geronimo!' one of them said suddenly and grinned like a child.

The ambulance arrived while the breathing was still shallow and reedy. 'He'll do,' the ambulance men said, and fastened an oxygen mask over Terry's mouth.

Suddenly Fran's legs gave way. She was always amazed when old wives' tales proved true: you did wring your hands at moments of stress, and your legs did fold at the knees when you had had enough. The policemen were looking sheepish now that the crisis was over, fastening buttons and donning their official positions with their helmets. 'We'll need a statement, miss,' one said and hauled her up the bank.

Margot was back to normal. 'Here's my card, officer. My home number's on the back. I saw it all. You did your best, but of course there'll be brain damage ... deprivation of oxygen ... I saw you counting. Still, jolly well done.' Suddenly her eyes flickered, checking the crowd, and Fran knew what she was thinking – *mustn't be seen to fraternize with the instruments of repression.*

As Margot reached for her arm, Fran leaned towards her. 'Fuck off, Margot,' she said, and felt an unholy satisfaction as the words went home.

She drove the Malones to the hospital and sat with them in the corridor. 'He was always a daring lad,' his mother said to no one in particular. 'He could never take a telling.' She still wore her pinny beneath her coat, and there were traces of flour around her fingernails.

It was getting dark outside and lamps sprang to life in the street. The doors swung open and the sister appeared. Her high-heeled shoes looked incongruous with the navy uniform, but her eyes were kind. 'Relax,' she said. 'He's young and strong . . . and lucky, according to our Registrar. You can go in for five minutes – two of you. Visit tonight and bring his gear.'

Mrs Malone stood up. 'Come on, dad.'

Mr Malone sat still. 'Better not, mother. We don't want to upset him. You go in on your own.'

He's frightened, Fran thought. After all that's gone on today, he's still afraid of being rebuffed.

She left him, weeping, in the corridor and went to tell Treesa all was well. Except that all was far from well when a father was crying for a son who might not want to see him, after all.

21

Saturday, 16 February 1985

Fran felt virtuous as she put a match to the fire. Eight-fifteen on a Saturday morning, and she was out of bed. She pulled her coat around her and watched the flames licking uninterestedly at the duff coal. 'Burn, damn you, burn!' Outside the world was in the grip of winter. Blizzards last week and two dogs drowned in an ice-covered pond the day before yesterday. General Winter had come, as Scargill had prophesied, but he was firing on his own lines. Everyone in Belgate was cold, which made their misery that much harder to bear. The flame flickered, and in desperation she covered the fire opening with a sheet of newspaper to act as a blazer. She kneeled to hold it in place and looked at the headlines. There had been a demonstration in the Commons over the bill on experimentation on embryos, and terrible violence at the Sunderland match the night before. She searched for something cheerful. The Bishop of Durham had opened his mouth again: that was always good for a laugh. And a lodge official wanted working miners banned from the streets of Easington. 'How bloody dare he!' she thought, and then had to snatch her hands away as the paper caught fire.

She carried tea up to Treesa and urged her to stay in bed till the house warmed up. 'I'll still be here at Christmas then,' Treesa said and struggled on to one elbow to drink her tea. Her nightdress was topped with a sweatshirt and cardigan, and beside her the baby was swaddled in blankets.

Fran bent to look at him. 'Wait till spring, little one. We'll have sunshine then.'

Treesa sighed. 'Sometimes I wonder if the sun'll ever shine again. It's been like a year of winter.'

Downstairs Fran put out cereal for Martin and let Nee-wan in from the garden. 'Sit down and be quiet,' she told him. 'I've got work to do.' She laid out her pens and pencils to write up her teaching practice: it had to be handed in on Monday and nothing must interfere. Her fingers were icy and she flexed them to warm them up. Cold as she was, she was faring better than most people in Belgate. She had never been used to fires roaring up the chimney winter and summer. 'There's grates in this village never gone cold till now,' Bethel had said the other day, and the perished faces on the streets of Belgate gave substance to her words.

At half-past nine the phone rang. 'It's only me,' Min said. There was an odd note in her voice that might have been glee. 'I won't keep you a second.' Fran's heart sank – that meant it would take at least till lunch-time. 'But I wanted you to be the first to know ... I'm pregnant! It was all the fault of Christmas.'

'You mean Santa Claus did it?' Fran asked, playing for time. Babies, babies, always babies. It wasn't fair.

'No, it wasn't St Nicholas,' Min was saying, 'it was St Dennis.'

Fran grinned. 'How's he taking it?'

There was a giggle from the other end of the line. 'As though it was the first ever. He's eating out of my hand.' Min's tone was triumphant.

'Is that why you did it?' Fran asked.

'How could you think such a thing!' Min said. 'It was an act of God ... I just pushed His hand a bit.' They rang off after Fran had agreed to come over for a drink after tea. 'Just you and me, Fran. Dennis is at a Round Table do and we don't want Eve. I've never had a chance to thank you for what you did, so tonight it'll be Moët et Chandon and we can really let our hair down. We can't talk freely if Eve's there ... she's still dying to know what happened, and you know how she agonizes over our feet of clay.'

Fran had just put down the phone when Bethel arrived. 'Get the tea on!' she said, walking through the living-room. Nee-wan had emerged from behind the chair to greet her, but shot back as the fire erupted and a piece of stone ricocheted around the room. 'Aye, mind, that Terry's got a lot to answer for,' Bethel said. 'I warned you about letting him smash that fireplace.'

Fran retrieved the stone and put it in the hearth. 'We'd have frozen without it, Bethel – especially Treesa and the baby. And don't forget he nearly lost his life for that fire.'

Bethel shook her head. 'He'd've been nee loss. It's his sort caused all the trouble.'

Fran went in search of the teapot. 'I'm not going to rise to the bait, Bethel. I've got work to do.'

She took the dog for a walk after lunch, avoiding the woodland and sticking to the streets. She could no longer bear the sight of butchered trees, and if there had been more petrol-bomb throwing she didn't want to know about it. She had pondered many times whether or not she should have dialled 999. The trouble was, you could never be sure you were not reporting your neighbour. Since the accident Terry Malone had been subdued but he was still militant ... not the type to throw bombs, but then which of the Belgate lads looked like would-be arsonists? Some of them must be.

As she turned for home she thought of last Saturday at this time. She had gone into Sunderland in search of shoes for Martin, and in the High Street had come face to face with Steve and his wife, Julie between them. The little girl had nudged her mother and whispered, and Steve's eyes had met Fran's in silent apology. Jean had been short and dark and older than Fran had imagined. She had waited for her heart to lurch at the sight of them together, and there had been nothing. Only a kind of pity.

She was crossing the top of Stafford Street when she saw the young policeman who had changed her tyre. He was in mufti and carried a holdall. Fran smiled. 'Been to see your mother?'

He gestured with the holdall. 'Been to board up her window. Some brave he-man put it in last night.'

They walked on, Fran seeking desperately for the right words. 'I wouldn't mind if they hit at me,' he said. 'OK, our lads haven't been perfect. They haven't been half as bad as they've been painted, but we've got our black sheep. Still, there's no excuse for taking it out on an old woman.' Fran smiled wryly. His mother looked all of fifty ... so that was old age.

'Are you still doing picket-line duty?' she asked.

He shook his head. 'Not at the moment. I was up at an opencast the week before last – we were there in force, and so were they. The lorries came. They pushed, we held firm. I could hear the vehicles thudding past behind me, and then I saw this bloke's face ... he was pushing forward and I could see it in his eyes: "That bastard's going to have me under the next lot of wheels," I thought. I tried to hold, but he was coming forward all the time. I felt the bonnet brush against me and I thought ... "I'm going to die." That was all. Not about me mam or me girl-friend or anything. Just ... "I'm going to die." And then the line broke and I thumped him. So I was sent home and suspended – no more gravy-train for a naughty boy. I've never been so pleased in me life.

'It makes you sick!' he went on. 'I watch the telly night after night, and we get a rollicking from the commentators. They don't say "police brutality", but they might as well. What do they expect us to do – stand bare-headed and let them pelt us? You should see some of the weapons they've used ... not just half-bricks, worse than that ... things they've spent time crafting, just so as they can do more damage. Over seventy of our lads injured. What came first, the riot or the riot shields? Then they say we've brought the army in. What a load of rubbish! I wish we had brought them in, let *them* take some of the stick. I was at an open-cast site not long since ... out in the wilds ... they dismantled a dry-stone wall and skimmed the rocks at us along the ground. You had police falling like nine-pins. But that doesn't make the papers ... oh no, it's all MPs on about police brutality and civil liberties.'

Fran stayed silent, unable to halt the flow of his frustration.

'Whose liberties? That's what I want to know. They say we're oppressing the miners: which miners? There's more miners back at work than on the pickets, far more. So who are we supposed to stick up for: them going in, or them standing outside the gates? Someone should tell us, because we can't win. There was this little lass the other day ... just knee-high. The lads gave her a bag of apples but I said, "You want to watch what you're doing. If she eats that lot and gets a bellyache, we'll be in more trouble!"'

He was into his stride now, not expecting answers. 'Why would I have it in for the miners? Me own dad was a miner; he died coughing up dust. Now I have to stand and take gobs of spittle off lads that's scarce seen the inside of the shaft. I'm not bitter – I'm sad!'

Fran tried desperately to divert him. 'Tell me something ... I've watched the battle-bus exchange on the car-park near the pit. A few hundred yards away at the pit gates there are hundreds of pickets yelling for blood. But none of them come to the car-park. When the buses get to the pit they'll try to wreck them, but they don't try to stop the exchange. It amazes me.'

For the first time his face lightened and his voice took on a note of pride. 'We saw to that. We explained to their leaders that rendezvous points weren't NCB land. They're public places, not the scene of an industrial dispute. So if they tried anything on public land, we'd have them. Our bosses have tried to cut out aggro where they could. Talk about the National Reporting Centre as much as you like, policing this area's a job for local forces and I think they've done a bloody good job.' Once more anger entered his voice. 'We're there to see that people can go about their lawful business unmolested. That's what we did! That's what I thought I joined the force for ... protecting people. Now I'm told I'm a puppet. Well, nobody's pulling my strings except the chief, and he's only doing his job. But who's pulling their strings, who issues the orders to them ... and finances them? Try asking that for a change, and you might get some surprises.'

They parted on the corner and she entered her own back street. Half-way down a group of lads stood grouped round a back door. She recognized one of them as the lad who lived there, a young miner. His mates were leaning against the wall and one had defied the frost and sat down on the edge of the kerb. Nee-wan rushed to greet them. 'Fed up?' Fran said. There was a chorus of assent. 'It'll soon be over,' she said.

One of them laughed. 'Seems like I've heard that before.'

Fran nodded. 'I know, it does seem to go on and on. But it can't last much longer. Were you for the strike?'

They shrugged defensively, reminding her of Martin when she asked him unanswerable questions. At last the boy in the gutter spoke. 'Put it like this, missus. There's 5 per cent at this end mad for Arthur ...' His left hand shot sideways. 'And there's 5 per cent at that end Maggie's men.' His right hand shot in the other direction. 'As long as they get their redundancy, they wouldn't care if the pit caved in. The rest of us are here in the middle, bleeding bloody bewildered.' There was another chorus of agreement.

'It's over but we can't go back,' a second boy added. 'You'd be marked for life if you went back now. It's really bitter.'

When Fran got into the house she put on the kettle and brewed tea. Seven mugs and a packet of biscuits, milk and sugar on a tray. She carried it into the street. 'Here's something to cheer you up. I'd invite you inside but it's no warmer in there.' She presided over the pot while they dished out the biscuits.

'Thanks missus, there's nothing like a cuppa.' The boy on the kerb lifted his mug. 'Here's to a settlement.' There were murmurs of disbelief. 'Sometimes I feel we'll never get back. No one thinks of us single lads with nowt coming in. They say it's all young 'uns on the picket, but we've got nee choice. That's the only money we can get, picketing fees.'

Fran filled the last mug. 'Don't you want to picket?'

There were shakings of heads. 'There's a few goes for it ... hot-heads. They're always looking for a punch-up, or running round in balaclavas causing trouble. But your average lad, he just wants a bit peace ... a few bevvies on a Friday night...'

There was a roar of laughter. 'And a nice bit of snogging on a Saturday, eh, Clogger?'

The boy blushed. 'Nee chance of takking a lass out nowadays.' He tried to change the subject. 'Any road, you've got to picket if you want your parcels. Look at Pearson's lad, he won't picket – he never liked trouble, not even at school – and he can't get for his bairn.'

Fran knew Paul Pearson. She had seen him about the streets during the strike, his baby in his arms. 'You mean they've refused him help because he won't picket?'

The boy nodded. 'If you don't picket, they mark you down, then when you turn up they say there's nowt left. You can't argue. No one knows what the Union men's got or not got. They're walking round with the funds in suitcases, dishing out here and there. If your face doesn't fit, you get nowt.'

Another boy spoke up. 'It was the same at Christmas with the toys. If your grandad was lodge chairman it was a bloody bonanza. If not it was, "Sorry pet. Santa's all cleared out."'

Fran could not contain herself. 'But why do you stand it?'

They shrugged. 'Nee option. They're running the Union, that's it. Anyway ...' The speaker looked a little ashamed as though they had all been guilty of betrayal. 'Anyway, we've got nee room for that other lot, Thatcher and MacGregor. It's not so much supporting the Union, it's standing up to the others. They'll not best the miner, not in the long run.'

There were murmurs of agreement. 'Miners have long memories. We won't forget Thatcher ... and we won't forget the pollis either. We'll never forget them!'

Back in the kitchen, washing the tea things, Fran thought over their words. Someone was going to have to heal the breach between miners and police, but it would need a Solomon. The sad thing was that individually the policeman and the miner were perfectly compatible; but in the mass, given rocks on one side and riot shields on the other, they were enemies. And there had been wrongs on both sides. Put people under pressure and cracks would appear – in Northern Ireland, or Belgate or anywhere else.

When she had wrung out the dishcloth and hung up the tea-towel she went to the corner shop. It was strange to be looking at baby foods again. They had changed since Martin's babyhood, become more exotic. She selected a dozen tins of Junior dinners and asked for a brown paper bag. 'A few things for the baby,' she told Paul Pearson when he opened his door. 'To tide you over till you're back to work.' As she walked away she decided it would be nice to see Min, tonight, to giggle and be daft for a little while. Living close to the nitty-gritty was becoming almost too much to bear.

Min did not disappoint. 'Come in. I've banished the kids to their beds so we've got the place to ourselves.' She was dressed in a georgette cat-suit with a gold lamé belt and sandals to match. 'Might as well dress up while I can – it'll be smocks and elasticated trousers soon enough. All the same, maternity wear's much more imaginative now, isn't it? Not that I'm going to overdo it. I'd like to get something lasting out of all this. Ma-in-law is simply over the moon, so I hinted I'd like a memento. And I've told Dennis I'd like a white gold choker. I've seen them in London. A kind of mesh so you can breathe, but quite savage-looking all the same. You know, the slave-girl effect. He hasn't said no, so I'm quite hopeful. If only your lot would get back to work! Dennis says business is in the doldrums because of the strike – they're not even replacing the company cars this year, that's how bad it is.'

Fran loosened her jacket in the over-heated room and wondered if she should try to convey the cold and desolation of Belgate. But this was another country. Instead she held out her glass for a refill. 'Tell me what Eve said when you told her.'

She felt mellow when she left Min's in spite of refusing too many refills. They had eaten Tandoori drumsticks and profiteroles, and reminisced about schooldays. 'Do you remember when David and Dennis shinned up the flag-pole and put up those psychedelic bloomers?' Fran asked. 'And Harold pretended he had to go home because he thought they'd be expelled?'

Min had left her seat and come to kneel at Fran's chair. 'I love it when you talk about David like that, as though you were glad he was once alive. I couldn't do it because I'm a weak bitch and if something hurt I'd have to run away. But I want you to know I admire you for doing it.'

Fran hugged Min for a moment and let her go. 'You're not as black as you paint yourself ... just a little bit grey round the edges.'

As she drove out of Sunderland she thought of the old days, and the six of them together thinking nothing would change, except to get better. They had been short-sighted but it was the only way to live. She was smiling at the remembrance of David when she saw the glow. At first she thought it was the pit, but then the wheel came clear against the skyline and she saw the fire was over to the west. A moment of panic came and went. Someone would have phoned her if the house had burned down.

She drove past the pit and, turning towards the house, saw the running figures before she heard the noise: the clanging of a fire-engine, the roar of voices, the crackling of flames that shot skywards. Ahead was an eddying, swaying mass of people, police and protesters locked in combat. The car slowed to a crawl as a police constable loomed up and slapped the bonnet to halt her. She wound down the window and a smell of burning filled the car. 'You can't get through here, miss. Someone's fired the pub. Best go back and take the high road.'

Fran shook her head. 'I live here ... a few yards on. I must get through.'

'Go back, miss. The road's closed.' Suddenly he lurched over the bonnet as something hit him in the back. He turned towards the crowd, Fran forgotten, and lunged forward. She realized she was pressing the accelerator, gunning the engine, and eased her foot. They had fired the Golden Hind, a pub that had closed last year. Of all the crazy things! Suddenly the crowd surged towards her, struggling and fighting. She wound up the window as the car began to rock. If she had dialled 999 when she'd found the fire-bomb site, none of this might have happened. But in her heart she knew she could no more have stemmed all this than stilled the North Sea.

Suddenly she realized someone was banging on the near-side window. A man, face anguished, was mouthing, 'Let me in!' through the glass. She saw the cameras round his neck and reached for the handle, but the door was held shut by the strug-gling bodies, both sides raining blows indiscriminately on any-thing that came within reach. She saw the photographer lift his hands to cover his head and then blood was running between his fingers. She pushed at the door and when it opened began to pull at the straps of his camera till he was in the passenger seat and the door was closed. 'You can't go forward, go back!' He was blinking through the windscreen as blood ran down into his eyes.

'I must go on ... my little boy's through there and this is the only road.'

She let out the clutch, praying as she did so that no one would fall under her wheels. She felt detached, quite ruthless and single-minded. She was going home! A man's face loomed through the windscreen, distorted with rage and mouthing like a fish. She trod on the brake.

'It's no use ... for God's sake ... you'll get us both killed.' The photographer was struggling to rid himself of the tangle of cameras so he could take over the wheel.

'I have to get through,' she said, wishing with all her heart she had not let him into her car.

'Go back. Go back!' He was trying to put the gear into reverse, treading on her foot as it guarded the clutch pedal. There was a banging on the roof and the car began to rock. 'Christ!' the man said and turned to open his door.

Fran clutched the wheel. They were all around her now. The car was no longer a haven, it was a trap. She glanced in the rear-mirror. The road behind was clear except for a single cavorting figure. He would have to take his chance. She threw the engine into reverse and pressed down the accelerator. The photographer pulled his door shut and the figure behind leaped away. A second later they were clear of the crowd and booling down the centre of the road. She changed into neutral and steered for the kerb.

'Are you all right?' In the light from the street-lamps she could see he was quite old and his face ashen beneath the blood. He looked back at the dancing figures, silhouetted against the flames. 'That wasn't protest,' he said. 'That was a bloody riot.'

'I've got to go, I'm afraid. I'll get through on foot,' she said, searching in her bag for a tissue to stem his bleeding. She wanted him out of her car.

'I've got a van back there somewhere,' he said. 'I expect I can find it. Ta.' He took the tissue and wiped his face. The tissue turned red under his fingers. 'Bloody hell, I didn't think it was that bad! It doesn't hurt much.' She was leaning past him to open the door, ready to bundle him out if she had to. 'Hold on . . . you don't want to leave the car here. They'll wreck it.'

She was torn between desire to reach Martin and fear for her precious Mini. If she lost it, there would never be another. She switched on the engine and reversed into a side road. 'That's it . . . right down. Away from the lights.' She made her good-byes and locked the car, trying desperately to remember the web of streets that lay between her and home. She could come upon the house from behind, through the allotments, but that would take time. Who knew where the rioters would go if the fire spread or police reinforcements appeared? She must be with Martin and Treesa and the baby if there was going to be trouble.

With a pang she realized she had never thought of Treesa and the baby until now, only of Martin, her own flesh and blood. She slipped the strap of her bag over her head so her arms were free and began to run. A blue police van passed the head of the side road, then another and another. With so many police about, it would be safe to go straight home.

She had worn her patent court shoes to Min's. Now she cursed them as the spindle heels wobbled beneath her. She tried running on the balls of her feet but the pavement jarred. Nothing for it but to run barefoot. She tucked one shoe in each pocket and set off again. She felt the feet of her tights hole, and ladders flickered up her legs. One shoe fell from her pocket but she did not falter. They had cost her fifteen pounds in the Dolcis sale, but what did that matter now?

As she drew near she could hear the crowd, distinguish faces. There was a sudden roar and a flame shot skywards, showering sparks. Helmeted police were trying to restore order, but it was useless. The shouting took shape: they were singing the song that Martin had sung that day in the kitchen. '*Burn, burn, burn the bastard. Burn, burn, burn the bastard. Burn, burn, burn the bastard, early in the morning.*' She could smell fire and the pavement was awash. You never thought of water in a fire, but it was there, swilling over her feet and running into the gutter.

People were dashing past her, young boys, faces alight with a strange excitement. 'Howay the lads!' They looked like football hooligans but it wasn't a game. A girl passed and caught Fran's eye. 'This'll learn the sods!' An elbow dug into her ribs, too hard to have been accidental. They're enjoying this, she thought.

There were firemen ahead, yellow legs gleaming. If she went on they would grab her, make her turn back. As she looked for a turn-off she saw terrified faces peering from windows. A door opened and a policeman shepherded out a family. 'Hurry along . . . fast as you can.' A little girl was crying and he scooped her into his arms. The man of the house carried a Jack Russell terrier, its eyes rolling with terror. The mother was holding a baby. 'My God,' she said bitterly, to no one in particular. 'My God . . . is this Britain?'

Suddenly the wall of the pub collapsed in an ongoing roar. It was still a hundred yards away but Fran felt the impact as the old bricks crumbled and fell and went on falling. She saw a car in the middle of the road, turned on its roof like a dead beetle. Flames appeared, the petrol tank exploded and the car was engulfed.

[192]

The flash caught her face, but it seemed not to matter. Perhaps that would happen to the Mini.

There was a crack as a window blew out somewhere, and unbelievably people were laughing and dancing with glee! Something flew past her ear and she heard her hair sizzle. Her ears throbbed with noise and her eyelids burned. This was what Hell would be, an escalating agony.

A voice boomed though a loud hailer and suddenly the crowd surged back, taking her with it. She struggled forward, beating them with her fists until she remembered the other shoe. When it was free of her pocket she held it by the toe and used the heel as a weapon.

Her nose started to run and she licked it into her mouth. Someone trod on her bare foot and smoke filled her lungs as she screamed in pain. The strap of her bag caught on someone's arm and she lashed out. 'Let go, damn you. Let go!'

'Steady on, lass. Steady on.' It was Fenwick, tall and gaunt in a shabby parka, but recognizably a friend.

Her arms fell to her sides and she dropped the shoe. 'Take me home, Mr Fenwick,' she said, and felt his arms go round her like a shield.

22

Sunday, 3 March 1985

'It's over, Terry. You might as well face it.'

Terry shifted the baby to his other shoulder. 'There now, pet, stop crying. You'll mak yersel' bad.'

Treesa shook her head in despair and looked at Fran. 'You tell him.' The baby whimpered again and Treesa held out her arms. 'Let me have him.'

Fran stood up. 'I think we'll all have a nice cup of tea.' The strike was over! Well over 50 per cent of the men were back, and the Durham NUM had backed the call for a return to work without a negotiated settlement. But still Terry stood firm. 'Are you well enough to go back?' she asked as she poured his tea. He was pale and his face was thinner, but they might be more the marks of maturity than of his ordeal on the embankment.

'I'll be well enough when the time comes,' he said and dipped his biscuit in his tea.

Fran felt a sudden pity for him. 'It's not exactly a defeat, Terry. You've all been brave.'

The biscuit threatened to crumble and he helped it into his mouth. 'We'd've won if we hadn't been let down. Trade-union solidarity? Don't make me laugh. They've produced more steel through this strike than they do when times is normal.' A picture of Bill Sirs, the steelworkers' leader, came into Fran's mind: a face tortured by the need to keep his own men in work. She wanted to point out that the miners had asked the impossible, and that they had continued to mine coal when the steelworkers were on the rack . . . but it didn't seem the time. Instead she said, 'You can't decide men's lives for them without giving them a chance to have a say, Terry. There should have been a ballot.'

He said nothing, simply shook his head as if in pity for her ignorance.

Terry left as Bethel arrived with the latest news. 'They say there'll be a march back on Tuesday. Behind the banner. But most of them are going in tomorrow to get a full week in. They're going round as though they've won the pools 'cos they'll get a pay packet next week. They've forgotten they'll have the butcher and the baker and the candlestick-maker down on them like vultures. They've hung back while there was nowt to get, but you wait till Friday . . . it'll be a massacree!'

Fran went for a walk after lunch. Walter was coming to tea and Bethel was pretending to be unconcerned but in reality cooking up a storm. 'I won't be long,' Fran said and turned up her collar against the cold.

They had boarded up the windows of the Golden Hind and nailed planks across the doors. What brickwork remained was blackened around every orifice, where tongues of fire had licked the outside walls. It had served its purpose, that last wanton act. As though all the pent-up animosity of a twelve-month had been consumed in one sacrificial flame, Belgate had been quiet since then, almost subdued. She walked up into the woods, devoid today of woodcutters. The trouble was, she was no surer now than she had been when it started. Hearts had been broken, the landscape scarred, and for what? It was noble to suffer for a principle, but had the principle been preserved? Had it been there in the first place? And more important, would Belgate recover? The coal industry was changing: whether or not they liked it they would have to face the fact. Nothing stood still for ever, however much you wanted it to. That was what frightened her most, that neither side seemed to have learned from the last twelve months. Instead, they seemed more confirmed in their entrenched attitudes and the words of the TV pundits still had the consistency of candyfloss.

The wider view was frightening and she narrowed her thoughts. How would Belgate be affected? The sea-coalers would return in the moonlight to take coal from the blast. The pit would continue to disgorge, but what of the heart of Belgate? She remembered Fenwick as he had half-led, half-carried her through the rubble of the riot and delivered her to her door that night. She had tried to thank him, to offer some hope for the future, but he had brushed it all aside. 'What's the use?' he had said and there was a note of finality in his voice. She had passed his house the next morning when she went to retrieve the Mini, but his windows were curtained and eyeless behind the boarded panes.

And what of Fran when the peace came? Treesa's affairs would be settled, she would have money for a home of her own. Without the baby the house would be empty once more.

She turned when she reached the top of the rise and looked back at the sea. It was flat and grey, no whitecaps to break the dark expanse. There were big ships on the horizon, leaving the Tyne or heading for the Tees, and two coasters waiting for the tide to turn so they could enter the port of Seaham. When she was a child her father had taught her to be proud of Sunderland, of being a Wearsider, but the mighty shipyards of the Wear were almost silenced. She felt afraid for the North-east, doubtful of Martin's future. And yet their history stretched back to Bede and before. Surely they would survive?

She was always afraid nowadays, but she was coming to terms with her fears. She knew now that she would love again because she had the capacity for loving. And she would grapple with her debts and pay her taxes and see Martin through to maturity, in spite of the pitfalls. But since David's death she had never felt safe and now she knew she never would feel safe again. That was the price you paid for leaving childhood.

Walter was already ensconced by the fire when she got home and his mood was sombre. 'There'll be worse trouble before long. They're all drawing breath and saying, "Whoopee!" – but watch out. The NUM's crippled, the whole trade-union movement weakened. When Scargill took over from Gormley he said he wanted to unite the Union ... and he's smashed it to smithereens. She must be rubbing her hands in Downing Street.'

Fran tried to console him. 'Well, at least it's the end of Scargill.'

Walter's snort held more sorrow than anger. 'You're wrong there, bonny lass. By next week he'll have convinced them he master-minded this lot. All part of the Grand Design. He's better at pulling rabbits out of hats than Paul Daniels.'

Bethel had come in from the kitchen, for once without the light of triumph in her face at Walter's admissions. 'You're mebbe right, but if they can't see what's in front of their noses they deserve no better. It'd never've happened if Gormley'd still been there. This one thinks he's the Messiah, never mind a union leader.'

Walter was shaking his head. 'The only mission he's got, Sally, is lust for power. He wants to see if he can make everyone dance to his tune and, by God, half the time he can. They've got a Star Chamber now to castrate anyone who disagrees with him. If you'd asked me twelve months since whether that could happen,

I'd've told you "Never". But I've seen a lot of things in this strike I wouldn't've credited. There's been more fiddling in the NUM than in the Royal Philharmonic. And not just the officials.' He leaned forward in his chair, eyes twinkling. 'If you don't laugh at this you get your money back...'

Fran felt a constriction at her throat. At least he hadn't lost his sense of humour.

'There's an open-cast site in Durham ... doesn't matter where ... and there was never a shortage of pickets. "Put me out there," they were all saying, "I'll shut the bugger down." Turns out they were picking up a fee from the Union to close the place, and a fee from the owner to keep it open. They stood there shouting "Scab" and shaking their fists while the lorries went in and out like yo-yos. Beat *that*!'

Fran shook her head. 'I don't believe it ... the picketing at the open-cast sites was savage!'

Walter sat back. 'Please yersel'. But I'd believe anything now.'

'Is there a cup of tea going?' Treesa looked tired as she came into the room and Fran made room for her at the fire.

'Sit here and I'll top up the pot. Is Christopher asleep?' Treesa nodded. 'Yes, he's dropped off. He's cried that much! Still, he's asleep now; I think he's worn himself out.'

As she plugged in the kettle Fran looked out of the kitchen window at the deserted yard. Nearly two years ago she had seen a mouse flow under the garage door and done nothing about it: so the saga of the mice had begun. She would know better now. She handed Treesa her cup and topped up Bethel's. It was growing dark outside, and she moved to shut the curtains. 'It'll be nice to have a proper fire again.' She went into the kitchen and drew the curtains, and then went up to the landing window. The moon was already up, a sliver in the west, and the sky was clear. Spring would be coming soon.

She drew the curtains in Martin's room, then her own, and tiptoed into the room Treesa shared with the baby. She knew before she crossed the room that something was wrong, was afraid before she touched the baby's brow and felt the dry heat. Its breath seemed to be drawn up from troubled lungs, an agon-

[197]

ized sound that seemed to grow worse even as she listened.

She knew she must go down, tell Treesa something was wrong, but she felt disinclined to do so. They would all look at her, expect her to take charge, and she was not up to it. She was tired of struggling with life, tired of being pushed to the limits. Except that limits, like everything else in life, were endlessly accommodating. You thought you could bear no more, but in the end you did. She picked the baby from the cot and wrapped it securely before she carried it downstairs.

She saw the faces turn to her, at first surprised and then perturbed. Terry was standing in the kitchen doorway, mouth already open. 'There isn't time to argue,' she said firmly. 'We have to take Christopher to hospital. Will somebody get my coat?'

As she drove through the darkening streets, lights were springing up in the houses. Treesa sat beside her, crying quietly as the troubled breathing came and went. 'I think it's diphtheria,' Fran had said to Bethel. 'Except that no one gets that nowadays. But that's what I think it is.'

Now she drove as fast as she could on to the Sunderland road, watching the signs flick past. Eight miles, seven miles, six. When David was dying they had lifted him into an ambulance and sent it jangling through the crowded streets. An ambulance man had held a mask to his face, and she had held his hand and asked him not to leave her. She had looked from the windows and seen the rush-hour traffic and known they would not get through. But the cars and buses had parted in obedience to the siren and David had died in an iron bed in a side ward five hours later.

This time she gave thanks for the empty Sunday roads, willing the baby not to give up. Diphtheria formed a web in the throat and closed the airway; they had to cut a hole in the windpipe and divert air to the lungs. People had done it with pen-knives before now, and the sufferers had lived. But Peter Lee had banished diphtheria from the streets of Durham when he gave them pure piped water. So why was it happening now? She heard Terry in the back seat, clearing his throat. 'Not much further now,' he said and she knew he was afraid.

[198]

They took the baby away through swing doors. 'Sit here,' the nurse said. 'I'll come back as soon as I can.' When she came back her face was expressionless. 'He's going up to Ward 5. There's no need to panic. Doctor just wants another opinion. You can stay, mum and dad. Your friend might as well go.'

Fran was glad to escape. Terry had not disclaimed parenthood, he was holding Treesa's arm and doing his best to console her. He was the proper person to stay. 'I'll come back if you need me,' she told Treesa. 'Maybe they'll let him go later on. Just ring me and I'll come.' They both knew it was nonsense but they nodded agreement.

It was Martin who comforted her. 'It's a strong little baby, mam. Remember what it did to the Poody dog. It won't die.' She cried then, and clutched him, and he did not draw away. 'It's all right,' he said, and she nodded. Babies who could pull the legs off Poody dogs could surely defeat diphtheria.

In the end it was not diphtheria after all. 'It's quinsy,' Terry said when the call-box pips stopped. 'It's only quinsy, and he should be all right. They've got him on antibiotics, massive doses. If he responds . . . and they say nine out of ten do . . . he'll be all right. If not, they can do an operation . . .'

'A tracheotomy?' Fran asked.

'Yes, that's it. They do that while they find out the proper treatment. But the main thing is, he's going to be all right. The doctor says it was the right thing to bring him straight in. It's made all the difference . . .'

'Thank God,' Bethel said when Fran went round and told her. 'I don't hold with praying for favours, but I've asked for a few tonight.'

Fran nodded. 'I should have prayed but I was too muddled up. Anyway, Treesa's staying till the baby settles and then they're coming home in a taxi. I offered to go for them but Terry said no.'

Bethel looked agitated. 'Will he have any money?'

Fran nodded. 'I gave him something before I left. I said we

could sort it out later.'

The older woman settled back in her chair. 'Quinsy. I haven't heard of quinsy for years. They used to wrap your throat in flannel but it still closed up. Many a one died of it, couldn't even open their mouths.'

Fran patted her arm. 'It's different now. They've got antibiotics, and all sorts of things. You'll have your precious baby back before you know where you are.'

As she went back to her own house she passed people scurrying here and there. She had forgotten the strike was over! There was a new air of activity, even at that time of night. In the darkness a woman was collecting washing from a line. 'I've just been airing his pit clays. They've been in-bye for a year, and they hum.'

When she'd switched on the immersion heater she looked in on Martin. 'Try and go to sleep darling. We know everything's going to be all right, and it might be ages before Treesa comes back. I'm going to have a nice bath and go to bed myself.'

He shuffled down under the covers but his eyes remained alert. 'Will the strike be over tomorrow?'

Fran nodded. 'All over bar the shouting. Some people ... the very strict Union members ... will stay out till Scargill says to go in, but most of the men will go back tomorrow.' She sensed he had something to add. 'Will Terry go back home now?'

Fran sat down on the edge of the bed. 'Do you want him to?'

He nodded. 'Yeah. Not just for Mike. I think it's better if families stick together.'

She wanted to reassure him but it wouldn't do. He trusted her to tell the truth. 'I don't know what'll happen. I'm fairly sure they'll get friends again, but once you've been away from home it's hard to go back. Anyway, when you get to Terry's age you'll want to leave home.'

His tone was confident. 'I won't. I won't ever get married.'

She felt the first frosts of panic as she stood up. If she got things right he would go: that was the irony of motherhood. If you did it properly you lost your stake.

She was in the bath before she realized how tired she was. It wasn't just today – it had been a hell of a year, and now it was catching up with her. Two years, really – a chapter that had begun with David's death. She would always date things from then. AD ... the year of David. There would not be a year of Steve. She would remember him only as an interlude.

But she would remember the strike, as a time of deprivation and anger and comradeship and tragedy. If there had been good leaders on both sides, it might have been different. Instead Mac-Gregor had been the urbane godfather figure, always saying he had nothing to give. And Scargill ... he had played his followers like a master puppeteer, but he had paid a price. Tonight, on television, the signs of strain had shown on him. A strike was like an atom bomb: you could drop it on your enemy, but you couldn't escape the fall-out.

When she was ready for bed she collected Walter's book on Peter Lee, turning once more to the marked page. *'Not only men but nations must realize that the human family is thus so linked together that we must work together in a co-operative spirit if civilization is to endure.'* If only she could spray those words on the walls of Belgate. If only Peter Lee were here today to draw the miners together once more. He had been ruthless in the pursuit of social justice but he had been a militant who preached conciliation, and she liked that. He had banished open drains from his county and with them the toll of infant deaths. No wonder they had named a town after him. Where was his like today?

It was two o'clock before the taxi drew up outside but she was still awake. She looked from the window and saw them facing one another, a foot apart. As though she had willed it, they moved forward and melded and clung. She let the curtain fall back into place and climbed into bed.

She was still awake when the first footfall sounded in the street. It was a trudging step, and those that followed were no more jaunty. She wondered if the lone footstep was Fenwick's, but dared not look. It would not be Terry Malone, that was sure. He would march in at the Union signal, not a moment before. But he would go back. Yesterday she had asked him a question she had never dared ask before: why he clung to a pit that had robbed him of his brother. 'Is it because there's no other work, Terry?'

He had not answered for a moment, and she wondered if she had gone too far. Then he looked up and smiled. 'It's just my place, isn't it? It's in the blood. Going down the hole, that's what Malones do. We're good at it. Pit ears, pit eyes ... we can read that bitch like a book.' There was affection in his voice and a kind of reverence.

'He's looking forward to going back,' Fran thought and was amazed.

But he would not go back today. A few streets away he would be lying, listening as she was listening to the halting return. Down below someone struck up a tuneless whistle. It was 'Colonel Bogey', but no one joined in. Fran felt her lips purse in sympathy as the lone whistle died away. There was silence for a moment, and she held her breath until there was an anguished stage whisper beneath her window. 'Howay, lads!' A voice picked up the 'Colonel Bogey' theme but the words were his own:

MacGregor has only got one ball,
The other is in the Albert Hall.
Scargill, dear Arthur Scargill,
Drives us all right up the wall.

One by one voices joined in, the tempo quickened. Fran lay, smiling, as the feet picked up rhythm, the drift back became a march. The Belgate men were going in! She turned on her side and made plans for the future as the heart of Belgate steadied and returned to its old, familiar beat.